SHAKESPEARE AND THE LOSS OF EDEN

The Construction of Family Values in Early Modern Culture

Catherine Belsey

First published in paperback 2001 by
PALGRAVE
Houndmills, Basingstoke, Hampshire RG21 6XS

ISBN 0–333–80184–9

This book is printed on paper suitable for recycling and
made from fully managed and sustained forest sources.

A catalogue record for this book is available
from the British Library.

10   9   8   7   6   5   4   3   2   1
10   09   08   07   06   05   04   03   02   01

Printed in China

To Alan and Cynthia
with love and thanks

Previously published books by Catherine Belsey

Critical Practice
The Subject of Tragedy: Identity and Difference in Renaissance Drama
John Milton: Language, Gender, Power
Desire: Love Stories in Western Culture

Contents

Illustrations

Acknowledgements

The author and publisher wish to thank the following for permission to use copyright material.

Figures 29, B. T. Batsford Ltd; 38, 39, 40, cliché Bibliothèque nationale de France; 36, 37, By permission of the British Library; 1, 9, 12, 32, By permission of the Syndics of Cambridge University Library; 13, 14, 17, 20, 21, 24, The Conway Library, Courtauld Institute of Art; 15, The Conway Library, Courtauld Institute of Art, Fred H. Crossley and Maurice H. Ridgway; 23, The Conway Library, Courtauld Institute of Art, Lawrence Stone; 3, 10, By permission of the Folger Shakespeare Library; 7, Glasgow Museums: The Burrell Collection; 11, 34, Kupferstichkabinett, Staatliche Museen zu Berlin – Preussicher Kulturbesitz; 8, The Metropolitan Museum of Art, New York, Gift of George R. Hann, 1960, and 35, The Metropolitan Museum of Art, New York, Gift of Irwin Untermeyer, 1964; 41, 42, Öffentliche Kunstsammlung Basel, Kunstmuseum. Photo: Öffentliche Kunstsammlung Basel, Martin Bühler; 43, Museo Thyssen-Bornemisza, Madrid; 26, By courtesy of the National Portrait Gallery, London; 31, From the Collection at Parham Park, West Sussex, England, open to visitors from April to October each year; 4, 5, 16, 18, 19, 22, 28, 30, Nicholas Prigg; 25, Tate Gallery, London, 1998; 6, 27, V&A Picture Library; 2, Warwick Castle.

Thanks also to Ron Koster for the Holbein decorated capitals used throughout the book via his website at: http://www.psymon.com/

Preface

'Families,' a friend once told me, 'are the people who have to take you in – whether they like it or not.' Families are places of warmth and support; they are a constant feature in an unpredictable world; we can rely on them. At the same time, proximity may nurture hostility in direct proportion to the love it is supposed to take for granted. Precisely because of the high expectations families generate, they can be deeply disappointing. Worse, they can be abusive, both physically and emotionally.

In the course of the sixteenth century in England, the developing state discovered an investment in keeping the population in its sights, encouraging people to settle in stable groups, their relationships recorded in the parish register. Meanwhile, the parish itself, responsible for the survival of the poor, increasingly recognized the advantage of inducing two parents to stay together and support their children by the fruits of their own labour. And in the same period the Reformation clergy found it necessary to identify a new way of perfection to replace the now discredited monastic celibacy. Family values became the object of intense propaganda, and of the anxiety that the reconstruction of any value system necessarily creates.

We are the direct heirs of the early modern construction of family values, incited by politicians and moralists to believe, in the teeth of considerable counter-evidence, that the family will make us whole, both as individuals and as a society. But at the same time we are also experiencing an unprecedented anxiety about family values, in the course of acknowledging the limitations of the proposition that there is only one proper way to arrange our sexual relations, and in the process of learning from the statistics how commonly unhappiness can follow from the obligation of loyalty to those who have the greatest opportunities for brutality towards each other. Love, attributed to nature, can be more oppressive and more coercive than convention or law.

This book has three main aims. The first is thematic: to historicize and thus denaturalize family values. Whatever is customary comes in due course to seem natural. Moreover, since in a free society the explicit imposition of norms and regularities appears authoritarian and thus elicits as much resistance as conformity, when we make rules we call them nature, so that nonconformity can be stigmatized as unnatural. The proverbial wisdom, currently backed by some versions of sociobiology and evolutionary psychology, naturalizes the ideal of the loving nuclear family and condemns its failures. But the laws of nature have no history: they do not change. The proposition that family values emerged at a specific moment in the history of Western culture represents a refusal to accept the inevitability of certain norms.

As the figures for marital violence and cruelty to children emerge in our own society, it becomes increasingly apparent that the loving family, our culture's most cherished institution, is also too often a place of physical and psychological torment. Conceived as a stabilizing element in society, the family can equally be a source of deep-seated emotional instability. The history of the emerging ideal of the affective nuclear family in early modern England suggests that these contradictions may be structural, the result not so much of individual human weakness as of a problem at the heart of family values themselves.

My second aim is to treat Shakespeare's plays as the location of cultural history. Rather than isolated works of art, to be explained by reference to their context, these fictional texts may be seen to participate in the construction and affirmation of meanings in the period. And cultural history is above all a history of meanings. It has been a critical convention that we should interpret fiction in the light of its context. Scholars have read sermons, marriage manuals or domestic conduct books in order to explain what happens in the plays. By a strange reversal of values, however, this 'background', invoked to validate a specific reading, too frequently turns into the foreground, and in the process obscures features of the plays themselves. Are women enjoined to submission in the homiletic literature? It seems to follow that we are invited to condemn women who assert a position in the plays, however little support we find for this view in the fictional texts themselves.

My intention, by contrast, is to treat the plays as the material of cultural history alongside non-fictional texts of the period, rather than identify one as explanatory background to the other. When it comes to accounts of the family, domestic conduct books are no more neutral, impartial or authoritative, no more representative of their culture, than fiction. Where, indeed, could we find more detailed attention to the ambivalences of courtship, marriage and parenthood than in works designed to enlist and hold the attention of an audience by dramatizing the intense and intimate emotions of love and hate? Without assuming that the plays 'reflect' the world that produced them, we can be sure that they explore the meanings of the terms they construct and reiterate in ways that were expected to be at least partially intelligible to their original audiences. Meaning is never either single or static. To participate in a specific culture is to understand, reproduce, modify or transform, whether consciously or not, the polysemic signifiers in circulation there, and the plays cannot fail to take part in this process. *Shakespeare and the Loss of Eden* is an attempt to interpret, from the present, the complex, plural, contradictory character of a past culture as this is displayed in its texts.

Third, my plan is to analyse visual and written materials side by side. Poststructuralist theory is often criticized for privileging language. In practice, however, its concern is the signifying process, semiosis, whether in visual or in verbal form. Like words, pictures signify, and their spectators are invited to make sense of them. When we explicitly read a visual image, translate its meanings into words in order to give an account of it, something is necessarily lost. But when we interpret a verbal construct in words other than its own, there is also a loss. No less a component of culture than writing, and perhaps prior to it, the visual throws into relief the inadequacy as well as the solicitation of the reading process.

In the light of what we know now, the book sets out to trace representations of the emergence of the loving family in three linked fields: Shakespeare's plays, English visual culture of the sixteenth and seventeenth centuries, and interpretations of the Book of Genesis in the period. As early modern popular culture recounts, the primary Scriptural vindication of family values, the first loving marriage, ordained by God in the Garden of Eden, also led to betrayal, exile and the first murder, when Cain killed his brother because God preferred Abel. In Shakespeare, while marriage is synonymous with a happy ending, married love is shown to give way to murderous jealousy, and sibling rivalry leads to violence and death. The story of the nuclear family told in these texts and images, from romance through marital conflict to parenthood and the relations between the children, is both idealistic and sceptical.

English family values emerged out of the religious, political and economic upheavals of the early modern period, when marriage based on love and consent was sanctified as a way of life for Christians, and the closeness of the family came to offer an alternative to the impersonal values of the emerging market. Many of the contradictions implicit in our own perception of the loving family were also evident at this inaugural moment: early modern accounts of the family put on display the twin possibilities of triumph and disaster. Precisely because of the promises it seems to make of perfect and shared happiness, now as then, the family also breaks hearts.

In the hope of naming something of this ambiguity, I have called the book *Shakespeare and the Loss of Eden*. Am I, then, charting a Fall? The answer is yes and no. I have no confidence in the myth that engrosses modernity of a lost golden world corrupted by time, or a founding moment from which the present has fallen away. The history of the transition from arranged to consensual marriage records, in my postmodern view, no moment of innocence, no high point of grace and no decline, but only specific joys and particular anxieties. On the other hand, family values *represent* for many people a utopian fantasy which, on closer inspection, is recognized as precisely utopian, realized nowhere. That recognition can bring desolation, the sense of exile from a destined happiness. But perhaps, the texts imply, Eden is an idea which in practice was always already lost.

I have incurred a great many debts in the course of writing, some very specific and some so extensive that my bare thanks here do not begin to balance the account. I am grateful to John Astington, Leeds Barroll, Judith Bennett, Peter Blayney, Kent Cartwright, Howard Cheetham, Stuart Clark, Peter Coss, James M. Dean, Alan Dessen, Cynthia Dessen, Tom Dawkes, Antony Easthope, Balz Engler, Geoffrey Fisher, Janette Graham, Stephen Greenblatt, Marshall Grossman, Richard Helgerson, Coppélia Kahn, Angela Locatelli, Lena Orlin, Elihu Pearlman, John Percival, Helen Phillips, Lois Potter, Susan Snyder, David Skilton, Yoko Takakuwa, Julia Thomas, Rachel Thomas, Ann Thompson, Charles Whitworth, Georgianna Ziegler. Helen Clifford has been a mine of information about material culture. I have borrowed shamelessly from Claire Connolly in my account of cultural history. I always come away wiser from my conversations with Barbara Mowat. And Susan Zimmerman has entered into the spirit of the quest with characteristic sympathy and enthusiasm.

I am grateful to the British Academy for support to attend the World Shakespeare Congress in Los Angeles in 1996, where I presented the first draft of Chapter 4, and for an award which made it possible to reproduce the illustrations. In June 1993 the University of West Virginia allowed me to explore some of the issues in a challenging and euphoric three-day Seminar. I am also grateful to the participants in a joint RCA-V&A seminar in May 1996: they taught me more about cultural history in a single day than I can possibly acknowledge. My MA students at Cardiff University and my graduate class at UNC-Chapel Hill came up with ideas that repeatedly made me rethink my own. I have benefited from the expertise of the staff of the Rare Books Room at the University Library in Cambridge. The Arts and Social Studies Library at Cardiff University has been a constant and sympathetic resource. In 1991 I chaired a seminar at the Folger Institute in Washington DC, which was where it all began, and when in 1994 I held a Fellowship at the Folger Shakespeare Library, the kindness and the intellectual generosity of the staff and readers once again made the pursuit of sources a pure pleasure.

For the sake of consistency, I have modernized the spelling, typography and punctuation of quotations from early modern texts.

Parts of Chapter 2 appeared in *Parallax*. An earlier version of Chapter 3 was published in *The Seventeenth Century*.

Catherine Belsey

Chapter One
Introduction: Reading Cultural History

I

n the Rhymney Valley, 15 miles north of Cardiff, just off the main road to Merthyr Tydfil, stands the manor house of Llancaiach Fawr. It was constructed in the sixteenth century for the ap Richard family, later the Prichards, Welsh gentry who married locally and whose eldest sons were alternately named either David or Edward. During the political upheavals of the 1640s, Edward Prichard initially pledged his support for the King and was put in command of Royalist forces. Later, he changed his mind: as a devout Puritan, who was being asked to pay more taxes than he liked, and who no doubt saw the way things were going, Prichard changed sides, and in 1646 he held Cardiff Castle for Parliament. On 5 August 1645, at what may well have been a critical moment in Colonel Prichard's struggle with his conscience over these matters, Charles I had dinner at Llancaiach Fawr on his way to Brecon. The reflections of the King's host on the occasion are not recorded.

Llancaiach Fawr is now open to the public, restored with a view to reproducing its condition at that historic moment. The award-winning 'living history museum' invites visitors to experience the past directly, as they are conducted round the house of the absent Prichards by their servants, dressed in seventeenth-century costume and speaking a version

of seventeenth-century English. The servants refer only to events and
places which could have been known in the period; they cook to reci-
pes from the time, and are unable to recognize the names of any modern
dishes that might resemble them; they prescribe herbal remedies for
visitors who cough or sneeze. The servant-guides question visitors
politely about themselves, and express astonishment that it is possible
to travel from Cardiff in such a very short time. There is a good deal of
ribaldry, no doubt licensed by the period. And the male servants are
all deeply resentful of their absent mistress, Mary Prichard, who is
forever, we are led to understand, discontented and peevish, laying
claim to higher breeding than her husband, and constantly indisposed.

The house is a domestic museum, and what it puts on display is a
seventeenth-century family. It is emblematic of the limitations of the
project that the Prichards themselves are away from home: how could
the early modern family be made present, after all, in a heritage spectacle which is, in certain ways, quintessentially postmodern?
Meanwhile, this book is also about representations of the early modern family, and the family 'itself' will be no more present in my account
than it is in the manor house. In both cases, all we have access to is the
trace of past meanings, and since, as Jacques Derrida explains, meaning itself is no more than the effect of a trace, cultural history can only
trace the traces of the family at a specific moment in the past. But my
interest in Llancaiach Fawr is motivated not only by its thematic over-
lap with this book, but also by the radical methodological differences
between the two projects, its and mine.

'History comes alive at Llancaiach Fawr', the Guide Book announces.
'From the moment that visitors enter the formal gardens, they are surrounded by the sights, smells and sounds of the past.' Some of the
sounds turn out to be tape-recorded: I was astonished to hear invisible
horses stamping in the adjacent stables. But some are not: the pea-
cocks screaming on the lawn are real. Modern standards of hygiene
prohibit the exact reproduction of the smells. Internal privies at
Llancaiach Fawr discharged into a diverted brook. (To the cultural historian the inclusion of *en suite* privies in a number of relatively modest
domestic buildings of the mid-sixteenth century in England, Scotland
and Wales shows a commitment to privacy considerably earlier than
other sources might have led us to expect.) 'Step over the threshold of
Llancaiach Fawr', invites a publicity leaflet, 'and travel back over 350
years.' The servants are happy to discuss the political situation as it

obtains in 1645, and to give their views, not all of them shared. But above all, the museum centres on domesticity: visitors can try on copies of clothes from the period, or handle replicas of the kitchenware. In other words, Llancaiach Fawr encourages us to cross a boundary between present and past, between one historical moment and another, into a vanished epoch. The project is to recover the life of an early modern household, to permit us to encounter cultural history as participant observers, by suspending our own interests, identities, commitments and convictions. 'In every respect', the Guide Book affirms, 'it should be an unforgettable experience.'

It is. I mean no disrespect to the Prichard family or their modern 'servants' if I say that what I found most unforgettable was my own acute embarrassment. This was not attributable to a sense of my superior knowledge of the period: on the contrary, I learned a lot. Where I did know – or thought I knew – about the cultural history of the mid-seventeenth century, I could not fault the account I was given. The problem was rather that I was asked to cross the boundary in one direction, and irreversibly, for the duration, to enter the past in a dialogue where, deprived of any intelligible reference to the present, I had no secure place to speak from. I felt tongue-tied, unfamiliar with the conventions of the time and unable to give an account of my own interest in what I was hearing. (How, for instance, could I possibly explain to a seventeenth-century steward that I wanted to see (but not to use) the privy in order to chart the emergence of privacy in the period?) They ask where you live; the place does not exist in their world and they shake their heads in bewilderment; alternatively, it does exist, but it is not the same place now as it was in 1645. The furniture and pottery of the period, displayed as exhibits in a glass case in a conventional modern museum, are objects of an always conjectural knowledge; conversely, when they are experienced, held, handled, they become irretrievably alien, as do the eating habits and the herbal remedies. To try on the clothes is to be 'dressed up', in costume. This was not 'costume' in the seventeenth century, however, but everyday dress, and people presumably knew how to inhabit it. When the familiar present ceases to be a secure foothold, the past becomes more remote, not less, harder to read because the only frame of interpretation available to a modern visitor is relegated to a distance, out of reach.

II

If the present is ruled out of order, translation of the past into the terms of the present is not an option. It was precisely in order to challenge the conventional idea of history as a process of translation that 'living history' was devised. Llancaiach Fawr is by no means unique, of course. The everyday life of Plimoth Plantation, where the original Pilgrims landed, is brilliantly replicated on Cape Cod; Colonial Williamsburg reproduces the life of a community in eighteenth-century Virginia. The Holocaust Museum in Washington DC is laid out experientially in chronological order. In the early days, visitors were offered a card which would give them the identity of an inmate of one of the camps. They were invited to insert the card at intervals into machines to find out what stage 'their' story had reached; in the end, they would discover whether 'they' had escaped or died. Meanwhile, the Globe Theatre in London promises the chance to see the plays of Shakespeare and his contemporaries performed in an 'authentic' setting.

Conventional historiography, on the other hand, translates the past into the present. Here too the project is recovery, but the idea is to make the past present to our *understanding*. An earlier epoch exists as a document written in an unfamiliar language for the linguistically competent historian to render in a language we know.[1] Traditional cultural history follows the same pattern. Ideas and beliefs are assembled, material objects decoded, letters and diaries analysed, all in order to offer the modern world an understanding of the values of the past. 'Living history' is synchronic: it isolates a specific moment of the past and erases, ostensibly at least, everything that has happened since. Conventional historiography, by contrast, locates the specific moment diachronically, charts its causes and consequences and, in the process, constructs a story. This narrative, intelligible, as Hayden White points out, generically as comedy or tragedy, romance or satire,[2] so that it 'makes sense' to modern readers, effaces its own genre, as well as the present from which it is recounted and the interests, convictions and commitments of the historian. Traditional cultural history, too, constructs a narrative – of origins and vestiges – in which the arrival of the present constitutes the end of the story, whether happy or tragic. The more totalizing the narrative, the more readable the history; but the process of translation itself, the act of *making* history, is erased. 'That', conventional history affirms, 'is simply how it was.'

Unlike history, legend draws attention to its own textuality: 'That's what they say,' it affirms; 'that's what we read'.[3] But at the same time, legend eliminates the difference of the past: even the most heroic of golden worlds exists in a kind of synchronic present as a model. History is born at the moment when textuality is effaced: 'that's what happened,' it says; the past is apparently recovered in its truth as an object of knowledge. But here too, paradoxically, since the translation takes the place of the event or the object, supplants the real and pushes it further away, what is lost is the pastness of the past, its otherness. This ordered, teleological, generic history can never resemble the past as it was lived. The project of 'living history', by contrast, is to recover the experience, to turn the detached analyst into a participant. In the first case, meaning is thought to defer experience; in the second, experience is offered at the expense of meaning.

It seems to me that neither project can deliver what it promises, that recovery of the past, whether as translation or experience, is not a possibility. In both instances, the present is all too present – apparent as the form into which the past is translated in one case, and as embarrassment in the other. Llancaiach Fawr invites us to cross the boundary between one historical period and another, to experience as participants a different moment of cultural history. I do not believe we can. Instead, I want to define a distinct practice, which I shall call history at the level of the signifier. This is a form of cultural history which involves neither translation nor experience, but depends on reading. Moreover, it is a material practice – as material in its own way as social history, to which it can be related. But it is not synonymous with social history nor, in my view, subordinate to it.

III

To distinguish history at the level of the signifier from social history is to make a methodological distinction which 'living history', like life, indeed, obscures. The kind of cultural history I am putting forward is a history of representation. An early modern funeral monument to a mother, for example, depicts her orphaned children as chubby and vulnerable. A century earlier, children were generally represented on tombs, when they appeared at all, as miniature adults, with no very notable distinguishing features except their smaller size, and even that was not always indicated. This does not imply that in practice children

changed shape. On the contrary, what it suggests is that the difference
between parents and children now signifies in a new way. A baby on a
tomb of 1631 fingers the decoration on her mother's bodice, just as
any modern baby might. The inference a cultural historian draws is
not that medieval babies did not in practice play with projecting ornaments, but that this habit was not widely thought worth representing.
Representational priorities change as values change, and history at the
level of the signifier records these shifts of value. A textual history of
the nuclear family is not to be conflated or confused with its social
history. The number of people sharing a house is not what is at stake
here; their 'experience' of each other is not accessible. We can, however, discuss and attempt to date the emergence of shared values and
the gradual spread of new ideals.

Social history gives priority to describing practices, while cultural
history records meanings. It is a relief to be able to differentiate, to
know that we no longer have to try to reconcile the sympathy Renaissance plays seem to evoke for young lovers who defy enforced marriage
with the widespread early modern practice of arranging partnerships
in the interests of property. Lawrence Stone's influential account of
The Family, Sex and Marriage disappoints to the degree that it fails to
distinguish between practice and values. Stone largely ignores fiction.
At the same time, the texts he invokes – letters, diaries, legal documents – are treated as broadly transparent. But analysts of texts know
that the values a society approves, endorses in letters and diaries, or
prescribes by law, may well differ very considerably from its day-to-
day practices, just as its practices may differ from the utopian or tragic
alternatives defined in fiction.[4] Nor does fiction 'reflect' practice. After all, people did not, as Jim Sharpe, the distinguished social historian,
once patiently explained to me, commonly take their sisters' hearts to
banquets on daggers, as Giovanni does in *'Tis Pity She's a Whore.*

Cultural history records meanings and values, which is to say that its
concern is not so much what individuals actually did, but more what
people wanted to do, wished they had done, what they cared about and
deplored. Not that a society's practices are irrelevant to history at the
level of the signifier. As Louis Althusser pointed out, stressing the
materiality of ideology, beliefs are inscribed in practices, particularly
ritualistic practices.[5] Where practices feature in cultural history, they do
so primarily in terms of their meanings – as customs or habits, for example, which demonstrate the values a culture subscribes to. If fiction
idealizes marrying for love while the majority of parents resolutely go

on arranging the unions of their children, cultural history recognizes a conflict between residual and emergent values.

The distinction I am proposing is not a binary opposition: meaning and practice inevitably inform and, indeed, invade each other. The meaning of the hall in the late medieval house changes as it ceases to be the setting for even ceremonial dinners, and the owners increasingly retreat with their children to a separate and relatively private dining room. It is important to be aware that, even so, 'the family' continues into the seventeenth century to include the servants, whose moral behaviour and religious observances are the responsibility of their master and mistress. Similarly, it helps to know that when, in Twelfth Night, Viola asks whether Orsino is still a bachelor, she is not simply identifying a possible husband, but establishing whether she can hope to join his household dressed as a lady, since Olivia's is closed to her. Because a bachelor's retainers would be male, an Elizabethan audience would understand, the only opportunities for a woman in his house would take the form of menial work. We misread fiction if we misunderstand the practices of the period. Social and cultural history are thus profoundly interrelated, but we stand to lose if we collapse one into the other, or efface the differences.

For cultural historians practices signify. Culture constitutes the vocabulary within which we do what we do; it specifies the meanings we set out to inhabit or repudiate, the values we make efforts to live by or protest against, and the protest is also cultural. Culture resides primarily in the representations of the world exchanged, negotiated and, indeed, contested in a society. Some of these representations may coincide with existing practices; they may determine or legitimate them; or alternatively, they may challenge them. Representations are not, however, purely discursive: they also have, in my view, their own materiality. That is to say, culture is in its way *lived*.

No sane person would now look to Hollywood movies for the truth of contemporary social practice; any future social historian who saw our advertisements as depicting our actual way of life would be seriously misled. At the same time, the popular appeal of film and advertising, and their corresponding commercial success, depend to a high degree on their inscription of widely shared ideals, fantasies and values. We live our lives in relation to these dreams, in self-congratulation, disappointment or resignation. 'Life', we recognize, is not like fiction. At the same time, however, fiction generates hopes, desires and aspirations, and these, too, are lived; popular texts affirm

norms and proprieties which we adopt, with whatever anxiety, or repudiate. Culture is lived as *a relation to* practice, as commitment or
resistance, or as an uneasy alliance between the two, an anxious, un-
decided ambivalence. If love has become a matter of free choice, is
Giovanni entitled to choose to love his sister? And if he can be said to
have his true love's heart, what exactly are the limits of that possession?

To affirm the relative independence of cultural history is not, I want
to stress, a covert way to denigrate social history. On the contrary, social history is an important and distinguished discipline, with its own
scrupulous standards of scholarship and accuracy. We should do well
to take account of it, and to emulate its meticulousness. But there may
be a substantial gap between the endorsement of a value and its widespread implementation, or between practice and the ambivalences
which attend it. This gap is of interest as evidence of conflicting values, but the discipline of cultural history need not depend for
confirmation on the research of social historians, any more than it supplants that research. And if this opposition is itself deconstructed in
different ways by the brilliant work of Natalie Zemon Davis, Carlo
Ginzburg or Stuart Clark, this only goes to show that our methodological distinctions are no more than that, frames which enable us to
isolate for study specific aspects of the vast and unfamiliar terrain that
constitutes the past.

History at the level of the signifier is decisively textual. Culture is
lived, but we have no direct access to early modern 'life'. The materials of cultural history reside in the signifying practices of a society,
and these include its fictions,[6] where meanings and values are defined
and contested for the delight and instruction of an audience which is
expected to understand a proportion, at least, of what is at stake. Meaning is value-laden: we learn the proper attitudes to good and evil as
we learn to understand the terms, or to recognize heroes and villains.
Culture is learned as well as lived, and we learn to live it as we learn
to speak, to follow stories, to read, write, interpret images, obey or
repudiate conventions. No human practice takes place outside it. Birth,
reproduction and death are probably as close to nature as most of us
come, but these events are undergone in culture – in all its uncertain-
ties and ambivalences. If we experience them as natural, that only goes
to show how thoroughly we have internalized the meanings culture
prescribes.

IV

The form of cultural history I am attempting to define acknowledges our distance from the past. In this respect, history at the level of the signifier is both more and less ambitious than 'living history'. Its project is not the recovery of the experience in its imaginary fullness, but the recognition of cultural difference. On the other hand, it asks questions that 'living history' cannot answer. As a historian of family values, I wanted to know more about the nature of the relationship between the politically astute Colonel Prichard and his 'peevish' wife, two of whose four children, both the boys, died young. The servants could not tell me. They could report on the behaviour of the couple when they were together, but this in turn would need to be interpreted, historicized, before it could become part of a history of the family. The Guide Book includes a photograph of the servants in bed, three of them sharing an attic. I wondered quite what exchanges occurred in that attic after dark. The modern impersonators of the servants might have answered my questions, but I'm not sure I would have trusted them to know any more than I did.

History at the level of the signifier looks at the residues the past has left – its documents, which I take to include fiction, sermons, pamphlets, maps, visual images, ornaments, the allocation of space, architecture, including the opportunities domestic buildings provide for privacy, and sleeping arrangements. To this extent, cultural history self-evidently resembles anthropology: it constructs a culture by reading its artefacts. But it differs from anthropology in its classic mode to the degree that it studies a vanished epoch. Unlike synchronic ethnography, the distance cultural history sets out to bridge is, by definition, chronological. In this respect, it resembles archaeology. History at the level of the signifier interprets the residues of the past explicitly from the present, and emphasizes the pastness of the past. It takes for granted that we *make* history, which is to say that we make a story which differs from the one contemporaries would have made.

We do not, that is to say, interpret another culture from what Clifford Geertz calls 'the Native's Point of View'.[7] There is a radical dissimilarity between, on the one hand, sympathetic, imaginative engagement with the perspective of a participant in another culture, a native speaker – or writer – and on the other hand, the abandonment of our own cultural location and the historically specific knowledges it entails. At

Llancaiach Fawr I inspected the privy, once I had finally prevailed on my hosts to allow it, alone and in silence. Only then could I take account of its location on the first floor, and note the ventilation arrangements; only then could I make a mental comparison with the provisions at Chenies Manor in Buckinghamshire and Castle Menzies on Tayside, and give due consideration to the fact that, in all these cases, the properties belonged to the gentry rather than the aristocracy, if Highland chieftains can be classified at all within this framework. The comparison led me to wonder whether courts of the period, with strong motives not to cultivate privacy, might positively discourage places of concealment. Few of these inconclusive reflections would have been possible from the native's point of view.

Meanwhile, in my experience at Llancaiach Fawr, dialogue was extremely restricted when I was denied access to my own culture. Dialogue is an exchange between subjects. The subject is what speaks or writes, and it does so in a language which is the inscription of certain knowledges – of a culture. As subjects, we have learnt to signify in a specific society, since signification always precedes us as individuals, and meanings pertain at a specific historical moment. To speak or write is to reproduce, however differentially, the meanings we have learnt. We participate in dialogue from our own moment, and it follows that we understand, if at all, from where we are. We interpret the past and its subjects from the present, since we have nowhere else to interpret from, and it follows that 'our situation can allow us to be familiar with their situation in ways other than their own ways.'[8] We read the documents of the past in order to produce the possible range of their meanings, which is not the same as the range of meanings that could consciously have been identified at the time. Cultural history does not inhabit the past and it does not share its frame of reference. We interpret, inevitably, from the present, and the present necessarily informs our account of a past that cannot speak for itself. In a conventional museum, we understand the objects in the glass cases to the degree that we are able to frame them with a knowledge, constituted in the present, of their purpose and use. 'Living history', by contrast, shows these same objects to be precisely unfamiliar: we have to learn in the present to handle them. Documents offer information which historians now sift, filter and reconstitute as narrative. The present disrupts the subject-object couple of empiricist knowledge: there is no 'objective' account of the past.

V

Does it follow, then, that if 'objectivity' is not an option, we not only make history, but we also make it up? Certainly, fiction (etymologically, 'making') invades the realm of 'fact'. Llancaiach Fawr is theatrical and the theatricality is part of the experience: we are guided round the manor house by actors, who play roles in a performance and interact with the audience of visitors. The visit itself is offered not only as instruction but also as recreation, a suitable activity for holidaymakers or family outings. But in this respect, as education in the form of entertainment, it hardly differs from conventional museums, television documentaries, popular history magazines or the accounts of the past that feature in the book-review pages of the Sunday papers. Public anniversaries memorializing historic events, however solemn, are also recreational as well as theatrical, and the occasions themselves to a degree construct the nature of the memory they reaffirm.

Moreover, the historical documents, too, are already the effect of 'making' in this sense, so that even the material on which history is based is not entirely independent of the fictional process. Written records from the period select, however innocently, the information worth preserving, to the degree that they choose what to exclude: even the most apparently indiscriminate chronicle leaves out a good deal more than it recounts. In an age of photo-opportunities we are conscious of the degree to which portraits and photographs from the past are also 'staged'. Self-representation is very often a 'performance': wills stand as monuments to the deceased, as well as dispositions of property; letters are exchanged not only within the framework of the epistolary conventions of the moment, but also in the light of expectations about what the recipient might want to know; diaries may present an image of the self to gratify or appal the reader, even when this reader is understood to be the author at a future date. And in turn, the process of representation inevitably invades the historian's narrative: the vocabulary in which it is written is necessarily value-laden; the story itself is told according to the conventions of narrative in general and a generic pattern in particular, whether the genre is comic or tragic.

Some empiricist historians take the view that to query the transparency of their work is synonymous with proposing that there is no difference between fact and fiction. Poststructuralist theory, they affirm, urges that we might as well read a novel as a work of history, or that history itself is pure invention.[9] It would be odd indeed if a theory which turns on difference should set out to erase differences. I take it for granted that the real exists, as distinct from invention, and that the past happened in a sense that the events of *Middlemarch* did not. Its residues testify in their stubborn otherness to the previous existence of a world that is more than the product of our current imagination. The texts, the documents, the material remains do not in practice always confirm our expectations. On the contrary, they surprise us, and elicit a corresponding modification of what we thought we knew. Familiar with the quite different arrangements in courts and palaces of the period, I had not expected to find *en suite* privies lower down the social scale.

In other words, the problem of history is not the real, but our account of it, our record of its past, which is always delimited by the signifier. We cannot know the past outside the residues it leaves, and these remains are always subject to our interpretation. Reflection, judgement, narration have no purchase outside language, and we have no independent guarantee that the differences inscribed in language map on to differences in the real. In consequence, while we owe it to the past to read as meticulously, assess as scrupulously and record as faithfully as we can, these virtuous practices, however rigorously carried out, cannot ensure the impartiality, the independence, in short, the truth of the stories we tell. We have no direct access to a past that exists outside the construction we put on it in the present.

To the degree that the present informs our account of the past, we make history *out of a relation, which is always a relation of difference between the present and the past*. I put it in these terms because I want to stress two points. First, a relation of difference is not full; it is not a thing; it has no content. Cultural history, as a relation between present and past, is neither a recovery of the past nor an affirmation of the present, but an acknowledgement of the gap that divides them from each other. And second, if the kind of cultural history I am proposing is not in consequence empty, a blank sheet, or a self-proclaimed fiction, that is because we *make* a relation, in both senses of that term, out of *our* reading practices and *their* documents. We produce, that is to say, a past which is both the consequence of our analysis and its motive. I take it for granted that the real existed then as now; but I take it equally for granted that the real was no more knowable then than it is now. All we can analyse is the signifier, in which not only the real, but meaning too, while not simply lost, is forever differed and deferred, relegated by signifying practice itself to uncertainty and undecidability, difficult, recalcitrant, evasive. Meanings do not, in other words, present themselves as fully formed, discrete objects of knowledge. Indeed, they do not *present* themselves at all. The idea, intelligibility, what we imagine as the concept, does not exist independent of the signifier itself, which both precedes and relegates the supposed pure signified.[10] The signifier, the place where meanings are made and also supplanted, is the material of our study – the signifier precisely in its materiality.

VI

History at the level of the signifier treats signifying practices – maps, houses, clothing, tombs – as texts. Such 'documents' from the past are both substantial and legible. We can read them, as much as we can ever read anything, to the degree that we are familiar with the signifying practices of their moment. And since signifying practice in general, like language in particular, is in the first instance public, conventional, shared, learned, there is no reason why we should not learn to read the meanings of the past by immersing ourselves in the documents, even though we shall never understand them as native speakers.[11]

Of course, not all instances of cultural history can or should do all this. Here I have chosen to dwell, in addition to Shakespeare's plays, on the visual imagery of the period, as this appears in forms not normally treated as great art: embroidery, furniture, tomb sculpture, woodcuts. Aware of my limitations as an art historian, I have paid very little explicit attention to technical developments and changes of convention, except in so far as these make possible the meanings I set out to identify. Techniques, materials and conventions do not change all by themselves. Plasticity develops alongside a desire for mimesis, and mimesis becomes an object of desire when there is a motive for setting out to reproduce the illusion of what the eye actually sees. Of course, there are differences of skill, but when early modern tapestries show apples larger than human heads, we construe that their symbolic role in the story counts for more than perspective. Conversely, the more fluid effigies that begin to appear on seventeenth-century tombs enable us to recognize a new interest in the depiction of emotional relationships.

In other words, I have tried to read closely, but not necessarily as an art historian would read. If we are to make history at the level of the signifier, we shall need to pay extremely close attention to all the documents in question. While I unreservedly welcome the rereading taking place in English departments – under headings like gender studies, queer theory, postcolonial analysis – I am uneasy about the predominantly thematic character of much of this work. I regret, that is to say, what I see as a neglect of the signifier, the basic material of the hermeneutic practice I am proposing. The decline of close reading is the result, of course, of a reaction against American New Criticism and practical criticism in the UK. I do not want to return to either of these activities, but I am occasionally unconvinced by some of the interpretations that are put forward in the name of recent approaches. At the end of the introduction to an anthology of new historicism and cultural materialism, Kiernan Ryan makes the point in these terms:

> Radical historicist criticism is undoubtedly the poorer for its reluctance to meet the complex demands of a text's diction and formal refinements; for in the end only a precise local knowledge of the literary work, acquired through a 'thick description' of decisive verbal effects, will allow the critic to determine how far the work's complicity with power truly extends, and how far beyond our own horizon it may already have reached.[12]

Theory is often blamed for bad reading habits, but it does not follow from the undecidability of meaning that inattentive readings are just as good as any others. The prime exponent of undecidability, Jacques Derrida, reads minutely, demonstrating in his mode of analysis a precision that would put many literary critics to shame. Exactly because meaning is not present to itself or the reader, because all we have is the signifier, we need to tease out, by detailed attention to the textuality of the text, its nuances and equivocations, its displacements and evasions, the questions posed there and the anxieties on display about the answers proffered.

What is at stake is not an empty formalism. But it is, in my view, imperative, if we are to make good cultural history, to take account of the modes of address of the texts we analyse. In written works it matters who addresses whom, in what situation and with what authority.[13] When the works in question are fictional, it matters that we differentiate between the fictional speaker and the text. The views of the villain are probably contrary to what the audience is invited to believe: Iago's racism and misogyny, for example, should not necessarily be taken for the play's. There is a pragmatics of the utterance within the world of the fiction: Hamlet, say, invites Horatio to endorse the promptings of his conscience; but the dialogue between them also sets up a relationship between the play and the spectators, and the nature of the ethical invitation there is altogether more elusive, not least because we have no access to the historical audience's reaction. Genre also delimits what is affirmed. A domestic conduct book sets out to overcome the anxieties about marriage that motivate its publication; a play, by contrast, foregrounds anxieties to sustain the plot for five acts, and a happy ending does not necessarily dispel them entirely. Moreover, in fictional practice genres are rarely pure. A familiarity with fairy tales might protect us from reading substantial areas of Shakespeare mimetically.

Difference is once again the critical term. In addition to their attention to the formal differences within and between texts, the readings that we make in the practice of history at the level of the signifier will also give full weight, I hope, to the reading process itself as a relation of difference. They will not claim, that is to say, access to the truth of the text, or the single, correct interpretation. They will acknowledge their own motivation and their own partiality and know that reading takes place from a position in the present. And they will also recognize the difference *within* the past and *within* the text: conflicts and inconsistencies of meaning that both reproduce and motivate debate, disagreement and struggle in the world at large.

VII

Current theory permits us to see meaning as heterogeneous to the point where an affirmation and its opposite, power and resistance, may share the same inscription. Dissension, in other words, inhabits discursive practice, characterizes it, and at the same time destabilizes it. Texts take issue with other texts, but they also differ from themselves, inscribe the conflicts they take part in. It is perhaps too easily assumed that other epochs were somehow simpler than our own, or that the cultural history of former periods is appropriately represented as ultimately unified. Our world, we allow, is divided, full of debate, culturally diverse and intellectually stratified, but nostalgia still tempts us to imagine a previous culture as a consensual realm, in which the important meanings and values could be taken for granted as shared, despite distinctions of language, class or gender. This seductive account of the past seems to me fundamentally misguided, and nowhere more so than as an interpretation of the early modern period, where virtually every topic was matter for dispute, much of it passionate, some of it violent. In my view, the century between 1550 and 1650 in England was one long moment of dissension, where radical shifts in economic and political relations were both the condition and the effect of fundamental challenges at the level of ideas, and these challenges in turn were the result of cultural exchanges between the present and a recovered classical past, among the emerging European 'nations', and between the Old World and the New.

But it is also, I believe, misguided, however tempting, to identify difference simply with conflict. Sometimes difference is synonymous with indifference. As I see it, the Renaissance was also a period when knowledges that were self-evident in one genre of writing might well be entirely ignored in another. Medical advice might be contrary to clerical instruction, for instance. Sometimes conflicting knowledges would compete for supremacy; but in other cases cognitive dissonance simply subsisted without closure. Incompatible convictions – rationalist on the one hand and magical on the other, profoundly sceptical in one instance and deeply sentimental in another – might survive alongside each other, sometimes contesting the same ground, sometimes without ever coming into contact. We do the period an injustice, I increasingly believe, if we try to make its meanings and values fit together to form an internally consistent totality, expecting physiological knowledge to 'explain' Shakespearean comedy, for instance, especially if to explain is to efface or resolve the discordant elements within the texts.[14] At the very least, physiology and comedy are different genres, addressed to different audiences on different occasions.

Everyday meanings are elusive, contradictory or undecidable. This implies a version of cultural history which takes account of the resistances, as well as the regularities, of the past. Like political, social or economic history, though in its own way, cultural history can be a record of oppressions inadequately imposed and proprieties acknowledged and then evaded. The project is not an account of a coherent 'world picture', but a record of the difficulties that arise when societies attempt to bring their members into line.

Dissent is the reason why things change, or one of them, at least: the one that is open to our appropriation, as the blind mechanisms of the market are mostly not. And the instabilities of cultures are the pressure points for change. If the future is also our concern, as current interest in gender studies, queer theory and postcolonial studies presumably implies, we need a version of cultural history that acknowledges incoherences and offers evidence that things change, so that we have grounds for hoping that, in the long term, injustice might be significantly reduced. Otherwise, there is no point in complaining. We need, in other words, a theory and practice of reading that foregrounds dissent.

Nowhere is cognitive dissonance more evident than in fiction. Part of our awareness of the density of some of Shakespeare's plays, part of their ability to make a sense, however varying, to succeeding generations or from distinct political positions, may be the effect of a conjunction within them of different knowledges, which precisely do not cohere into a single, decipherable, decodable, thematic *message*. Fiction, which may have no design on its audience but to entertain, can afford to mingle the propositions currently in circulation, without any obligation to rationalize them. As a space of play, where some of the prohibitions of the symbolic Law are temporarily suspended, fiction can permit inconsistency without irritable reaching after resolution. Fiction, then, and Shakespeare's fiction no less than any other, is a crucial element in the cultural history we produce.

VIII

It follows that there are certain critical differences between the form of cultural history I am proposing and the practice of new historicism. I value the break new historicism has made with a literary paradigm that no longer challenged us on its own terms, and I share its commitment to extending our attention beyond the purely literary, but the highly sophisticated work of Stephen Greenblatt and his colleagues differs from the model I am putting forward in three specific ways.

First, new historicism seems to me to treat texts as relatively transparent: not, that is, to look for the inconsistencies and instabilities of meaning which are my primary concern. In consequence, second, the cultural moments it depicts are seen as more unified, more harmonious, more homogeneous than they are in my account. In this, new historicism borrows, as I see it, from its anthropological model, though I understand that anthropology too is becoming more interested in dissent and the struggles that go on within the cultures it studies.[15] However, in its homogenizing impulse new historicism also reproduces

the values of American functionalism, which implies that the local features of a society all work, in the last analysis, to maintain the social
order as a whole. In my own view, derived from Foucault's, power is
always and necessarily coupled with resistance as its defining difference. Third, and closely linked with my reservations about
functionalism, it is important to me that I tell a story. This is not the
same as recounting an anecdote from the period nor, on the other hand,
do I want to revert to traditional metanarrative, to repeat a totalizing
history of progressive development or emancipation. (New historicism
has never been guilty of this.) But I do want to emphasize change – as
evidence that the way things are is no more natural or inevitable than
the way they used to be. New historicism takes over from anthropology an inclination to isolate synchronic moments rather than situate
them in a differential relation to what came before and after. In this
respect, too, new historicist practice differs radically from the work of
Foucault, to whose influence it is so widely attributed. Foucault commonly contrasts one epoch with another. My own interest, like his, is
in the reasons why certain cultural values – and certain cultures, indeed – do not survive, or survive only with difficulty by effacing their
own internal differences.

The distinctions I have made are refinements. What I share with the
project of new historicism is a commitment to cultural history itself, to
the recognition of the otherness of past cultures, the inclusion of fictional texts in the category of cultural artefacts, and a corresponding
refusal of the categories of foreground and background, text and context. New historicism has done more than most recent schools of
thought to transform, modernize and politicize the agenda for English
departments throughout the world, and it has done so with great flair
and style. In that enterprise it has my unqualified support.

IX

What is it, to return to my projected cultural history of early modern
family values, that I expect to find? What, in other words, is the nature
of the story my patient attention to the texts of the period makes possible? Not 'living history': not an experience my readers are invited to
share. But not an ordered, teleological account of causes and consequences which effaces its own textuality, either: not mastery. Distinct
from social history, my account, as history at the level of the signifier,

draws on the texts to argue that family values as we understand them have nothing to do with nature. They arose (and were natural-ized) in the period in question, and are therefore subject to change. Reading from the perspective of an ambivalent present, when the close-knit, supportive nuclear family can also appear as a form of heterosexist oppression, and begins to be seen as the location not only of affection and support, but also of domestic violence and child abuse, I find in the early modern texts a story of ambiguities, riddling paradoxes and contradictions: a desire to possess (wife, children, property) which acts by destroying, predicated on a lack which fills the vacancy with fearful imaginings, including marital jealousy and sibling rivalry. The loving family, our culture's most treasured institution, turns out, then as now, to intensify the options for tragedy.

We have been familiar, at least since the 1930s, with the story of the Reformation replacement of Catholic asceticism by the progressive idealization of the conjugal relation during the first 100 years of the Anglican Church. In *The Allegory of Love*, C. S. Lewis showed the Renaissance romance of marriage triumphant over the medieval romance of adultery.[16] Lewis's account was subsequently confirmed from a rather different perspective by the Hallers in their influential essay on the Puritan art of love in 1942.[17] The general case has been contested, of course, usually from the point of view that the romance of marriage had medieval antecedents; it does not follow from the fact that most noble marriages in the middle ages were arranged in the interests of property and lineage that they were therefore loveless. But the Lewis-Haller account of the emergence of a widely shared ideal has probably represented the dominant view, nevertheless, for the last 60 years.

Medieval Catholicism regarded celibacy as the way of perfection. The monastic ideal of chastity was a renunciation of the flesh and of the values of this world; priests were also expected to be celibate. Marriage was not condemned, but it was seen as second best, in line with St Paul's view that it is better to marry than to burn. The Reformation, however, changed the position radically. Monasticism was no longer an option; and in order to integrate the clergy more fully into the community, the Reformers advocated marriage for them too, as the foundation of parenthood. The result was a celebration of family values which sometimes reached rhapsodic rhetorical heights. There were, of course, dissenting clerical voices, but they were residual. In England the earlier Pauline position was still audible well into the seventeenth century, most notably in Donne's sermons on marriage, but it was in the process of giving way to a radical new orthodoxy of wedlock as a terrestrial paradise, where the love between husband and wife is an analogue for the love of God. The conjugal relationship is now properly romantic, erotic and companionable, and it duly leads on to the rich fulfilment of family life. By 1638 Robert Crofts was to write:

> There is no pleasure in the world like that of the sweet society of lovers in the way of marriage, and of a loving husband and wife. He is her head; she commands his heart; he is her love, her joy; she is his honey, his dove, his delight. They may take sweet counsel together, assist and comfort one another in all things; their joy is doubled and redoubled. By this blessed union the number of parents, friends, and kindred is increased. It may be an occasion of sweet and lovely children, who in after times may be a great felicity and joy to them ... A multitude of felicities, a million of joyful and blessed effects, spring from true love.[18]

Meanwhile, in the fiction of the early modern period, adultery progressively loses its romance, and figures like Tamora, Marlowe's Isabella or Webster's Vittoria offer to excite horror rather than sympathy. Even the relationship between Antony and Cleopatra can be seen as more tawdry than heroic. Courtship leading to marriage has become the most appropriate place for love. Tristan and Isolde yield to Orlando and Rosalind, and marriage is now synonymous with a happy ending. Childhood, newly vulnerable, is valued for its innocent charm, and the family becomes a seminary of good subjects, where children learn at their mother's knee the fear of God, obedience to the laws of realm, and the rules of good conduct.

The seamless narrative recounted by C. S. Lewis and his successors is not inaccurate, but more recent and more sceptical accounts indicate that it lacks nuances.[19] Early modern culture did not emerge into the sunlit uplands Crofts describes without a passage through much darker terrain. In our own period Shakespearean critics, eager to embrace family values, have sought in the wisdom of Shakespeare's plays an authority for their own optimistic conviction that the proper outcome of true love is a lifetime of marital and parental concord. Recent disclosures, however, have subjected this belief to severe testing, as it becomes apparent that the privacy of the family home can shelter physical and emotional cruelty, as well as domestic felicity. In the light of what we are now beginning to know, the story we have told of early modern marriage is gradually being refined.

Reformation clerical imperatives coincided with the desire of the developing state to pin down the whereabouts and stabilize the behaviour of the population. Parish registers recorded births, marriages and deaths, and armed with this information, the ecclesiastical authorities did their best to bring marriage under church control, and to restrain those nomadic fathers who proved so ready to leave their wives and children to the support of the parish. Subject to proper rules themselves, parents were increasingly seen as the origin of propriety in their children: in due course the home came to be understood as a place of self-discipline and instruction, both founded on affection. This ideal of the loving nuclear family reached its fully developed form in the eighteenth century and was sanctified in the nineteenth. The best things in life, moralists reminded the victims of an emerging capitalism, are free. However humble the circumstances, happiness is available to all, in the relationship between a faithful husband and wife, who care more for their children than for wealth or pleasure. A loving, supportive home produces well-ordered, happy children, who grow up to become citizens of a properly regulated society. Even now, governments continue to insist that only the restoration of family values can save us from soaring crime rates and the threat of civil disorder.

Proponents of family values insist that the loving nuclear family is ordained by God – or his Enlightenment surrogate, nature – as the only proper location of desire. Like all value judgments, this ostensibly innocent proposition can have coercive consequences. Not only does the affirmation of the ideal set out to corral all decent citizens of the Free West into heterosexual monogamy; it also obscures the degree to which the family is the place where we learn to reproduce other oppressive norms of Western culture, including the norms of gender itself. At the individual level families can, of course, be warm and nurturing, and it is worth bearing in mind that unpaid parental labour, supremely the work required for the socialization of children, saves the state a great deal of money. Meanwhile, however, family values are invoked politically to justify imposing financial penalties on single mothers; they allow governments to blame families for the rise in crime and increasing illiteracy, both, it might be argued, direct effects of their own economic policies. And they legitimate the withdrawal of state provision for the elderly and the infirm. Meanwhile, empirically,

at our own historical moment, the Western family enclave, we are finally compelled to acknowledge, all too commonly conceals behind
closed doors all kinds of subjugation and suffering, not to mention ill-
treatment of the elderly and infirm.

I cannot speak for God, who may well have ordained the nuclear
family for the rest of us, though he noticeably did not choose to belong
to one himself. Recent research in anthropology and sociobiology, however, indicate that, contrary to the prevailing image, the nuclear family
has very little to do with nature. Both social history and cultural history are now contributing to a mounting scepticism about family values,
as the analysis of their emergence in the early modern period helps to
historicize an ideal which had come in the West to seem so inevitable
that it passed for universal. My own contribution to this process consists in an attention at the level of the signifier to the unresolved
ambiguities in the representation of the emergent nuclear family.

The official Reformation view of marriage is clear. According to *The
Book of Common Prayer*, it is 'an honourable estate, instituted of God in
the time of man's innocency'. This is what legitimates holy matrimony
as a proper way of life for Christian people: when Adam was without
sin, God himself gave him a wife who would perfect his happiness.
Thomas Becon defines the married state as 'an high, holy and blessed
order of life, ordained not of man, but of God'.[20] 'In Paradise also, that
garden of pleasure, was it instituted, yea and that before any sin reigned
in this world, to show that it bringeth to man great joy, wealth, felicity
and quietness.'[21] A great many Puritan divines were to reiterate this
account in their own words, both from the pulpit and in print. 'Marriage is a merri-age, and this world's Paradise where there is mutual
love', Rachel Speght insisted, defending women against an anti-femi-
nist pamphlet in 1617.[22] As a minister's daughter, she could evidently
take for granted the connection between matrimony and the Garden
of Eden. Popular poetry reaffirmed the analogy. Sylvester's best-selling translation of *The Divine Works and Weeks* of du Bartas exclaimed
in successive editions from 1605 on:

> O blessed bond! O happy marriage!
> Which dost the match twixt Christ and us presage!
> O chastest friendship, whose pure flames impart
> Two souls in one, two hearts into one heart!
> O holy knot, in Eden instituted.[23]

And, of course, the whole tradition finds its culminating moment in Milton's epic celebration of the wedded love between Adam and Eve.

But the story of the first marriage is also a record of deception, exile and loss. The serpent beguiles Adam's God-given helpmeet and companion, so that she eats of the tree of the knowledge of good and evil. When Adam also consumes the forbidden fruit, the disobedience of the first couple is complete, and God drives them from the Garden. Their punishment is not only exile, but also labour in both senses of the term, as Adam is compelled to till the soil for sustenance and Eve brings forth children in sorrow. The Fall is also the origin of death. The sinful progenitors of the human race will die: in due course, Adam and Eve will now have to return to the dust from which they were taken. But even before they do, Cain, the eldest child of this first union, will grow up to murder his brother, so that the blood of the innocent Abel cries out to God for redress. The family turns out to shelter tragic betrayal and unmotivated violence. Radically heterogeneous to itself, the biblical account invoked by the Reformers to authorize the new ideal of the loving family also exposes the deepest misgivings about conjugal and sibling relationships. The Genesis story, so widely illustrated in the early modern period, commonly makes little effort to separate these antithetical implications, and its repeated inscription in the sermons and the visual culture of the time may be read as radically complicating the cultural history of the family still widely taken for granted.

Meanwhile, recent work on representations of domestic crime in the period confirms the impression that the family was a source of anxiety. Frances E. Dolan, for example, looks at treatments of familial homicide, especially in the pamphlets, and the power relations they imply between married couples, masters and servants, parents and children. She goes on to show how these accounts illuminate *The Tempest, Othello, The Winter's Tale* and *Macbeth*.[24] Though Dolan's main concerns are with hierarchy and its subversion, my own firm impression is that there is also a direct connection between the emergence of family values and the increasing perception of the loving family as a place of danger. The greater the emotional investment and the more intense the commitment, the more profound the fear of betrayal and suffering.

Shakespeare and the Loss of Eden, no less selective than any other historical narrative, is not offered as a comprehensive account of the emergence of family values in the early modern period. Instead, in an

effort to focus in detail on specific instabilities at the level of the
signifier, I have chosen, perhaps arbitrarily, to isolate visual representations of the biblical story of the first family in relation to some of
Shakespeare's plays, linking these in turn with other instances from
the image repertory of the period. Chapter 2 explores Adam's loneliness in the Garden before the creation of Eve. Paradoxically, the lack
which instigates desire was already in evidence in the pastoral setting
created to satisfy the innocent Adam's every need. This lack, redou-
bled in a fallen world, also unsettles the celibate academy of *Love's
Labour's Lost* and the golden world of the Forest in *As You Like It*.
Courtship progressively 'civilizes' the heroes of these plays, teaching
them to perform the identities their culture prescribes: romantic love
turns out to be a recruiting ground for good subjects. Chapter 3 relates
Cymbeline to the Fall as it is represented in sermons and on marriage
furniture. Posthumus and Cymbeline himself are alike unable to 'read'
the wives they love any better than Adam reads Eve, and the
undecidability which characterizes both passion and signifying practice is here shown to be radically destabilizing. In Chapter 4 I relate
The Winter's Tale to the domesticity offered to Adam and Eve and their
two young children as compensation for the loss of Eden. But in Shakespeare's only full-length dramatization of relationships within the
loving family, affection unaccountably gives way to murderous violence. Meanwhile, tragedy enters into representations of the family in
the monumental sculpture of the period, as more lifelike representation of the figures replaces traditional formality. And finally, Chapter
5 draws a parallel between *Hamlet* and the first murder. The fratricide
which inaugurates the plot of the play explicitly repeats Cain's crime,
and propels the next generation into a *danse macabre* which recalls the
sequential violence chronicled in the remainder of the Old Testament.
The Ghost appeals to Hamlet in the name of family values, and the son
longs to avenge his dead father. But like the figures of the living in the
Dance of Death, Hamlet also hangs back, afraid of the secrets with-
held from flesh and blood, the knowledge of what lies beyond the
grave. Hamlet seeks ethical grounds for action in order to be sure of
his immortal destiny. What he reaches, however, is not certainty, but
the mysterious terrain of death itself, propelled there, it seems, by a
loving father. A place of intense emotion, the family, designed, then as
now, to domesticate desire and stabilize society, also proves in its early
textual inscription to be radically precarious, lawless and deadly.

In reading the texts, I have drawn on current theory: Michel

Foucault's identification of the coercive potential of norms, Jacques Derrida's analysis of meaning, Jacques Lacan's account of the human condition. Deprived of the vocabulary of the present, I should, as at Llancaiach Fawr, have nothing to say. In one obvious sense this is anachronistic, but what else can we be? In another, however, there is, it seems to me, a relationship of similarity, as well as difference, between these post-Cartesian (and to a degree anti-Cartesian) theorists and the (just) pre-Cartesian culture of Shakespeare's moment. Early modernity and postmodernity share certain perceptions. What divides them from each other is the intervention of modernity itself, the Enlightenment and its heritage. Moreover, Lacan, in particular, seems sometimes to reproduce earlier insights. There is, I believe, a line of descent from St Augustine through Montaigne to Lacan, despite the self-evident differences between these three figures from radically different cultural and historical moments.

Any essay in cultural history is subject to the inadequacy of all interpretation. My account of family values will attempt to represent, with whatever limitations, the incursion of anarchy, cruelty and death into what is legal, affectionate and life-giving, the element of suffering in felicity. The limitations of cultural history are not, or not only, however, a matter of ignorance, but also an effect of representation: the past necessarily exceeds our depiction of it. Meanwhile, we too are participants in our own continuing history. The presence of our historical moment in the processes of both interpretation and representation means that we are necessarily implicated in the stories we tell, to a degree that neither 'living history' nor conventional historiography are able to acknowledge. There is no place outside history from which to make what sense we can of the past.

Chapter Two
Desire in the Golden World: 'Love's Labour's Lost' and 'As You Like It'

I

he youngest of three sons is neglected by his brother, who inherits the estate when his father dies. Though the heir was charged by their father with his education, the younger brother is treated, he complains, like a servant, or worse. The second son has at least been sent to school, but the third is barely distinguished from the farm animals:

> he keeps me rustically at home, or, to speak more properly, stays me here at home unkept; for call you that keeping for a gentleman of my birth, that differs not from the stalling of an ox? His horses are bred better; for besides that they are fair with their feeding, they are taught their manage, and to that end riders dearly hired: but I, his brother, gain nothing under him but growth, for the which his animals on his dunghills are as much bound to him as I.
>
> As You Like It (1.1.6–15)[1]

Even the horses are trained, exercised, put through their paces, Orlando points out, but he is left without the instruction that befits his place in society, his noble birth undermined by the lack of cultivation. What is at issue is the upbringing appropriate to a gentleman (1.1.66–72), the training in civility that will add the practices of courtesy to an already virtuous nature. If Oliver will not provide this, Orlando insists, he will take his own small inheritance and go off to seek his fortune (1.1.73–4).

Families can be difficult. As the well-known story of the Prodigal Son repeatedly reminded early modern society, elder brothers may easily resent their younger siblings (1.1.37–9), and the equally familiar story of Cain and Abel was a constant reminder of the murderous lengths to which such fraternal rivalry might go. Oliver comes close to having Orlando killed, but – this opening indicates – *As You Like It* (1599) is structured like a fairy tale, and the audience may guess that in the end, it will be the youngest son who marries the princess and lives happily ever after. He will acquire such civility as he needs, no doubt, in the course of the story.

A few years earlier, the same audience had had the opportunity to watch four young men dedicate themselves, with whatever reservations, to study, in order to make the Court of Navarre 'the wonder of the world' (*Love's Labour's Lost* (1594–5), 1.1.12).[2] Subjecting themselves to the most rigorous discipline, forswearing the company of women, fasting, and sleeping very little to pursue their education, they will renounce 'barbarism' (1.1.112) to become 'heirs of all eternity' (1.1.7), graced by fame and honour, their court 'a little academe, / Still and contemplative in living art' (1.1.13–14). Renaissance academies, whether in theory or in practice, devoted themselves to cultivating philosophical knowledge, discussing the nature of virtuous government and the proper relations between the estates of the realm. They also fostered chivalry, as well as poetry, music and masques – the arts of civilized living.[3]

It won't work, of course. Not only is their projected asceticism hopelessly utopian, as Berowne makes clear; in addition, the French Princess and her ladies are expected on an embassy from the King, and the young men must immediately break their oath or betray the very values it stands for. Moreover, the unreconstructable Costard has already been caught with a woman, Jaquenetta the dairymaid, 'a child of our grandmother Eve' (1.1.252). The dramatic ironies are readily apparent: a misplaced idealism has led the King and his companions to choose quite the wrong way to civilize the court. They will learn, the audience might construe, a good deal in the course of the play about the civility that distinguishes human beings from the beasts, but not by repudiating the physiological appetites they share with the animals. What is more, the children of our grandmother Eve may have more to contribute to the civilizing process than the lords imagine.

II

During the course of the 1590s Shakespeare's comedies put romantic courtship on the popular stage for the first time, and in the process created a new genre.[4] It is difficult for us, as inheritors in a line of descent that passes through *She Stoops to Conquer*, Jane Austen's novels, *The Importance of being Earnest* and *Four Weddings and a Funeral*, to recognize the novelty of this invention. There were, of course, antecedents, networks of intertextual affiliation that made the new genre both possible and intelligible. The *commedia dell'arte* took love as a frame for the interaction of a series of social types. In this it drew on Roman comedy, a staple of early modern grammar-school education, where love stories formed a scaffolding for the play of social satire and intrigue. Ovid, equally part of the syllabus, was a master of the tears and torments of desire, as well as the ironic distance which shows them to be absurd. A heritage of medieval romance made the anguish of extramarital passion familiar, and Petrarchan poetry defined the paradoxes of unsatisfied desire, while contemporary prose romances specialized in long-separated couples and the ruses, including crossdressing, employed by virtuous heroines to follow their chivalric lovers. During the previous decade, Lyly's elegant and sceptical fantasies had subjected the plaints of lovers and the antics of Venus and Cupid to delicate dissection on the courtly and 'private' stage. But only Shakespeare's plays set romantic love leading to marriage at the centre of the action, anatomizing the relationships between lovers.

The project must have been easier defined than accomplished. What, after all, was this 'love' that the plays would put on display? High emotions, intense sensations, and in the end, mating? The problem of dramatizing love as reciprocal feeling and sexual exchange is that there is very little to show for it: even when the sexual act is simulated on the modern stage, the experience of desire and the sensations of passion are not necessarily made present to the audience. And if the play is to last for the duration of five acts, and if the desire in question is to be vindicated as true love, the proper basis of marriage, the end had better not come too soon. Courtship is mating deferred, and the practice

of procrastination, in conjunction with the promise of a happy ending,
offers the audience the specific form of pleasure we know as romantic
comedy. Shakespeare's plays celebrate the deferral of consummation
that is romance; love is symbolized, indicated in the form of sighs,
complaints, apostrophes, declarations, appeals, demonstrated by teasing and coaxing, and postponed by absences, misunderstandings,
errors of judgment.

The human being is always an organism-in-culture, driven to formulate its basic impulses as demands, and in the process, necessarily
submitting to the cultural dictates inscribed in the signifier. Culture is
as formative, as determining, as the organic: the symbolic Law imposes
the order of culture on a nature which cannot thereafter recover an
imagined wholeness, the integrity of pure sensation. Nor can signifying practice alone satisfy the requirements of the desiring human
animal, which oscillates restlessly between the organic and the symbolic in quest of a gratification it cannot name.

And yet to name it seems imperative. Like their predecessor,
Astrophil, seeking to define and fulfil desire, Shakespearean lovers
become, in the first instance, poets.[5] *As You Like It* shows Orlando
hanging verses on trees, while Phoebe writes to Ganymede in rhyme,
and also cites Marlowe (4.3.40–63; 3.5.81–2); Armado in love prepares
to 'turn sonnet' (*Love's Labour's Lost*, 1.2.175–6; 4.1.87–92), and the four
lords compose lyric poems, invoking Petrarch and Ovid; even Bottom
plans to ask Peter Quince to write a ballad about his night with the
Queen of the Fairies;[6] Falstaff ends his love letter in verse; and poor
Slender, who longs to be in love with Anne Page, wishes he had his
book of songs and sonnets (probably *Tottel's Miscellany*) with him.[7]

Romantic love is represented in lyric form, but in all these cases the
overflow of powerful feelings is to varying degrees borrowed from
another: in drawing on the poetic conventions of their culture, lovers
assume an alien identity, reproduce an already familiar rhetoric and
vocabulary, and put on display the inevitable citationality of desire.[8]
Slender, who is not in love, but feels he ought to be, seeks confirmation in the words of others; Bottom will get someone else to write what
he feels. But the intertextual dependency of all love poems ensures
that these are only extreme versions of a process of naming by reference to existing instances. Love made present to the lover is thus in
more than one sense a *re*presentation; the declaration of love is a form
of impersonation, derivative. As Touchstone insists, comparing himself to Ovid, 'the truest poetry is the most faining/feigning' (*As You*

Like It, 3.3.5–6, 16). The Folio text effaces the aural pun, available to a theatre audience, on 'feigning', but the same play on words also appears in Egeus's accusation against Lysander: 'Thou hast by moonlight at her window sung / With faining voice verses of feigning love' (*A Midsummer Night's Dream*, 1.1.30–31).[9] In Touchstone's account the most real, the most valuable poetry is truest because most desiring (faining), longing, most truly felt; it is truest as poetry because most imaginative (feigning), inventive; and also, paradoxically, truest to the nature of love because most dependent on the fiction (feigning) that the lover *is* or is like Ovid, Petrarch, Marlowe or the poets of *Tottel's Miscellany*.

Shakespeare's comedies defer consummation by representing this *re*presentational character of romance, specifying the citationality and the impersonation which characterize its display. Love, experienced as unique and personal, is shown to be at the same time a matter of convention, offering the audience the dual pleasure of recognition and distance. Here is Dumaine, who has promised to eschew the company of women for three years of unremitting study, in love none the less with Katherine:

> On a day – alack the day! –
> Love, whose month is ever May,
> Spied a blossom passing fair
> Playing in the wanton air.
> Through the velvet leaves the wind,
> All unseen, can passage find;
> That the lover, sick to death,
> Wished himself the heaven's breath.
> 'Air,' quoth he, 'thy cheeks may blow;
> Air, would I might triumph so!
> But, alack, my hand is sworn
> Ne'er to pluck thee from thy thorn.
> Vow, alack, for youth unmeet,
> Youth so apt to pluck a sweet.
> Do not call it sin in me,
> That I am forsworn for thee;
> Thou for whom Jove would swear
> Juno but a Ethiop were,
> And deny himself for Jove,
> Turning mortal for thy love.
> *Love's Labour's Lost* (4.3.98–117)

The medieval lyric tradition is cited in the analogy between the lady
and the flower of spring; Elizabethan convention is accountable for
the conceit, which momentarily evokes the lover, somewhat oddly, as
a zephyr with puffed cheeks and pursed lips; Ovid is recalled in the
allusion to Jupiter's metamorphosis; and the poem reproduces the conventional repudiation of dark skin in an epoch when fair is
beautiful.[10] Dumaine's pastoral poem is, in other words, both representative and mannered. But could it be otherwise? At the end of the
play, Berowne, on behalf of the four young men, renounces the rhetoric of courtship, 'speeches penn'd', wooing in rhyme, 'spruce affection/
affectation',[11] in favour of 'russet yeas and honest kersey noes' (5.2.402–
13). But as G. K. Hunter has brilliantly argued in an essay on 'Poem
and Context in *Love's Labour's Lost*', the play does not unequivocally
endorse this affirmation of the plain style. On the contrary, affection
and affectation share a root and a meaning in the period. 'What the
play asks', Hunter continues, 'is whether one can ever *profess* such
affection without moving towards affectation.'[12]

The love poems of Dumaine, Longaville and Berowne all reappeared
as miscellany pieces in *The Passionate Pilgrim*, an anthology of poems
by various authors printed by William Jaggard in 1599, four or five
years after the first performance of the play, and Dumaine's was printed
again in *England's Helicon* (1600). As Hunter points out, while this constitutes evidence that they were capable of standing alone as love
poems, it also encourages comparison between the effects of their different contexts. Read as numbered contributions to a collection of lyrics,
the poems are conventional declarations of love, whether real or fictional; in the play these same declarations are read out, overheard,
derided, condemned as inadequate, and thus made to seem parodic,
absurd. But they are not, Hunter argues, dismissed in consequence as
mere comedy: 'The energy of the poem does not simply drain away
into the context of the play; it remains obvious enough to challenge
us, as it were, to remember its anthology potential.'[13] Circumscribed
by Berowne's mockery, Dumaine's poem nevertheless retains the lyric
quality of a profession of forbidden love which longs for the innocence of nature. The figure of the unseen passage through velvet points
to love's sensual project, while the comparison with Jove invests desire with divinity and with the archetypal character of mythology.

Moreover, Dumaine's next speech immediately draws attention to
the artifice of the poem, and the difference feigning necessarily imposes between faining and its representation: 'This will I send, and

something else more plain, / That shall express my true love's fasting pain' (4.3.118–19). The plainer 'something else' is not specified, but in Berowne's later version, the plain style is simply less articulate, not more expressive: 'wench, so God help me, law! / My love to thee is sound, *sans* crack or flaw' (and even then Rosaline objects to '*sans*') (5.2.414–16). Romantic love, which cannot show itself except as representation, at the same time necessarily exceeds whatever representation is designed to make it evident. Dumaine will send his poem, and a supplementary demonstration that the poem is more than feigning. But what will supplement the supplement? Love as art is no less love; how else can it make itself apparent?

If the recognition of his poem's inadequacy paradoxically reaffirms Dumaine's sincerity, it also underlines the citationality of *that* idea. Longaville has already prefaced his own recitation by a similar reservation:

> I fear these stubborn lines lack power to move.
> O sweet Maria, empress of my love,
> These numbers will I tear and write in prose.
> *Love's Labour's Lost* (4.3.52–4)

Berowne's apology, meanwhile, is built into the text of his poem: 'O, pardon love this wrong, / That sings heaven's praise, with such an earthly tongue' (4.2.117–18). In a sense, hearing the four poems declaimed in relatively rapid succession does, after all, offer the audience access to a kind of oral 'anthology', invites them to 'mark how love can vary wit' (4.3.97), with all the repetitiveness, as well as the variety, that that implies.

Self-criticism imposes a distance between Longaville and Dumaine as lovers, on the one hand, and as authors of their own love poems, on the other. Their poems, they complain, conventionally enough, are precisely not 'expressive'. No stage direction indicates how the poems might have been pronounced. With conviction? or with the kind of hesitation that would emphasize the element of self-doubt? or perhaps both in succession? In any case, these poet-lovers evidently find themselves to a degree outside the representation which is the best attempt they can make to put their inner state on display. The lover who features in his own love poem is not, it appears, wholly synonymous with the lover who loves and reads out the verses.

The circulation, publication or, indeed, performance of a love lyric paradoxically makes public what is understood to be a private meditation. The audience is there as the addressee of the process of representation, but only in the same way that the spectators are understood to be in attendance at a classic realist play, invisible and silent, beyond the awareness of the fictional characters. We have the illusion that we are made privy to the intimate reflections of solitude. *Love's Labour's Lost* shatters this illusion, and thus parodies the genre, by making its fictional audience invisible and inaudible only to the poets themselves. The attention of the *play's* audience is thus divided between the love lyrics and Berowne's derision, romance on the one hand and scepticism on the other:

> All hid, all hid, an old infant play.
> Like a demi-god here sit I in the sky,
> And wretched fools' secrets heedfully o'er-eye.
> More sacks to the mill. O heavens, I have my wish!
> Dumaine transformed! four woodcocks in a dish!
>
> (4.3.75–9)

That Dumaine's imagined secrets are about to be exposed to ridicule frames his poem in advance with irony, and brings out the speciousness of its invocation of Jove as a moral example. How could Jupiter, as a notorious and compulsive traitor to his marriage vows, successively denying his own identity to pursue the objects of his desire, constitute a precedent that would justify Dumaine's abandonment of his own vow of celibacy? At the same time, however, Berowne's jubilation at Dumaine's arrival with yet another piece of paper is ambiguously motivated: the 'wish' that is so gratifyingly realized is not only to triumph over his friend's absurdity but also, just like the King's (4.3.46) and Dumaine's own (4.3.120–21), to find a further companion in love, betrayal and folly: he himself is one, after all, of the four woodcocks caught and cooked.

Derision and sympathy are entwined here. To dismiss Dumaine as ludicrous is also, by implication, to dismiss Berowne, and this is rendered the more difficult by the fact that Berowne has anticipated any judgement the audience might be tempted to make in his self-ridicule for his own submission to the power and absurdity of love:

> This wimpled, whining, purblind, wayward boy,
> This Signor Junior, giant-dwarf, Dan Cupid,
> Regent of love-rhymes, lord of folded arms,
> Th'anointed sovereign of sighs and groans.
>
> (3.1.174–7)

Berowne has already disarmed the audience by judging the folly of love and its representation, and by acknowledging at the same time how little influence that judgement has on desire:

> Well, set thee down, sorrow, for so they say the fool said, and so say I, and I the fool ... I will not love; if I do, hang me! I'faith, I will not. O, but her eye! By this light, but for her eye, I would not love her – yes, for her two eyes. Well, I do nothing in the world but lie, and lie in my throat. By heaven, I do love, and it hath taught me to rhyme.
>
> (4.3.3–12)

Berowne's is the only poem that seriously miscarries; Berowne's is the only poem that is read out by another, the singularly unromantic curate, Nathaniel. By this means the play seems to treat Berowne's love most ironically. But then Berowne's poem alone is criticized by a figure whose judgement elicits no confidence whatever, the pedant, Holofernes. Does this, paradoxically, invite the audience to sympathise with Berowne? Possibly, except that it is also Holofernes who rightly specifies the derivativeness and the corresponding banality of Berowne's perfectly exemplary love poem: '*Imitari* is nothing. So doth the hound his master, the ape his keeper, the tired horse his rider' (4.2.125–7).

Laughter and sympathy pursue one another in rapid succession, each without erasing the trace of the other. The placing of the poems, in other words, changes the signifying possibilities of the text, but does not determine them; here context opens alternative options and closes none. And meanwhile, context itself is polysemous in its turn, requiring interpretation. In *Love's Labour's Lost* the settings of the poems ripple outwards, multiplying the ways an audience might understand the nature of the love the play depicts. Romantic love is shown as intimate, unique, familiar, impersonal, banal, absurd and engaging all at once. In this way the play teases and tantalizes, offering its audience an experience that in some ways resembles the pleasure of seduction itself. Shakespeare's new genre of romantic comedy postpones consummation by deferring the finitude of definition.

III

Orlando, we are to understand, festoons the Forest of Arden with love poems:

> From the east to western Inde,
> No jewel is like Rosalind.
> Her worth being mounted on the wind,
> Through all the world bears Rosalind.
> *As You Like It* (3.2.86–9)

Shakespearean comedy does not repeat itself. This play's subjection of love poems to ridicule is much more condensed, their romantic idealization immediately parodied by Touchstone:

> If a hart do lack a hind,
> Let him seek out Rosalind.
> If the cat will after kind,
> So be sure will Rosalind.
> (3.2.99–102)

The witty fool, whose materialism so delights Jaques (3.3.28), reduces love to mating by eliminating the romantic courtship that distinguishes human behaviour from the animals'. His own object of desire is not, it will turn out, 'poetical' (3.3.9–23). Jaques, too, watching the lovers assemble for the final scene, insists on the animal implications of marriage: 'There is sure another flood toward, and these couples are coming to the ark. Here comes a pair of very strange beasts . . . .' (5.4.35–7). But however the scepticism of Touchstone and Jaques might delight some recent sociobiologists, it is not widely shared in the early modern period.

Most editions printed in the 1570s of the popular 'Bishops'' Bible place at the head of the Book of Genesis a woodcut depicting the moment, recorded in Chapter 2, verses 19–20, when Adam named the animals (Figure 1). Sometimes, the image is inset into a pictorial narrative showing key moments from the stories Genesis tells; sometimes,

Figure 1   Adam naming the animals, 'Bishops'' Bible, 1578

the naming scene stands alone. An elaborate decorative border encloses
the first man, sitting with his back against a tree. His left hand is raised,
as if he is telling off the names of the beasts, who go contentedly about
their business before him. The sun, moon and stars shine at once above
them all, and at the top centre, the Tetragrammaton, the four letters of
the name of God in Hebrew, authorizes the proceedings from behind
the veil of a cloud. God is represented by the Divine Name, since the
Reformation did not allow the deity to be shown as a person. Adam
shares a grassy bank with a squirrel in the tree above him, as well as a
monkey, a frog and a lion. The plain beyond is occupied by a range of
animals, some of them, like the elephant and the camel, familiar only
from other representations, and some, like the mountain goat and the
heron, rare enough, especially to the London readership which must
have constituted the first market for an illustrated Bible. The woodcut
thus offers the spectator the chance to repeat Adam's own activity by

identifying the animals portrayed. The newly created world includes a selection of natural features, and further in the background, the sea reveals the heads and tails of fishes.

In the woodcut Adam's difference draws attention to his isolation: his size distinguishes him from the other creatures, and his nakedness makes him appear more vulnerable. He is very much alone. Some of the animals are in pairs: there are two swans, legendary for their life-long fidelity to one another, two sheep, and one horse bounding after another, for all the world like the courser and the jennet in Shakespeare's *Venus and Adonis*. Most of the beasts are shown as grazing or drinking from the stream, apparently oblivious of the man who watches them. Before the Fall a human being is no threat to them, of course, but they are also indifferent to his presence. Adam's naming arm reaches into the visual space of the plain, as if in the hope of touching a fellow-creature. His gaze, if we didn't perceive it as knowing, might equally be wistful: there is no fit companion for him here.

God's newly created world is not, it appears, altogether perfect, after all. In the translation given in the 'Bishops'' Bible,

> And the Lord God said, It is not good that the man should be alone: I will make him an help like unto him. And so out of the ground the Lord God had shaped every beast of the field, and every fowl of the air, and brought it unto man, that he might see how he would call it. For likewise as man himself named every living thing, even so was the name thereof. And the man gave names to all cattle and fowl of the air, and every beast of the field; but for man found he not an help like unto him.
>
> Genesis (2.18–20)[14]

The naming process authorizes the human being, investing Adam with knowledge and agency, but it also isolates him from the organic world and throws into relief the limitations of his solitude: 'It is not good that the man should be alone.' Reformation opinion varied on the reason why it was not good. Most evidently, Eve was necessary to generate the human race,[15] but her creation also promised mutual society, companionship,[16] 'a singular union of hearts and wills',[17] solace and rejoicing,[18] 'the conjunction of both their bodies and minds'.[19] As a suitable support for Adam, she would provide all the joys of marriage, including an early version of care in the community: 'Her help consisteth chiefly in three things: in bearing him children, the comforts of his life, and stays of his age, which he cannot have without her.'[20] Alone, Adam lacked the elementary pleasure of mating available to the animals, and more: the affection, warmth and succour that the family affords.

The story of the family begins at the very beginning, when God created the heavens and the earth, differentiating the formless chaos of the void to make darkness and light, evening and morning. His work in the following days was a process of separation – of the dry land from the waters, the sun from the firmament and from the moon and stars. Next, God filled the waters with swarms of living creatures, and made every species of bird to fly across the firmament and multiply their distinct kinds. The earth, too, was impelled to bring forth life, first the plants, and then the animals and creeping things in their variety. Finally, on the sixth day God created a man and a woman to have dominion over all this and blessed them. They were to multiply their own kind and fill the earth with their progeny. And at every stage of this creative labour, God saw that it was good.

The newly formed earth, we are to understand, was a place of plenitude. Out of darkness and depth, God summoned up difference as the basis of presence. This is what demonstrates his omnipotence: only a divine power, moving on the face of the waters, could separate and distinguish in order to produce life from the deep. Creativity evidently abhors a vacuum. On God's command, the firmament is filled with stars and birds, as well as the two great lights that mark the distinction between day and night; the waters come to teem with all kinds of fish and sea monsters, and the earth is populated with a diversity of creatures. Moreover, the plants provide sustenance for the animals and the human beings. No wonder that on the sixth day, when God saw all that he had made, 'behold, it was exceeding good' (Genesis, 1.31).

The second chapter of Genesis, however, records an alternative (and earlier) version of the myth. In this account the sequence of Creation is different, and one thing is not good. Before there could be plants and herbs, God needed someone to till the soil, so he made man in the dust and breathed life into his nostrils. Then he put the man in a garden in Eden, full of trees that were both beautiful and nourishing, to cultivate the plants and to live on the fruit of all but one. Reflecting on the situation, however, 'the Lord God said, It is not good that the man should be alone: I will make him an help like unto him.' It was at this stage that God made the animals out of the ground, and Adam named them, 'but for man found he not an help like unto him.' At the heart of

God's Creation, in this version of the story, resides not plenitude but a lack. It is not good for Adam to be alone, but the animals are not fit company for him, not meet to provide the right kind of help, not *like* him. In consequence, imperfection inhabits God's perfect world. As Henoch Clapham explained in his summary of the story for children, published in Edinburgh in 1596,

> Having created man, Elohim bringeth all inferior creatures before him to see how he will call them: who in the depth of his understanding mind willeth and uttereth such names as the Lord approved. But every living thing having his yoke-fellow, man was alone and therefore imperfect.[21]

The Creation itself is a process of differentiation, but to name is also to differentiate. Adam, invited by God to name the animals, repeats that element of the Creator's work by distinguishing between species, but in the process, he also encounters his own difference and the sense of incompleteness that is the cause of desire. He identifies the animals authoritatively to the degree that he gives them such names as God approves, (re)producing an authorized vocabulary. Submitting in this way to the symbolic Law, Adam becomes an organism-in-culture; made in God's image on the one hand, and sharing with his fellow creatures an impulse to mate on the other, dissatisfied with the limited prospect of the beasts' society, he seeks the kind of companionship that will make him whole. Neither self-sufficient nor capable of fulfilment in God's newly created world, Adam is at odds with the plenitude that surrounds him. When God makes a human being, difference – the condition of identity – enters into identity itself and generates a want that is an effect of the human repetition of God's own differential work.

In *Paradise Lost*, when Milton's Adam learns that Eve has eaten the forbidden fruit, he instantly recognizes the magnitude of the crime and its fatal consequences. Nevertheless, he knowingly chooses to share the death she has incurred, rather than return to the loneliness he remembers from before her creation:

> How can I live without thee, how forgo
> Thy sweet converse and love so dearly joined,
> To live again in these wild woods forlorn?
> *Paradise Lost* (9. 908–10)[22]

As an adjective, 'forlorn' characterizes the woods which, without Eve, would be abandoned, cheerless, desolate. But the inclusion of 'again' may be taken to indicate that in their figurative dejection, the woods would offer no more comfort than before, when Adam had previously lived there without 'converse and love'. Moreover, 'forlorn' can also be read as an adverb qualifying the verb: 'To live ... forlorn'. Deserted by Eve, Adam would live alone and utterly lost – again.

In Book 8 Adam recounts to Raphael, in the first person, what he remembers of his own creation. Waking, as it seems, from sleep, he rejoiced in the creatures, his body and his power to speak. God delivered the prohibition on the fruit of the tree of knowledge, but declared that he gave the whole earth to Adam and his race. As a sign that he possessed all things, Adam recalls, God brought him the animals to be named. They came in twos, and yet, he tells the angel, 'in these / I found not what me thought I wanted still' (8.354–5). This is the first mention of wanting. He turned to God to explain:

> Thou hast provided all things: but with me
> I see not who partakes. In solitude
> What happiness, who can enjoy alone,
> Or all enjoying, what contentment find?
>
> (8.363–6)

It was hardly solitude, God insisted, with all these living creatures for company. But Adam was not persuaded. Deferentially but decisively, he went on to make his case. The other creatures were inferior, he argued, and there could be no true society between unequals (as the God who had endorsed the English Revolution must have known). What was at stake, Adam explained with proper respect, was more than the pleasures the animals shared with each other:

> ... of fellowship I speak
> Such as I seek, fit to participate
> All rational delight, wherein the brute
> Cannot be human consort; they rejoice
> Each with their kind, lion with lioness;
> So fitly them in pairs thou hast combined;
> Much less can bird with beast, or fish with fowl
> So well converse ...
>
> (8.389–96)

God was not, Adam recalls, entirely displeased by this reply, and congratulated him on his discernment:

> A nice and subtle happiness I see
> Thou to thy self proposest, in the choice
> Of thy associates, Adam, and wilt taste
> No pleasure, though in pleasure, solitary.
>
> (8.399–402)

Milton's God, it turns out, was just testing. He had known all along about the lack which would leave Adam wanting and had planned the remedy. He would now present Adam with an altogether different kind of creature:

> What next I bring shall please thee, be assured,
> Thy likeness, thy fit help, thy other self,
> Thy wish exactly to thy heart's desire.
>
> (8.449–51)

And yet the problem remains of the imperfection at the heart of the divine Creation. On his own, Adam is defective. God has put the case that he too is alone, since as God he can have no equal, but Adam's counter-argument depends on his own deficiency:

> Thou in thy self art perfect, and in thee
> Is no deficience found; not so is man,
> But in degree, the cause of his desire
> By conversation with his like to help,
> Or solace his defects.
>
> (8.415-19)

The problem of Adam's deficiency had troubled several generations of clerics eager to explain to the laity why the Reformation attributed such a high value to married love. Medieval romance had tended to locate sexual desire outside marriage: as C. S. Lewis knew, the classic love stories of the middle ages were extramarital. Meanwhile, the Catholic Church reluctantly included desire within marriage, conceding that it was better to marry than to burn. The project of the Reformers, however, was to extol desire as divinely endorsed, and marriage as the gift of God to further his Creation. Desire, of course, is predicated on lack: we want what we don't have. And the Bible indicated that there must have been a lack in Paradise before the Fall, a want which the creation of Eve would supply. According to John Wing, who in 1620 published two sermons on the happiness of Christian matrimony under the title *The Crown Conjugal*, Adam had perfection, but he still wanted one thing. He was immortal, the image of God, sovereign over all creatures in a Garden specially prepared for him.[23] 'In a word, he was every way so absolutely happy that unless a man had his perfections, it is scarce possible to make complete relation of his glorious condition.'[24] But amid all this, God said,

> One thing is yet wanting; what is everything, where this is not? Paradise and all the prerogatives royal of the earth are but one half (if so much) of man's temporal happiness; the best blessing is yet behind. Adam is alone: he hath not a mate, a woman, a wife, a female to himself.

His most wise Creator 'discerned this want'.[25]

It is hard to avoid the conclusion that there is a structural paradox here. Adam, Wing says, was absolutely happy. And yet his happiness was not absolute: on the contrary, it was incomplete. God made Adam, and he made him perfect, absolutely happy – and wanting. The process of legitimating desire by locating it in an unfallen world also threatens to display that world as initially insufficient. A similar paradox worried Thomas Gataker, who published two sermons on the theme of *A Good Wife Gods Gift* in the same year. Gataker's argument, too, grapples with the problem of the degrees of happiness available in God's perfect Creation:

> The woman was God's own gift to Adam; and she was God's gift bestowed on him to consummate and make up his happiness. Though he were at the first of himself happy, yet not so happy as he might be, until he had one to partake with him in his happiness.[26]

By now, however, Ester Sowernam had taken witty advantage of what seems a logical lapse to support, in her refutation of Joseph Swetnam's misogynist pamphlet of 1615, the case for the superiority of woman, as God's last and most excellent creature:

Yet Adam was not so absolutely perfect but that, in the sight of God, he wanted an helper. Whereupon God created the woman, his last work, as to supply and make absolute that imperfect building which was unperfected in man, as all divines do hold, till the happy creation of the woman. Now of what estimate that creature is and ought to be, which is the last work, upon whom the Almighty set up his last rest – whom he made to add perfection to the end of all creation – I leave rather to be acknowledged by others than resolved by myself.[27]

Henry Smith's earlier *Preparative to Mariage* (1591) is apparently untroubled by the logical difficulty, but this text produces an oddly deprived version of prelapsarian solitude in consequence:

> like a turtle which hath lost his mate, like one leg when the other is cut off, like one wing when the other is clipped, so had the man been, if the woman had not been joined to him: therefore for mutual society, God coupled two together.[28]

To be human is to be mutilated, wanting, and the remedy is coupling, reciprocal society, love in marriage. Married love is uniquely human and humanizing. In the encyclopaedic text that may well be regarded as the most popular poem of the early modern period, first published in an English translation by Josuah Sylvester in 1605 and reissued in five subsequent editions by 1630, Guillaume de Saluste du Bartas recounted the daily work of the Creation and went on to trace God's Providence in the story of the Old Testament as far as the Babylonian captivity. Du Bartas considerably amplified the biblical record, but very much in the spirit of the Reformers. The Sixth Day of the First Week celebrates the capabilities of the newly created human beings, made in the image of God: the soul, though imprisoned in flesh, can fly to the heavens and seek out knowledge; painting can frame another nature; we make machines to represent the stars in their courses. 'Oh complete creature!', the text exclaims. Thus we bear witness to our high descent.[29] And yet this same complete creature is, it will shortly appear, inadequate without the woman God made from his rib. Like Henry Smith and, indeed, like Calvin, Sylvester's du Bartas treats the solitary Adam as defective, and his descendants ('here') as no more than semi-human:

> You that have seen within this ample table,
> Among so many models admirable,
> Th'admired beauties of the king of creatures,
> Come, come and see the woman's rapting features:
> Without whom, here, man were but half a man,
> But a wild wolf, but a barbarian,
> Brute, rageful, fierce, moody, melancholic,
> Hating the light; whom nought but naught could like;
> Born solely for himself, bereft of sense,
> Of heart, of love, of life, of excellence.
> God, therefore, not to seem less liberal
> To man, than else to every animal,
> For perfect pattern of a holy love,
> To Adam's half another half he gave,
> Taen from his side, to bind through every age
> With kinder bonds the sacred marriage.[30]

The divine gift of human love makes Adam whole, and wholly human; it transforms his successors into complete men, civilizes them, cures their brutish, bad-tempered selfishness, and releases their capacity for excellence. Paradoxically, by giving to the man the mate every animal already has, God liberates him from subjection to his animal nature and makes him fit for specifically human society.

From 1608 onwards, editions of Sylvester's du Bartas included, as the frontispiece to *The Second Week*, the woodcut of Adam naming the animals that had appeared in the 'Bishops'' Bible in the 1570s (Figure 1, p. 37), though without the frame of stories from Genesis. Evidently that depiction of Adam's difference, with the authority-and-wistfulness that it seems to indicate, appeared to correspond with du Bartas's account of the human condition. To be human is to be subject to desire, but it is also, and by the same token, to be uniquely capable of holy love and the civility it inculcates. This is not in the early modern texts a question of the redeeming influence of a good woman, a Victorian Agnes or Dorothea: du Bartas is at least as misogynistic as most of his contemporaries.[31] Nor is the love at issue purely a matter of minds, spiritual: Eve, made out of Adam's rib, is explicitly reunited with his flesh and bone in marriage. It is by acknowledging Adam's physiological kinship with the beasts that the text affirms a mysterious transcendence which is the God-given source of a new completeness:

> No sooner Adam's ravished eyes did glance
> On the rare beauties of his new-come half,
> But in his heart he gan to leap and laugh,
> Kissing her kindly, calling her his life,
> His love, his stay, his rest, his weal, his wife,
> His other self, his help him to refresh,
> Bone of his bone, flesh of his very flesh.
> Source of all joys! sweet he-she-coupled-one,
> Thy sacred birth I never think upon,
> But, ravished, I admire how God did then
> Make two of one, and one of two again.[32]

Married love is the basis of civil society. It is the main reason, Luther affirms, why men choose to live in fixed habitations, tilling the soil and bringing up children.[33] After the Fall, Adam and Eve cultivate in exile the arts of living, sharing the disciplined practices of God-fearing partners and parents, and teaching their children by precept and by example.[34] In a sermon on Genesis 2.18, John Donne indicated that out of the apparent defect in the Creation, God created the social world, since

> both of civil and of spiritual societies, the first root is a family; and of families, the first root is marriage; and of marriage, the first root that grows out into words is in this text: 'And the Lord God said, It is not good', etc.[35]

IV

Solitude is not good. In the early modern period the family becomes 'the fountain and seminary of all sorts and kinds of life, in the commonwealth and in the church',[36] and not only for the children, who internalize at their mother's knee the norms and values of their culture. Romantic love and the process of courtship also integrate the young, and young men in particular, into their society, teaching them to reproduce, with whatever extravagance, the conventions of civility. From Ovid onwards, love is an art, to be acquired in the Renaissance by practising the arts. The lover, emerging from boyhood to sigh 'like furnace, with a woeful ballad / Made to his mistress' eyebrow' (*As You Like It*, 2.7.148–9) learns to perform an identity which takes its place in a sequence leading on to full participation in the commonwealth, first as a soldier and then as a magistrate (149–57). Love recruits good subjects.

The melancholy Jaques, by contrast, who records this process in the speech on the seven ages which has become so dear to anthologists, himself prefers to castigate courtly manners from a place outside their constraints. Jaques opts throughout the play for solitude and in the end for monastic celibacy. In what is probably no more than a coincidence, the audience first hears of him lying under an oak tree and contemplating the animals, though rather than name them, he moralizes their behaviour (*As You Like It*, 2.1). 'Compact of jars' (2.7.5), imaginably capable of transformation into a beast (2.7.1), fascinated only by folly and absurdity, Jaques resembles a version, appropriately softened for inclusion in a romantic comedy, of the loveless, self-absorbed outsider du Bartas so graphically describes:

> But a wild wolf, but a barbarian,
> Brute, rageful, fierce, moody, melancholic,
> Hating the light; whom nought but naught could like;
> Born solely for himself.

The lovelorn Orlando, who engages in a series of comically uncivil exchanges with Jaques (3.2.249–89), is also to be found stretched under an oak tree (3.2.230–37). Orlando, however, is not railing, but practising the performance of civility, by composing love poems:

> Why should this desert be,
> For it is unpeopled? No.
> Tongues I'll hang on every tree,
> That shall civil sayings show.
>   (3.2.122–5)

There was, as Orlando complained in the opening scene of the play, room for improvement by the addition of nurture to an already gentle nature. At his first encounter with Rosalind, he is speechless, unable to thank her for the chain she gives him, and painfully aware of the inadequacy of his behaviour (1.2.239–48). In the forest Duke Senior reproaches him for demanding food with drawn sword:

> Art thou thus bolden'd man by thy distress?
> Or else a rude despiser of good manners,
> That in civility thou seem'st so empty?
>   (2.7.92–4)

(This time, however, Orlando affirms that he knows 'some nurture' (2.7.98).) These are, of course, very venial failures of courtesy and accountable to the circumstances, but they serve to sustain a theme established at the beginning of the play. In due course, Rosalind-as-Ganymede will train him in the proprieties of courtship,[37] most notably the importance of punctuality (4.1.36–50), so that the next time he is delayed he is careful to send a (bloodstained) message.

As well as an art, love is thus a discipline, which tames and domesticates the human animal: desire is co-opted by social regulation. Touchstone knows this: 'As the ox hath his bow sir, the horse his curb, and the falcon her bells, so man hath his desires, and as pigeons bill, so wedlock would be nibbling' (3.3.71–3). The remedy for desire is marriage, and marriage, divinely endorsed, is a social and civil institution, an alternative to barbarity, the seminary of good subjects. Is it possible, then, that in *Love's Labour's Lost*, where scatological word-play and innuendo repeatedly emphasize the human-being-as-organism,[38] when Berowne's companions ask him for a rationalization of their apostasy, the case he presents is more than simple sophistry? The lords have made, he argues, a vow to study, but 'leaden contemplation' could never have taught them to write the 'fiery' poems they have now produced. Love, he continues, drawing on another set of conventions, this time courtly and Neoplatonic, sharpens the senses, increases valour, refines oratory and intensifies poetic skill. It follows that women's eyes are the source of the true 'Promethean', or civilizing, fire:

> They are the books, the arts, the academes,
> That show, contain and nourish all the world;
> Else none at all in aught proves excellent.

Women's eyes, inspiring love, make the world more visible; they include but also, perhaps, circumscribe it; and they nourish it, both by stimulating propagation and by nurturing excellence. And so, Berowne urges, 'Let us once lose our oaths to find ourselves, / Or else we lose ourselves to keep our oaths' (*Love's Labour's Lost*, 4.3.285–339). Self-evidently, Berowne here offers the 'salve for perjury' that his friends have demanded (4.3.285), but if the argument he produces cheers them up, it does so on the basis of its plausibility. Moreover, to a degree it also vindicates its own position: Berowne, for all his wit, has never shown himself more fluent, more eloquent or more persuasive.

V

But while Berowne's speech is arguably neither wholly specious nor wholly serious, it is certainly and above all playful, an exercise of wit designed to 'cheat the devil' (4.3.284). Love in the comedies is an art, and if it is also an education, it exerts its discipline by means of games and contests. Shakespearean lovers, in various forms of disguise, tease, tantalize and compete to outwit each other, usually, it has to be said, at the eventual expense of the men. Both men and women play at love, while fully understanding that the stakes are high. This sense of love as a game would largely disappear from the fully domesticated, fully moralized version of courtship familiar to us from Victorian fiction, as would the acknowledgement of romance as masquerade on which it depends. Early modern stage lovers perform an identity by citation, impersonation, theatricality itself, practising identifications by enacting their parts as other than they are in what is, or pretends to be, 'a pageant truly play'd / Between the pale complexion of true love / And the red glow of scorn and proud disdain' (*As You Like It*, 3.4.48–50).

Once Berowne has duly rationalized their perjury, the four young men promptly resolve to win the women with 'entertainment' (both hospitality and pastime) in the form of 'revels, dances, masques' (4.3.347, 353). Their first effort in this line involves impersonating Muscovites. Forewarned, however, the Princess and her ladies adopt vizards to tease them, so that the men pay court to the wrong women. Possibly, this is a variation on the confusions of identity already experienced in 2.1, where in the 1598 quarto version of the play, Berowne briefly pursues Katherine and Dumaine Rosaline by mistake. Finally, the men offer the Pageant of the Nine Worthies, in which others flatter the Princess on their behalf, while they mock the acting, rather than address the ladies. Romance is sustained by a succession of charades which defer direct interaction between the lovers.

A Midsummer Night's Dream (1595–96) integrates the impersonations, and the postponement they ensure, more closely into the plot of the play, as the lovers' identities are transformed by Puck's magic juice, while in Twelfth Night (?1601) Viola becomes Orsino's friend and trusted companion disguised as Cesario. The Merchant of Venice (1596–97) shows Portia and Nerissa in the guise of a young lawyer and his clerk, putting the fidelity of their new husbands to the test, and securing a tactical advantage in the process. But it is perhaps As You like It that most fully explores the seductive possibilities of masquerade. Orlando is captivated by Rosalind cross-dressed as Ganymede, and inhabiting the identity of a mischievous boy so convincingly that Celia reproaches her for betraying women (4.1.191–4). Rosalind's saucy lackey, the arch-seducer, Jove's own page,[39] displays a relentless scepticism about lovers, men, women, fidelity and marriage which challenges Orlando to ever greater idealization. And yet both the comedy and the romance depend on a certain undecidability about the identity of the speaker, as the woman-playing-the-knave is now cynical, now enticing, now reproachful, now encouraging. Evidently Ganymede, who has never been in love, and whose youthful impudence is his charm, is responsible for the affirmation that love stories are all lies, and that 'men have died from time to time and worms have eaten them, but not for love' (4.1.89–103). Is it Ganymede, however, or Celia's cousin, a teasing boy or a woman in love, who insists, 'I am your Rosalind' (4.1.62), and invites, 'Come, woo me, woo me' (4.1.65), or who exclaims, 'Alas, dear love, I cannot lack thee two hours' (4.1.169)? Sliding between different versions of the masquerade, different subject positions, distinct modes of address, Rosalind-Ganymede is 'changeable, longing and liking, proud, fantastical, apish, shallow, inconstant, full of tears, full of smiles' (3.2.398–400) to a degree that, far from curing Orlando, deepens his desire by so thoroughly keeping him guessing. And if the boy-actor playing a girl-protagonist impersonating a boy pretending to be a girl keeps the audience guessing too, the play offers to share with the spectator something of the pleasure of romantic seduction.

Lovers come to reproduce the conventions of their culture by learning to enact the identities it prescribes. We are what we are, twentieth-century psychoanalysis maintains, in response to the gaze of other people who have us in their sights, though what we are also exceeds their expectations. Awake, we play our assorted parts before the audience of the world, however much in dreams we resist our own capture by these roles. But romance introduces another dimension in the notion of identity as performance. Drawing on accounts of sexual display in animals, Jacques Lacan treats seduction as a kind of masked theatre, or a shadow-play against a screen which intervenes between us and the demanding gaze of the world. Dressed up, on show, on our best behaviour, performing, we become other than we are. How else can two organisms-in-culture construct between them a unique, idealizing relationship, which at the same time releases the strange impersonality of desire? 'It is no doubt through the mediation of masks that the masculine and the feminine meet in the most acute, most intense way.' But if that is the ultimate object of the exercise, are we simply animals after all? Lacan thinks not. Unlike the beasts, he urges, human beings are not entirely caught up in the display, not at the mercy of their own performance: on the contrary, always resisting the script we also follow, we know 'how to play with the mask as that beyond which there is the gaze'.[40] This game, this enactment or transformation, which knowingly cheats the coercive gaze of the everyday world, is the pleasure of romance. Feigning, like faining indeed, is uniquely human.

VI

The masquerade exhibits the playfulness, both sport and theatricality, contest and impersonation, that constitutes romance, and at the same time defers the moment of consummation that marks its closure. *Love's Labour's Lost* is sustained by masques and charades; the seduction of Orlando depends on the *fort/da* games of Rosalind-as-Ganymede. But all good things must come to an end and audiences have to be permitted to leave the theatre. How, then, is the deferred mating to be staged?

When Orlando 'can live no longer by thinking' (5.2.50), *As You Like It* solves the problem by personifying Hymen, who 'peoples every town' (5.4.142). The first recorded anatomical use of the term in 1615 is later than the play,[41] but in Greek mythology and, indeed, in Ben Jonson's *Hymenaei*, the god of marriage carries a torch and a veil, which very clearly point to his sexual meaning. Mating is staged as a masque, foregrounding both the question of representation in the theatre, and the theatricality of representation.

Love's Labour's Lost, meanwhile, concludes by postponing the moment yet again, in order to continue the civilizing process. As the Princess points out, young men so perjured cannot expect to elicit much confidence in yet another oath (5.2.784–8). Instead, she and her ladies will test the fidelity of their lovers for a year before consenting to marry them. In addition, love will curb the lords' linguistic exuberance: the derisive Berowne is to try his wit on the sick and dying, and if he cannot bring them to smile, he is to purge his mockery of its excess (5.2.829–57). Even Armado, the most rhetorically extravagant of them all, has undertaken to make himself socially useful for Jacquenetta: subdued by the child of our grandmother Eve, he will obey the work ethic for three years for her sake (5.2.871–2). By these means the men will prove themselves fit to be husbands. Appropriately chastened, disciplined by the imperatives of courtship to perform yet another identity, brought into line, they have no choice but to submit to the prescriptions of their society, to become in its terms good subjects.

Such was now the socializing virtue of marriage that some of the reformers believed it should be compulsory. Gervase Babington, Bishop of Llandaff and then Exeter, insisted that everyone – without exception – ought to marry, on the basis of God's pronouncement that it is not good for man to be alone.[42] Nicholas Gibbens, preacher of the Word of God, following Calvin, was inclined to be cautious: celibacy is right for some, though marriage is certainly honourable for all.[43] The matter was the more eagerly contested because Genesis 2.18 was so readily appropriated as a stick to beat the Catholic clerical and monastic ideal. Babington advanced his argument, he claimed, against all heretics, popes or papists whatsoever.[44] In Andrew Willet's version in 1605,

> we enforce this text against the popish forced virginity: for whereas God saw it was not good neither for Adam, then present, nor for his posterity, which should have more need of the remedy, to be alone, they contrariwise constrain their priests and votaries to live alone, depriving them of that mutual help and society which God hath appointed for their comfort, and to be a remedy against sin.[45]

Luther, who had himself once been a monk, of course, and then married, became increasingly vehement on the question. In a plea which might be taken to anticipate *Love's Labour's Lost*, he urged his readers not to fool themselves about their capacity for celibacy, 'even if you should make ten oaths, vows, covenants, and adamantine or ironclad pledges'. Moreover, he went on, 'should you make such a promise, it … would be foolishness and of no avail …. No vow of any youth or maiden is valid before God.'[46]

But the same Reformers who insisted on marriage were not always by any means utopian about the actual experience of conjugal life in a fallen world. What, in its turn, does marriage itself teach? Its most enthusiastic defenders not uncommonly conceded that it was above all the misery of the married state that would prove so educational, inculcating stoicism in unhappy circumstances: 'wedlock is unto the Christians as a school wherein they are godly instructed that in tribulation and adversity they faint not, nor be discouraged.'[47] *As You Like It*, too, is at moments remarkably cynical about the joys of the condition it equates with a happy ending, seeming almost preoccupied by the likelihood of unfaithfulness.[48] And the first marriage, divinely ordained precedent in Paradise for all human marriages, led directly to Eve's betrayal, followed by the couple's joint exile and death.

There was, then, the possibility in the period of a less optimistic account of the plight of the human animal as an organism-in-culture, made in God's image, but sharing the nature of the beasts. In this alternative version, while to be human is to be subject to desire, the remedy for desire may be at least as painful as the condition. It was Lyly in *Loves Metamorphosis* (1580s), perhaps the most sceptical of his romantic comedies, who offered the sharpest formulation of this alternative account of the divided human predicament. When Silvestris, who is in love, maintains nevertheless that he can see no spark of divinity in the condition, and no good reason to pursue it with such intensity, his friend Ramis replies:

> We have bodies, Silvestris, and human bodies, which in their own natures being much more wretched than beasts', do much more miserably than beasts pursue their own ruins. And since it will ask longer labour and study to subdue the powers of our blood to the rule of the soul than to satisfy them with the fruition of our loves, let us be constant in the world's errors and seek our own torments.[49]

To be neither a beast nor a god is to confront perpetual division, which love cannot allay. Here desire's gratification seems to be synonymous with suffering, and the object the lovers seek produces not wholeness but ruin. To a degree the play confirms this account. While the plot shows love as arbitrary and unstable, the happy ending attaches such reservations to its four marriages that there is no sense of reciprocity, but only a grudging submission on the part of the nymphs and an acknowledgement of the conditional character of love by their forester husbands.

Early modern culture, which embraced love as a humanizing force, marriage as the divinely endorsed remedy for desire and the family as the source of civil society, also recognized passion, even in its socially approved form, as all too human, and potentially dangerous and destructive. That ambivalence is the theme of the rest of this book.

Chapter Three
Marriage: Imogen's Bedchamber

I

ne taper burns in the bedchamber. It is almost midnight, the audience is invited to believe. Imogen puts down her book and, dismissing her servant, commends herself to the protection of the gods. In a silence broken only by the song of the crickets, an intruder raises the lid of a trunk. As Iachimo creeps towards the sleeping woman, he speaks of rape, invoking the notorious tale of a faithful wife violated in her bed by her Roman guest:

> Our Tarquin thus
> Did softly press the rushes, ere he waken'd
> The chastity he wounded.
> *Cymbeline* (2.2.12–14)[1]

Imogen has been reading Ovid's *Metamorphoses*, he reveals, stopping at the point in the story where Philomel submits against her will to the rapist Tereus, her sister's husband (2.2.44–6). But Iachimo's purpose in approaching Imogen's bed is not rape. Busily, he makes notes on the furniture, the tapestries, the bed itself and then her body, including a mole on her left breast. Without waking her, he slips off her bracelet. As the clock strikes three, he climbs back into the trunk and closes the lid.

The plot of *Cymbeline* (1610–11) turns on marital jealousy. For the sake of a bet, Iachimo persuades the exiled Posthumus that his wife is unfaithful to him in his absence. And he does it by spending the night concealed in Imogen's bedchamber, ready to offer Posthumus a lubricious account of his exploits, which sets out to convince by means of its circumstantial detail. Iachimo's process of persuasion occupies about 90 lines of text (*Cymbeline*, 2.4.40–129). Although Posthumus puts up an initial resistance, it seems remarkably easy to induce him to believe the worst of his innocent and devoted wife. Why?

The evidence which convicts Imogen of infidelity in the eyes of her husband begins with the description of her bedchamber. Iachimo's account of the furnishings is surprisingly specific in a play which elsewhere depends on a broad generic distinction between court and countryside, punctuated by brief excursions into an equally stereotypical Machiavellian Italy. The specificity of the inventory helps, of course, to render the credulity of Posthumus intelligible to the audience, but its effect in the play goes beyond a proto-novelistic *vraisemblance*. These decorations also signify. The bedchamber of the newly married Imogen is, appropriately, a setting for love, as the andirons indicate: they are silver Cupids leaning on their torches (*Cymbeline*, 2.4.88–91). But it is also a place where the dual meaning of the feminine in the period is put on display, as modesty on the one hand and sexual invitation on the other. The chimney piece, Iachimo claims and Posthumus confirms, shows 'Chaste Dian, bathing' (2.4.82), and if the Ovidian allusion hints at the fate of the watching Actaeon, turned to a stag and torn to pieces by his own hounds, as the proper punishment of Iachimo, another secret voyeur of feminine chastity, the primary association of Diana for the audience is surely with Imogen herself, who chastely resists the adulterous overtures of her Roman visitor. Meanwhile, the hangings depict Cleopatra's first encounter with Antony, a scene whose erotic intensity was already familiar from Sir Thomas North's Plutarch and Shakespeare's own play, probably first performed only a year or two earlier than *Cymbeline* itself. Cleopatra represents the exact antithesis of Diana: she is seductive, passionate, sexually knowing, adulterous – and consequently dangerous to men in a different way.

Though the text of *Cymbeline* repeatedly invokes the parallel between Imogen and Diana (2.4.159–60; 5.5.180–81), the design of Iachimo's description is evidently that Posthumus should infer an analogy between his wife and the Egyptian Queen greeting *her* Italian guest on the tumescent river. The chamber, he reports,

> ... was hang'd
> With tapestry of silk and silver, the story
> Proud Cleopatra, when she met her Roman,
> And Cydnus swell'd above the banks, or for
> The press of boats, or pride.
>
> *Cymbeline* (2.4.68–72)

Iachimo's strategy is not immediately successful, of course. These furnishings are widely spoken of, Posthumus insists. But when Iachimo produces her bracelet and describes the mole on Imogen's breast, Posthumus is ready to denounce his wife as a whore (2.4.128).

Posthumus believes himself betrayed by his faithful wife. Meanwhile, ironically, Cymbeline in his turn is captivated and ensnared by a wife who seems honest and proves false. The Queen, she finally reveals, has never loved him; but in the mean time she has endangered his relationships with his daughter, his court and his kingdom. Her mode of deception, in Cymbeline's account, is, of course, characteristically feminine and erotic:

> Mine eyes
> Were not in fault, for she was beautiful:
> Mine ears, that heard her flattery, nor my heart
> That thought her like her seeming.
>
> (5.5.62–5)

While Cymbeline too easily takes his wife's sexuality for virtue, Posthumus surprisingly readily interprets *his* wife's chastity as lasciviousness. 'Who is't', Cymbeline helplessly wonders, 'can read a woman?' (5.5.48), and in one sense his question might stand as an epigraph for the whole text. Two feminine stereotypes are invoked, both by the furnishings of Imogen's bedchamber and in the plot of the play. The difficulty for the male protagonists is to distinguish one from the other.

If Cymbeline is deluded by beauty, however, Posthumus is convinced of Imogen's infidelity by words. Iachimo tells two lies: that Imogen gave him the bracelet and that he kissed the mole. The remainder of the seduction process depends largely on equivocation, the exploitation of an excess of meaning which leaves open the possibility of more than one reading. Iachimo did not sleep in Imogen's bedchamber, he

maintains, but instead he 'Had that was well worth watching' (2.4.68).
For the audience, as witnesses to his purely voyeuristic relish of Imogen's beauty, the line can be said to lay claim to no more than the strict
truth. At the same time, however, the assertion also invites Posthumus
to draw the inference that Iachimo has taken possession of a woman
who made staying awake well worth his while. A descendant of the
morality Vice, Shakespeare's villain easily moralizes two meanings in
one word, and in the process enlists his victim in the active production
of his own deception. In a similar way, meaning both affirms and contradictorily exceeds what we know to be the case when Iachimo urges:

> Had I not brought
> The knowledge of your mistress home, I grant
> We were to question farther; but I now
> Profess myself the winner of her honour,
> Together with your ring; and not the wronger
> Of her or you, having proceeded but
> By both your wills.
>
> (2.4.50–56)

Here too equivocation makes possible two contrary readings: the information Iachimo brings back can also be read as carnal knowledge;
in saying that he professes himself the winner, he strictly lays claim to
no more than a simple performative, though he also seems to affirm
Imogen's infidelity; and it is surely true that he has wronged neither
Imogen nor Posthumus in the sexual sense of the word, although in
saying so he surely invites Posthumus to believe exactly the opposite.

At the moment when Iachimo tells the strict truth, his words become most evidently dangerous. 'By Jupiter', he insists of the bracelet,
'I had it from her arm' (2.4.121). Posthumus instantly construes this as
proof of betrayal:

> Hark you, he swears: by Jupiter he swears.
> 'Tis true, nay keep the ring, 'tis true: I am sure
> She would not lose it: her attendants are
> All sworn, and honourable: – they induc'd to steal it?
> And by a stranger? No, he hath enjoy'd her.
>
> (2.4.122–6)

Thereafter, he is deaf to rational doubt and gives instructions for Imogen's murder. Can Posthumus here properly be said to be reading or misreading? What is the *meaning* of Iachimo's words? Is it in the truth of the event or the intention to deceive, in the reference to the world or in the mind of the speaker? Or is it, conversely, in the duplicity of signifying practice, which would vindicate either reading, or both? And when Posthumus initially refuses to draw the obvious inference, is he *then* reading or misreading? Where is meaning to be found? Ultimately, the undecidability which permits equivocation resides in signifying practice itself, in the excess which allows and justifies contradictory constructions.

II

The play insists from the beginning on the honourable nature and virtuous disposition of Imogen's unjustly banished husband (1.1.40–55). This, we are to understand, is a marriage of true minds, based on long familiarity and the recognition of genuine worth (1.2.74–8). And yet, as in *Othello* (?1604) and *The Winter's Tale* (1609–10), conjugal love proves readily vulnerable to a wholly unsubstantiated fear of female infidelity.[2] Neither Othello himself nor Leontes, neither Posthumus nor Cymbeline, can reliably understand a woman. We may, if we wish, seek out explanations or excuses at the level of individual character. Critics of *Othello* have been exceptionally inventive here, but the case of Posthumus is more difficult. As for Leontes, his jealousy generally seems unmotivated either by events or by personal psychology.

An alternative possibility, however, is a precariousness in the early modern account of marriage, an instability in the cultural meaning of the institution itself, which might leave seventeenth-century audiences less mystified than we are by the incapacity of these husbands to read their wives with confidence. The documents of the period repeatedly compare the state of matrimony to life in the Garden of Eden: marriage based on true love is an earthly paradise, a glimpse in a fallen world of a happiness otherwise irretrievably lost. The comparison offers an ideal and idealizing account of the conjugal relation. At the same time, however, it brings with it an excess of meaning which calls into question the very ideal it proclaims.

When God gave Adam a wife meet for him, made out of his rib, and thus flesh of his flesh, bone of his bone, he ordained in the process the

institution which would legitimize sexual pleasure. God made marriage, and he made it innocent. In this context, it is perhaps mildly
surprising that *Cymbeline* so clearly locates true innocence elsewhere,
in the homosocial 'family' of Belarius and his two adoptive sons, who
keep house (or rather, cave, 3.3) so equably and so affectionately among
the pastoral landscapes of Wales. The details of their domestic economy
constitute evidence that hard primitivism is ethically superior to courtly
luxury.[3] In a similar way, *The Winter's Tale* invokes innocence, this time
as an explicitly theological category, and locates it in a homosocial,
pre-sexual childhood, when Polixenes and Leontes were 'as twinn'd
lambs that did frisk i' th' sun'. 'What we chang'd / Was innocence for
innocence: we knew not / The doctrine of ill-doing' (1.2.67–70).[4] There
follows a series of exchanges between Polixenes and Hermione in which
it is marriage that is characterized in terms of 'temptations', 'offences',
'sin' and 'fault' (75–86). This is courtly wit, of course, a sustained conceit, perhaps mildly scandalous, designed to induce Polixenes to stay,
and to give pleasure to the audience into the bargain. But the events of
the play will go on to confirm a parallel with the divine comedy, an
association between marriage and a radical error of judgement, followed by death, and in the end, a long-delayed redemption. The
exchange on marriage as a fall from innocence is the immediate prelude to the first unaccountable onset of intense sexual jealousy in
Leontes. If the clerical accounts of the first marriage turn out to be
shadowed by a knowledge of the short-lived character of the innocence they invoke, Shakespeare's plays, it seems, are still less optimistic
about the stability of the institution in a fallen world, repeatedly linking conjugal desire with danger and sorrow.

An elaborately carved and inlaid chest, currently in Warwick Castle, bears the following inscription:

> Izaak Walton Rachel Floud
> Joined Together in the Holy Bonds of Wedlock on the 27th Day of
> December AD 1626
> We once were two: we two made one;
> We, no more two, through life be one.

The central panel on the front of the chest depicts the earthly Paradise
(Figure 2). The garden is fruitful and prolific; the creatures Adam has
named are represented. But a large serpent uncoils from a branch above
Eve's head as she hands Adam an apple. Innocence is about to be

Figure 2   The Fall, marriage chest, 1626

surrendered: the serpent hangs menacingly over the couple, ready to teach them the nature of error and loss.

What are the implications of a relief, given a central place on a decorated marriage chest, showing the moment of the first temptation and Paradise in the process of being lost? Is the chest simply the work of a craftsman no longer permitted to display his skills in a church and impelled to reproduce his favourite scene wherever possible, even if the only option is a secular domestic setting? Or is the motive perhaps less arbitrary, an invocation of the official position on marriage as an honourable estate instituted of God in Paradise, but complicated by the iconographical tradition? Countless existing representations of the Garden of Eden gave prominence to man's first disobedience as a critical moment in Christian history. Was it perhaps too great a challenge to depict an identifiable Paradise, recognizable to the spectator, without allusion to the Fall?

Or, alternatively, is it possible that the early modern account of the conjugal relation in the culture at large is less naive, less utopian, than the official position might lead us to suppose? There were, after all, other ways of representing the relationship between Adam and Eve which might seem more obviously appropriate to a celebration of marriage. The creation of Eve from Adam's rib is common in both medieval and Renaissance iconography, and indeed is depicted in a woodcut placed immediately before the first chapter in the 1546 edition of the influential *Christian State of Matrimony* (Figure 3). While Adam sleeps, oblivious of God's intervention, the Creator summons the woman into his new-made world, where sun, moon and stars shine all at once. A sinless Eve looks up at her maker, her hands clasped in prayer. The process of Eve's birth showed her to be literally flesh of Adam's flesh, bone of his bone.[5] As another option, there is also a recognizable tradition of representations of the first marriage, performed by God himself.[6] In a mid-sixteenth-century French engraving of Adam and Eve by Jean Duvet, God wears the regalia of a bishop to join their hands in the presence of the heavenly host.[7] Naked and beautiful, the human figures stand out against the background of a densely populated heaven. Duvet was a Calvinist and his image reproduces, in visual form, Calvin's own account of the divine endorsement of conjugal love and companionate marriage.[8]

Figure 3   The Creation of Eve, 1546

The Ancient High House at Stafford, built in 1595 for John Dorrington, who was evidently a citizen of some substance, now contains an early modern four-poster bed with an elaborately carved wooden headboard. At the edges of the headboard are large and very nearly freestanding figures of Adam and Eve, while the panel between them depicts two symmetrically placed trees supervised by angels. Both trees are fruiting prolifically and exotically. On one side, the Tree of Life bears apples, pears and grapes simultaneously, and at the top is a pomegranate. But twined in the branches of the Tree of Knowledge on the other side is a strikingly large, scaly and venomous-looking serpent. This is not the conventional representation of the Fall derived from the iconographical tradition, and the eccentricity of the image makes it seem less likely that the bedhead is the work of a craftsman reproducing a familiar scene in an unfamiliar place, or a carving looking desperately for a location.

The Stafford Eve is, in her own way, a seductive figure (Figure 4). She is naked and, as in *Paradise Lost*, her long hair, uncovered and flowing, is a mark of female sexuality. Her left hand is lost: we cannot be sure what it might have been holding, though we can probably guess. The fig leaf indicates that she may be already fallen, though this is not a reliable indication of the Fall in the period. Adam is undoubtedly fallen, however: he has bitten into the apple he holds, and beside him are the spade and pickaxe with which he will from now on produce his own subsistence in the sweat of his brow. Beneath his feet is a skull, symbol of the mortality that constitutes his primary punishment (Figure 5).

Beds were important and valuable pieces of furniture. They were listed first in inventories,[9] and bequeathed in wills from generation to generation. And they were dynastic in the other sense too: the place where generation occurred. Beds constitute marriage furniture as centrally as wedding chests – perhaps more so. What would it mean to climb into the conjugal bed past a substantial and prominent image of Adam or Eve? The Stafford bedhead carries something like the same imbrication of contrary meanings as the Warwick chest: pleasure associated with fecundity in the profusion and vigour of nature; the serpent, threatening tragic error, exile and death; a wife, God-given, sensual and fertile, but at the same time dangerously seductive, and thus equivocal, her meaning, both to her husband and to all human beings as her descendants, finally unresolved.

Figure 4 Eve, bedhead

Figure 5 Adam, bedhead

There is reason to suppose that Izaak Walton knew the Ancient High House in Stafford and lived there for a time in later life. The house belonged to his relations. Had the bed been there in his day, he might well have approved it. Without doubt, he recorded a certain scepticism about marriage, which runs counter to the newfound idealization of the conjugal institution. Of John Donne's clandestine betrothal he was to write:

> love is a flattering mischief, that hath denied aged and wise men a foresight
> of those evils that too often prove to be the children of that blind father, a
> passion, that carries us to commit errors with as much ease as whirlwinds
> remove feathers, and begets in us an unwearied industry to the attainment
> of what we desire.[10]

Moreover, his account of the consequences of Richard Hooker's unfortunate and turbulent alliance figuratively invokes the Fall: 'And by this marriage the good man was drawn from the tranquillity of his college, from that garden of piety, of pleasure, of peace, and a sweet conversation, into the thorny wilderness of a busy world; into those corroding cares that attend a married priest, and a country parsonage.'[11] Is Izaak Walton's wedding chest no more, then, than the effect of a personal eccentricity, a resistance to the prevailing view?

The Stafford bedhead suggests not, and indeed there is evidence that the association between marriage furniture and the Fall may be more' than coincidental. Visitors to the Victoria and Albert Museum can see a brilliantly coloured earthenware dish, about two feet across, dated 1635 and bearing the initials T. and T. M. (Figure 6). According to the Museum's own caption, the initials indicate that this was probably a wedding or betrothal gift. The dish depicts the Fall, and if the work is less elegant than the carving on the Warwick chest, and if Eve is less immediately seductive to modern eyes than her counterpart on the Stafford bedhead, her golden hair curls just as sinuously, and the serpent is no less evident, and equally threatening. (The placard makes no comment on the relationship between the story of the Fall and the marriage it was here designed to celebrate.)

Meanwhile, in 1610 Dame Dorothy Davenport, of Capesthorne Manor in Cheshire, had embarked, presumably quite independently, on a labour which was to occupy 26 years of her married life, a tapestry covering the entire headboard of her four-poster, and a valance

Figure 6   The Fall, wedding or betrothal dish, 1635

above to match. This is explicitly a marriage bed: the valance bears the initials of Dorothy on the right and her husband William Davenport on the left. The background colour of the whole tapestry is still a warm gold: it must originally have been still richer. Light and vitality dominate the work, which shows plants and animals bathed in brilliant sunshine. The inscription on the valance urges, 'Fear God and sleep in peace.' It goes on to mention the 'joy and happiness' promised in heaven, but also the 'grief and sorrows' of hell which are the consequence of succumbing to sin, the world and the devil.[12]

The main panel, designed to cover the headboard, shows the Garden of Eden highly lit. Paradise is a prolific place, full of flowers and fruit, birds and animals. An ornate peacock struts on the lowest level; in the tier above, a furry caterpillar, nearly as big as Eve, approaches a sunflower. Unhampered, like most home-embroiderers of the period, by questions of scale or perspective, Dame Dorothy filled her Garden with engaging creatures, all in harmony with each other. A hare and a tortoise, who coexist without competing, are placed symmetrically at the bottom of the panel.

The tapestry also tells a story, however, and it is, of course, the story of the Fall. The human figures are not shown enjoying innocence. In the first picture, at the top left-hand corner of the panel, Eve takes a disproportionately large apple from the serpent twined in the Tree of Knowledge; she hands another to Adam. The Tree of Knowledge appears again in the centre of the panel. To one side of it the newly fallen Adam and Eve, now wearing aprons of fig leaves in token of their shame, reluctantly encounter the Tetragrammaton. Here, we are invited to suppose, God reproaches them for disobeying his commandment, and allots their punishment. The serpent, triumphant, slithers away. Meanwhile, on the other side of the tree, at the centre of the tapestry, a skeletal figure of Death stands behind them as they look back with regret at the Garden. Below they reappear, now clothed, with Adam delving and Eve apparently pregnant, about to undergo the pain of childbirth that would constitute her punishment. Prohibition, sin and suffering turn out to inhabit a world of pleasure and delight. Once again tragedy is seen to reside at the heart of the first marriage.

By the time Dame Dorothy Davenport began her long and dedicated work, there was already an established tradition of marriage furnishings recording the story of the Fall. The earliest case I have found was made in Wales and is now at the manor house of Cotehele in Cornwall.[13] In 1532 Sir Piers Edgcumbe of Cotehele married Katherine, widow of Sir Griffith ap Rhys, and she brought with her the elaborately carved tester of a four-poster bed which survives in Dyfed. One of the carved panels of the tester depicts the Expulsion of Adam and Eve from the Garden. The panel is clearly an interpolation: it does not quite fit the space available. The style of the figures shows equally clearly, however, that they are the work of the same craftsman, or of his workshop. Unless Katherine brought with her another unrecorded piece of furniture, the rest of which has been lost, it would therefore seem likely that the Expulsion scene was part of the bed by 1532.

Meanwhile, an embroidered Scottish valance, depicting the Temptation and designed to fit at the foot end of a four-poster bed, probably dates back to the mid-sixteenth century (Figure 7). It shows the respective arms of Colin Campbell of Glenorchy and his second wife Katherine Ruthven at the centre. Above this heraldic invocation of dynasty are the initials of the couple, CC and KR, linked by a truelove knot. To the left, Adam and Eve occupy a Garden filled with flowers. They stand on either side of the Tree of Knowledge, where the serpent, who has a human face, searches with scaly claws among the blossom. On the right, an angel with a flaming sword drives the erring couple from the Garden and Adam holds his arm above his head, as if to ward off the divine wrath. The valances designed to hang along the sides of the bed show more Campbell heraldry with fruit, flowers and animals, while, on one side, there are mermaids, emblems of feminine seduction and danger, and on the other, adolescent male love-gods, astride remarkably phallic twigs.

This set of hangings links dynastic marriage with love and sexual pleasure, as well as fertility and the Fall. Colin Campbell and Katherine Ruthven were married in 1550 and he died in 1583. In 1640 the valance

Figure 7 The Fall and the Expulsion, bed valance

was apparently still on a bed at Balloch, the home of the Campbells of Glenorchy, but by 1679 it had been stowed away in a chest.[14] Evidently it was no longer fashionable – or perhaps by then the moment of its complex and contradictory meaning had passed.

III

In Shakespeare, sexual jealousy introduces death into the enclave provided by loving marriage. Posthumus gives orders for Imogen's murder; Othello strangles his wife in their wedding sheets; in *The Winter's Tale* Hermione is lost, to be resurrected only after 16 years by what seems a miracle. Adam's disobedience, meanwhile, understood as a surrender to sexual desire in marriage, brought death into the world, and all our woe.[15] Perhaps coincidentally, the frame of the Cotehele tester with the panel depicting the Expulsion also includes a skeleton with a dart; it is no coincidence, however, that the Stafford Adam stands on a skull; Dorothy Davenport's embroidered bedhead includes the figure of Death in the Expulsion scene; and a set of late-sixteenth-century English or Scottish valances representing the Fall shows a bony figure triumphing over the banishment of Adam and Eve (Figure 8). As the angel, surrounded by flames, brandishes a sword over the rich vitality of the Garden, the skeleton, its arms above its head in glee, interposes itself between the couple as they look back at the Paradise they have lost.

These images put on graphic display the intrusion of mortality into the first marriage. While much of the early modern iconography of the Fall is familiar from the Middle Ages, the skeleton that helps the angel to drive the couple from the Garden is not a traditional motif. The common source of the two bedhangings depicting Death was almost certainly one of a set of woodcuts by Bernard Salomon, which first appeared in Lyons in 1553 as *Quadrins historiques de la Bible* and was translated in the same year as *True and Lively Historic Portraitures of the Whole Bible*.[16] Salomon's illustrations were reproduced in a number of Bibles issued in the course of the sixteenth century by the Protestant press of the same Lyons printer, Jean de Tournes, and later from Geneva, when his son was driven out of France by religious persecution. Salomon's figure of Death, which pursues the fleeing couple remorselessly in the Expulsion scene, appears to have been borrowed in turn from Holbein, whose biblical woodcuts were also printed in Lyons six

Figure 8 Death and the Expulsion, bed valance

years earlier, and translated as *Images of the Old Testament*. Holbein's woodcuts of the Creation and the Fall are simply transferred, presumably in the interests of economy, from his own earlier sequence of the *danse macabre*, where the skeleton appears alongside Adam, triumphantly mimicking his flight (Figure 9).[17] If Salomon appropriated the idea, however, his representation nevertheless transformed Death into an avenger who relentlessly pursues the fallen couple. The bedhangings bear only a trace of Salomon's Mannerist intensity, but the relative naivety of the images does nothing to diminish the sense of menace to conjugal love.

Figure 9   Hans Holbein the Younger, The Expulsion, 1538

Eve's punishment, meanwhile, was to be the pangs – and the perils – of childbirth. The Capesthorne Tapestry, following Salomon, shows Eve pregnant in the final image of the sequence. The marriage furniture I have described depicts the Fall with a frequency that indicates the existence of something approaching a convention, and the convention has the effect of linking marriage with pleasure, but also with danger and death. At the same time, however, it is important to recognize the limits of this claim. On the one hand, quite different stories commonly appeared on marriage furniture, including wholly secular Ovidian narratives. On the other, the Fall was by no means confined to marriage furniture. Indeed, the single, familiar image of the Tree of Knowledge, with the serpent twined in its branches and Adam and Eve on either side, was widely reproduced in Bibles and on samplers, embroidered book covers, chair backs, chests and plates.

The image itself was evidently satisfying, both in its formal symmetry and as a moral warning. But it rarely appears gratuitously or inappropriately. On the contrary, one eccentric continental instance demonstrates very precisely the way visual representation may link Temptation and Fall, death and the dangers of childbirth (Figure 10). A skeleton forms the trunk of the Tree of Knowledge, with its outstretched arms as the leafy, fruiting branches. The serpent twines around its ribs and the bones of its upper arms, in its mouth an apple gripped by the stalk and held above Eve's outstretched hand. The position of the skeleton's legs and head indicate that it is dancing. This paradoxical image, combining fruitfulness with the *danse macabre* and centring both on the Fall, appears on the opening page of Chapter 1 of Jakob Rüff's copiously illustrated treatise on childbirth.[18] Chapter 1 is about conception. The English translation is less lavishly illustrated and discards the woodcut of the Fall, but a preface by the anonymous translator retains from the original, perhaps inadvertently, a part, at least, of the connection of ideas that the image represents: the work of midwives, the preface maintains, relieves and succours 'all the daughters of Eva, whom God hath appointed to bear children into this world', and it is important that midwives should be fully informed, because the process of childbirth is such a perilous one.[19] Here Eve and the sexual act are linked with fertility on the one hand, and danger and death on the other.

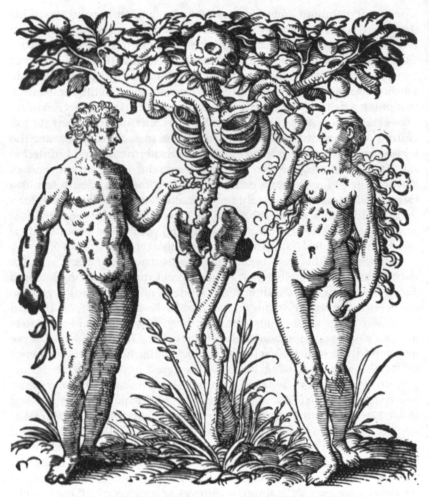

Figure 10 Death and the Fall, Jakob Rüff's treatise on childbirth, 1580

IV

The theological sequence that associates the first marriage with the Fall
and death is traditional. But the marriage furniture relocates the familiar narrative in a new context, bringing the stories into direct relationship
with the emerging ideal of conjugal love. Here again, as in Iachimo's

words to Posthumus, meaning tends to bring with it an excess. This time there is not necessarily any deliberate equivocation, nor even any projected ambiguity, but the duplicity of signifying practice is not a matter of intention. When the Reformers invoke it as the justification of marriage, Paradise means innocence, but it is very difficult to exclude the exact opposite meaning, the loss of innocence. From the perspective of a fallen world, and the early modern period had direct access to no other, Paradise is always lost, and the loss is part of the meaning of the word. Protestant divines alluded to Paradise in order to guarantee the innocence of marriage, but the meaning of the term they invoked necessarily brought with it an excess which reintroduced the very meanings it was their project to exclude. Donne's Twicknam Garden resembles Eden to the degree that it contains a snake: 'And that this place may thoroughly be thought / True Paradise, I have the serpent brought.' Is it possible that the serpent cannot in (cultural) practice be kept out of either Eden or the institution set up to resemble it?

Something of this excess, the return of the excluded term, also occurs in the clerical delineations of marriage. Distinctions are established in order to arrive at a definition of the ideal, only to collapse again as the repudiated value reappears to trouble the ideal itself, leaving an instability in the logic of the text. Marriage is Paradise, but Paradise is the place of loss; Adam was created happy, but not happy enough to manage without a help meet for him, a mate like him; the woman God made to supply what Adam lacked endangered and destroyed his God-given happiness; marriage both repairs and reaffirms the originary loss.

Whatever the theoretical difficulties involved in defining the place of lack in a state of perfection, marriage, it was resolutely affirmed, supplied what was wanting – and still does, in a fallen world where lack is the inevitable human condition. Marriage for love is the remedy for desire. Henry Smith, whose account of Adam's solitude was so strangely bleak, sees marriage as a happy ending. 'So', Smith triumphantly insists, 'shall that man be pleased which finds a wife according to his own heart. Whether he be rich or poor, his peace shall afford him a cheerful life and teach him to sing, "In love is no lack".'[20] But, of course, this gratifying state of affairs depends on the choice of the right partner. Instructions on how to distinguish a good wife from a bad take up a substantial proportion of the sermons and treatises on the conjugal relation. There are occasional concessions to the idea that marriage based on true love implies that women also make a choice, but the primary addressees of these texts are, of course, men. Marriage,

then, is both godly and joyful to the degree that a man selects a wife
who is pious, faithful and a fit companion for him; conversely, a corrupt, vexatious wife can turn his house into hell.

The problem is that the model for both is Eve, made by God as a
help meet for Adam and thus an ideal of feminine virtue and suitabil-
ity, but at the same time the cause of the Fall and thus the prime instance
of female vice and unsuitability. According to *The Christian State of
Matrimony*, the proper basis for a good marriage is 'the same heart,
disposition and love that Adam bore toward his Eva.'[21] Similarly, in
the view of William Whately, 'God himself hath set us the best copy of
marriage that can be: he made Eva meet for Adam; she answered him,
and he her in age, birth, and all things. He shall speed best that follows nearest this first precedent of matrimony.'[22] At the same time,
however, Whately sees marriage as full of afflictions. John Wing in *The
Crown Conjugal* is also uncertain whether Eve was a blessing or a curse.
If Adam's Paradise was less than absolute for want of a gracious wife,
Wing insists, 'then the enjoying of her is the having of the happiest
blessing under heaven'.[23] On the other hand, the greatest danger to
Adam's happiness was Eve. Men should therefore take care to choose
wisely when they select a wife. Look, Wing also and contradictorily
insists, at the case of Adam:

> foiled in his full strength and infected, yea poisoned, and that in the perfec-
> tion of grace, by his woman, whom the devil thought ... more meet and
> likely to overturn him than himself or any other instrument could choose, or
> use. And if he, who was without sin, and had armour of proof upon him,
> even the power of created grace, was yet wounded to death, what man or
> son of man that will come near her can hope to be out of her gun-shot and
> battery?[24]

Urging women to turn to God for help in becoming good wives, Wing
invokes Eve as simultaneously, and in a single sentence, both an ideal
and a warning:

> The time was when once it was natural to your sex to be so excellent, but she
> that first enjoyed it destroyed it, altering the property and losing the pre-
> rogative belonging to you all.[25]

In practice, then, careful choice might help, but it could not be guaranteed to resolve the deeper problem of the human being who is an organism-in-culture. As the clerical contradictions indicate, the difficulty is structural. Once desire exists as the defining condition of Adam's difference, it cannot be satisfied once and for all simply by the creation of a suitable mate. Desire is a perpetual condition, repeatedly dictating choices. In the event, unfallen Adam chose Eve and disobedience, as God must have known he would, for fear of a return to forlorn prelapsarian solitude. Paradise's greatest blessing was also its greatest danger: the very figure who supplied the perfection Adam lacked was also responsible for the loss of perfection. John Wing's *Crown Conjugal* is compelled by the logic of its own argument to a pessimism which seems to work directly against the explicit project, defined on the title page as 'A discovery of the true honour and happiness of Christian matrimony.' Since things went so badly wrong even in those ideal circumstances, Wing reflects, the chances of success in a fallen world are not high:

> If the Paradise of God may (possibly) yield a bad wife, what probability is there that any prohibited place can yield a good? And if the first man did fall there, how can any hope to stand upon this unholy ground?[26]

The text fails to produce the answer which would justify its own enthusiastic affirmation of marriage as 'the happiest blessing under heaven'.

Adam's God-given desire, these texts indicate, perhaps in spite of themselves, was dangerous. If solitude makes perfection imperfect, marriage, meanwhile, imperils the perfection it (re)creates. Adam's desire is primordial, prelapsarian, the effect of his difference from the animals and his consequent loneliness; it is within the moral Law and is met by the legality of marriage. But Eve, who is necessary to ensure his happiness, also destroys it; the woman created in order to contain desire within the Law proves to be herself anarchic. No wonder women cannot be read: the good and bad wife are one and the same person. Even the woman that God made specially for the purpose betrayed her husband. Marriage, which is a terrestrial Paradise, is after all inseparable from error, loss and death.

V

Recalled later in the scene in *The Winter's Tale* where Polixenes invokes their shared childhood to the proprieties of social exchange after his first outburst of jealousy, Leontes reintroduces the theme of boyhood innocence:

> Looking on the lines
> Of my boy's face, methoughts I did recoil
> Twenty-three years, and saw myself unbreech'd,
> In my green velvet coat; my dagger muzzl'd
> Lest it should bite its master, and so prove,
> As ornaments oft do, too dangerous.
>
> (1.2.153–8)

The child is protected from the unintended effects of the weapon he carries merely for ornament. Later, the dagger will be necessary as a means of defence, but the possibility remains that were it unmuzzled, it might damage the very person whose safety it was designed to guarantee. As the play makes clear, unmuzzled sexual desire also represents a possible threat, not only to others – as Hermione and Mamillius die, and Perdita is exposed to death – but also to the desiring subject, Leontes himself.

Not everyone at this historical moment was convinced by the utopian, if contradictory, clerical vision of conjugal happiness as the remedy for desire. Other accounts identify a radical discrepancy between the unpredictable, uncontrollable nature of desire and the stability of marriage. In St Augustine's broadly Platonic version of the relationship between the Fall and sexuality, Adam's original disobedience to God's command was directly punished by the subsequent disobedience of the penis, which seemed to live a life of its own, refusing to obey the fallen human will.[27] Sexual desire was thus not amenable to conscious control, not subject to regulation. Montaigne, following Augustine, also locates the anarchic restlessness of desire, which he attributes equally to women, in the unruly human sexual organ:

> The gods, saith Plato, have furnished man with a disobedient, skittish, and tyrannical member which, like an untamed furious beast, attempteth by the violence of his appetite to bring all things under his beck. So have they allotted women another as insulting, wild and fierce.[28]

It follows, Montaigne reasons, that love and marriage have wholly different projects, the one undisciplined and inconsistent, the other stable, substantial and constant. We are mistaken if we suppose that we do honour to marriage by uniting it with love.[29] Love is indifferent to reason and law. 'Cupid,' Montaigne insists, 'is a roguish God; his sport is to wrestle with devotion and to contend with justice.'[30] And, more tersely: 'Love knows or keeps no order.'[31]

His point is not the same as the medieval and Pauline concession that if sexual desire cannot be resisted, it had better be contained within marriage. Montaigne's argument, on the contrary, is that desire, which knows no law, has no place within the legality that is the matrimonial bond. As for the fear of cuckoldry, that is more or less inevitable, Montaigne affirms – though it is certainly best not to surrender to the misery of this vain and turbulent affliction.[32] Montaigne's *Essays* first appeared in Florio's English translation in 1603, and a new edition was published in 1613.[33]

Alongside a residual medieval asceticism, in other words, there emerged a humanist scepticism, which indicates that Izaak Walton's view of love as 'a flattering mischief' was not especially eccentric after all. According to Francis Bacon's account in his own essay on love, first published in 1612, within a year or two of the first performances of *Cymbeline* and *The Winter's Tale*, love similarly 'doth much mischief'. Dangerous and destructive, 'sometimes like a siren, sometimes like a fury', but always 'the child of folly', love is best avoided, Bacon urges, by people with serious aims in life,[34] and he is not much more enthusiastic about marriage.[35]

Much of the ambivalence towards love and marriage that characterizes early modern culture finds a focus in Robert Burton's *Anatomy of Melancholy*. This huge compendium of observations, quotations and allusions devotes one of its three 'Partitions' to 'Love Melancholy'. The context does not always indicate whether Burton is writing about love in general, or love in its pathological manifestation as melancholy; indeed, the text does not maintain a consistent distinction between the two, so that love itself commonly appears as a pathology. Broadly, *The Anatomy* offers a sustained denunciation of love's tyranny over what might otherwise be reasonable human beings. 'I had rather', Burton affirms, 'contend with bulls, lions, bears and giants than with love; he is so powerful, enforceth all to pay tribute to him, domineers over all, and can make mad and sober whom he list.'[36] Love extinguished

Solomon's wisdom and depleted Samson's strength; it overcame the piety of Lot's daughters. In general, this invincible force brooks no resistance:

> Human, divine laws, precepts, exhortations, fear of God and men, fair, foul means, fame, fortunes, shame, disgrace, honour cannot oppose, stave off, or withstand the fury of it.[37]

Love is full of doubts, anxieties and suspicion; it effeminates; even the most staid and discreet people are absurd in love.[38] It is inordinate: it begets rapes, incests, murders.[39] Burton is extraordinarily fluent – and copious – in his accounts of love's folly, blindness, dangers and excesses. Love knows no bounds, and commonly leads to madness, or suicide, or both. Within marriage it produces jealousy, a topic which occupies a section of its own.

In consequence, wedlock, Burton maintains, is to be undertaken only reluctantly: 'In sober sadness, marriage is a bondage, a thraldom, an yoke, an hindrance to all good enterprises . . .' And then it is as if the author suddenly remembers in mid-sentence what, as a good Anglican divine, he ought to say, and hastens to correct his position:

> not that the thing is evil in itself or troublesome, but full of all contentment and happiness, one of the three things which please God, when a man and his wife agree together, an honourable and happy estate.[40]

Elsewhere, after all, he has already invoked the official position, sounding remarkably like Thomas Becon nearly a century earlier:

> this nuptial love is a common passion, an honest, for men to love in the way of marriage ... You know marriage is honourable, a blessed calling, appointed by God himself in Paradise; it breeds true peace, tranquillity, content and happiness ... when they live without jarring, scolding, lovingly as they should do.[41]

An encyclopaedic text, a patchwork of authorities, ancient and modern, Burton's *Anatomy* inherits two conflicting traditions, one derived from classical and Catholic authors, including the Church Fathers, and the other from his own immediate predecessors in Protestant orders. And it shares this heritage with early modern culture in general, reproduces, indeed, the incompatible knowledges and cognitive dissonances the period took for granted. *The Anatomy of Melancholy* thus puts magnificently on display the contradictory values in circulation in its own era, the 1620s and 1630s,[42] demonstrating in the process something of the difficulty of constructing an 'accurate' cultural history of what was evidently still a highly charged topic. But though Burton hastens to correct his most obvious deviations from Anglican orthodoxy, in the matter of love there is no doubt where *The Anatomy*'s real sympathies lie: while it can bring joy, 'yet most part, love is a plague, a torture, an hell, a bitter sweet passion at last ... the Spanish Inquisition is not comparable to it; a torment and execution it is'.[43]

Impervious to rational argument or authority, beyond the reach of Law, desire has its own relentless imperatives and anxieties. Medieval romance acknowledged this: it was while they were reading the story of Lancelot and Guinevere that Dante's Paolo and Francesca embarked on the adultery that would lead them irrevocably to hell. Part of the project of the early modern romance of marriage was to bring desire in from the cold: to moralize and domesticate a destabilizing passion, confining it within the safety of the loving family. Dynastic marriage must have been an anxious business, especially with so many adulterous love stories in circulation idealizing unfaithfulness. The romance of marriage would turn matrimony itself into an adventure, while holding the couple together in lifelong fidelity based on mutual love.[44]

Shakespeare's accounts of marriage, particularly in the Last Plays, suggest that the plan to bring desire within the conjugal relation might have unforeseen consequences, intensifying the anxiety by unmuzzling a threat which would operate within the institution it was designed to make safe. The serpent appears to Leontes inside the conjugal garden, and it tells him lying stories of love and dynasty both betrayed in a single act. In *Othello* the serpent is personified as Iago, who lures the hero to his own deception. Iachimo exploits the excess of meaning to reintroduce precisely the anxiety that the romance of marriage was designed to exclude.

The marriage furniture, the sermons and the secular texts together suggest that the analysis made in the plays is not all that surprising, that there is a structural anxiety at the heart of the early modern celebration of conjugal love. To counter the dangers intrinsic to the married state, some of the clerical treatises and the domestic conduct books of the period recommend unceasing vigilance, as if a contradiction could be overcome by an effort of will. A good deal of attention is devoted to the duties of married people: marriage guidance comes into existence in the inaugural moment of the loving nuclear family itself. No one, the divines insist, should expect marriage to be easy. To avoid discord, the husband should learn to be tolerant, correcting his wife's faults with love and gentleness. The wife should learn patience, curbing her will in the interests of harmony. William Whately's two books on marriage are devoted primarily to the inevitable difficulties, and *A Care-cloth*, printed in 1624, specifically concerns itself with the troubles of conjugal life, because 'likely none do meet with more crosses in marriage, or bear their crosses more untowardly, than those that most dream of finding it a very paradise'.[45] The text omits to mention that anyone naive enough to dream of finding it a paradise would almost certainly owe this illusion to the writings of Whately's own clerical colleagues.

The problem with the moral prescriptions, however, is that they make no allowance for the irrational character of the desire which is now to be incorporated into the marital relationship. Desire is fearful, possessive, proprietary, outside rational control. Moreover, beyond the pleasure principle, it is easily transformed into deadly hatred. The plays take full account of what, in the twentieth century, Jacques Lacan calls 'the dark god in the sheep's clothing of the Good Shepherd, Eros'.[46] Desdemona is not a bad wife, but Othello is easily convinced that she is. Imogen is chaste, but once he is persuaded of her infidelity, Posthumus's certainty outruns Iachimo's equivocations. Error infects and poisons wedded love, bringing loss and death in its wake. Leontes, obsessively jealous, is not open to reason or authority; he is deaf to his counsellors, his Queen and the oracle. Posthumus rejects out of hand Philario's plea for patience: 'Never talk on't: / She hath been colted by him' (*Cymbeline*, 2.4.132–3). Desire is absolute: it knows no Law; passion cannot be rendered dispassionate by rational intervention or an act of will.

The anxiety evident in the inaugural texts of the loving family is not to be allayed by the moral discipline those texts prescribe, because what is at stake is not simply the need for vigilance in defence of a fragile institution, but a defining paradox in the ideal itself. Meaning brings with it its own inevitable excess. Just as Paradise means both happiness and loss, innocence and the serpent, just as Eve means both partnership and betrayal, so marriage based on love means the conjunction of contraries, peace and anxiety, completeness and lack, companionable tranquillity and danger. Introducing desire into marriage is evidently a bit like inviting a bandit in as chief of police to defend law and order: it might work, but it's a risky strategy.

VI

The clerical treatises set out to invest marriage with a meaning which the character of language itself is unable to hold in place: even where there is no intention to equivocate, excess unfixes the most resolute of affirmations. Equivocation, it might be argued, is the paradigm case of all signifying practice. Meanwhile, the plays make explicit the impossibility of domesticating desire merely by the repeated assertion of its legality. Imogen's bedchamber is watched over by golden cherubim carved on the ceiling (*Cymbeline*, 2.4.87–8), but they cannot exclude the contrary meanings inscribed in the furnishings, or keep at bay the serpentine intruder who so easily converts her husband's love into murderous hate. Marriage is finally saved in Shakespeare's romances not by vigilance, but by coincidences, by miracles, by divine intervention. The reunions of Imogen and Posthumus in *Cymbeline* and of Leontes and Hermione in *The Winter's Tale* are an integral part of the happy endings of these plays. We are invited, in my view, to believe in them. The official position is that marriage is an earthly paradise. But at the same time, the clerical texts, as well as the marriage furniture and the plays, can all be read as indicating that the conjugal bedchamber, like the God-given Garden, turns out to be a good deal more dangerous than the official analysis was formally willing to allow.

Chapter Four
Parenthood: Hermione's Statue

I

ine, meticulous pen-and-ink drawings depict a succession of episodes recounted in the book of Genesis, from the Creation to the Tower of Babel. The 20 illustrations made in 1607–8 by the Flemish engraver, Jan Wierix, exist in three separate series, with individual images differing from each other only in detail. Immediately after the Expulsion from the Garden of Eden, Wierix shows the construction of domesticity out of the wilderness (Figure 11). Before a background of mountainous crags, Adam props a ladder against the wooden frame of a house. Holding two bundles of reeds for thatching, he puts his foot on the first rung; a donkey, with more reeds strapped to its back, munches a thistle in a plot that is evidently beginning to be a farmyard. Chickens peck about among the logs and a boar shows a sidelong interest in a pile of vegetables. Protected by what is already a stable, Eve sits with a child on her lap, watching the cooking-pot on the fire.

Sylvester's du Bartas recounts the story in verse in *The Divine Weeks and Works*. Once the Fall has overthrown the beneficent order of God's Creation, Adam and Eve find hostility wherever they turn: plants and animals are dangerous to them; sickness threatens to subdue them (and the text lists with some relish the symptoms of various fevers, tumours and skin diseases[1]); psychological disorders wait to entrap them. After a whole Book describing the appalling consequences of the Fall, the Fourth Part of the First Day of the Second Week begins with an invocation

to peace, and goes on to show Adam and Eve beginning to take charge
of their new life with all the dedication and ingenuity of the Swiss
Family Robinson. While Adam seeks nourishment amid 'craggy moun-
tains', 'thorny plains' and 'bristly woods',[2] Eve learns to make clothes
for them both. These are not adequate for the winter, however, so at
this stage Adam provides himself with sheepskin slops, hats and dou-
blets.[3] When the natural shelter of caves and hollow trees also proves
inadequate, they build a lodging for themselves, with tree trunks for
support and oak crossbeams, using mud and reeds to make walls. A
door is tied on in the absence of hinges. Adam discovers how to strike
fire from flint, and Eve learns to blow the kindling into life. Then they
have children.

Evidently, the first couple are duly punished: in the Wierix drawing
Adam labours; Eve has already undergone the pains of childbirth. But
there are clearly compensations too: parenthood elicits responsibility,
and diligence is rewarded by the emergence of order, as well as the
establishment of the unified family, in the process of taming a hostile

Figure 11   Jan Wierix, Taming the wilderness, 1607–8

world to produce the essential elements of a simple but civilized way of life. Isolated and vulnerable, but resolute, the first family creates an enclave in which affection and mutual support can flourish. Wierix's image of motherhood without luxuries, set in a stable among domestic animals, points forward to another idealizing image of the family, the Nativity, as it appears in the countless representations that were already thoroughly traditional by the time Wierix completed his drawings.[4]

These were executed in Antwerp, but visual images circulated relatively freely in Europe at this time. One set of the *Creation* drawings was listed in the inventory of Archduke Leopold Wilhelm of Austria in Vienna in 1659.[5] In any case, Wierix simply developed in mimetic detail the portrait of postlapsarian domesticity that had become increasingly familiar in the course of the sixteenth century. Holbein's

sequence of *Pictures of Death* begins with four woodcuts of the Fall, which reappeared in his *Images of the Old Testament*. The fourth of these, immediately following the Expulsion, shows Adam digging, mocked by Death (Figure 12). In the background, Eve holds a distaff while she nurses a baby. The gender roles of the adults are clearly differentiated; the child, meanwhile, is chubby and vulnerable. This is already a loving nuclear family.

Figure 12   Hans Holbein the Younger, The first family, 1538

Holbein's *Pictures of Death* was widely circulated: there were 11 authentic versions and many spurious editions and imitations before the end of the century.[6] Certainly, a set of seventeenth-century embroidered pillowcases, now in the Victoria and Albert Museum, although it takes the initial Creation images from Salomon, draws on Holbein for its representation of Adam delving while Eve spins and suckles the first baby. Thomas Harriott's account of Virginia, printed in 1590, includes an engraving by Theodor de Bry from a drawing by John White, showing the Temptation. In the background Adam digs on one side of the picture, while on the other a diminutive Eve holds an infant under a makeshift shelter.[7]

Nuclear domesticity as a sequel to the Fall is a common motif in engravings of the period.[8] The image was evidently familiar enough to generate inventive variants. The late-sixteenth-century English or Scottish bed valances have accumulated enough detail to locate the fallen couple in what is clearly a domestic setting (see Figure 8, p. 71). Evidently melancholy and perhaps exhausted, Adam sits with his head on his hand, but he still clasps the familiar shovel, while Eve, childless in this instance but probably pregnant, sits and spins. In addition, however, the two figures are shown enclosed by a picket fence, where chickens perch at intervals. Between Adam and Eve stand a flagon and a goblet. It is possible that these are designed to refresh Adam after his labours; it is equally possible that they signify a fallen decadence; in either case, however, they are household objects, rudimentary indications of a newfound domesticity. The individual plot of land, duly fenced in evidence of ownership, represents a humble compensation for the lost walled Garden;[9] the loving family reproduces in miniature the love between God and his creation. Perfect reciprocity is beyond recovery, but some sparks of the original ideal subsist from before the Fall. In Luther's account, 'This living-together of husband and wife – that they occupy the same home, that they take care of the household, that together they produce and bring up children – is a kind of faint image and a remnant, as it were, of that blessed living-together.'[10] The warmth and companionship, and the sense of a shared project, are a consolation for the loss of the pure and intimate relationship they might have had with each other and with God.

At about the same time, loving nuclear families gradually begin to supplant the dynastic family in English Renaissance drama. Oddly enough, *Cymbeline* offers one notable instance of family values at work. When the fortunes of Posthumus reach their lowest ebb, as a result of his failure to sustain what is evidently a marriage of true minds, his father, mother and two brothers rally round in a dream and appeal to Jupiter to intervene on his behalf. Their prayers are granted and the devotion of the family is seen to be instrumental in bringing about the happy ending. Less happily, however, these figures are all dead and the apparitions explicitly proclaim themselves ghosts (*Cymbeline*, 5.4.88).[11]

Coincidentally, perhaps, England now had a recognizable nuclear royal family for the first time in a century, and if perfect marital harmony was too much to expect, the royal children certainly elicited the hopes and fears of a nation. Mourning for the tragic death of the young Prince Henry in 1612 was not wholly dispelled by the festivities in honour of his sister's marriage the following year.

As a play about the relationship between a married couple and its repercussions for their two young children, *The Winter's Tale* (1609–10) constitutes Shakespeare's most detailed depiction of the affective nuclear family. While the play thus contributes to the early modern development of family values, it also anticipates our own concerns about domestic violence, emotional and physical. The unreasoning rage of Leontes apparently causes the death of his loving wife; Mamillius, whose childish precocity is invested with its own innocent charm, dies of grief for his mother; and his baby sister, her vulnerability repeatedly stressed in the play, is exposed to die on the strict instructions of her father. Moreover, these tragic events are shown as the direct consequence of the intensity of the marital relationship itself. Romantic love is attended by anxieties that imperil the family it produces; anarchic desire destabilizes the institution it also founds.

This close attention to the nuclear family is eccentric, however, in the Shakespeare canon. Apart from the cameo of the Macduffs, where love evidently characterizes relations between the couple and between mother and children, it is hard to think of affectionate families in Shakespeare, though there are a good many fathers preoccupied by lineage. Like Capulet and Egeus, parents are more commonly seen coercing their children into arranged marriages than rejoicing in a loving relationship with them. Although the Pages of Windsor are a happy couple, with two engaging children, the parents disagree with each other about who will make the best son-in-law, as well as with their daughter herself, who wants to marry for love. While the plays focus repeatedly on family relationships, they most frequently isolate for our attention fathers and daughters (Prospero and Miranda, Lear and his children), or mothers and sons (Volumnia and Coriolanus, Cymbeline's Queen and Cloten).[12] Sibling rivalry in the tragedies and sibling resemblance in the comedies are sometimes important elements of the plot. Marriage, when it constitutes the theme, is often childless, or effectively so – to sidestep the classic question, 'How many children had Lady Macbeth?' Nuclear families with two affectionate parents and two lovable children are sufficiently rare in Shakespeare to suggest that at the end of the first decade of the seventeenth century the ideal is new enough not to be taken for granted.

The nearest theatrical parallel, chronologically and thematically, is probably *The Duchess of Malfi*, a play which, whether coincidentally or not, was revived several times in the final decade of the twentieth century. *The Duchess* was first performed within a few years of *The Winter's Tale* in 1613 or 1614. Here, where the protagonist marries in accordance with the emerging values, for love and not for lineage, and is explicitly identified as a caring mother to her young children, the plot of the play depends on the collision between this sympathetic affective ideal and an older, overtly dynastic and patriarchal model, in which the male head of the family expects to control his sister's sexual alliances.

II

Outside fiction, however, we may turn for corroboration of a story of changing values to what is probably the period's most widespread art form. Early modern tomb sculpture put on display, across the broadest geographical range and on behalf of a spread of classes – nobles, merchants and gentry, as well as others from time to time – in the place where they were most regularly visible to the whole parish, the changing meanings of the family in its various ideal forms. Funeral monuments of the period project for the world to see the self-image that the family wished to record for posterity, often including the grand marriages of the children, as well as the memory of those who died in infancy. Individual resemblance was not important: what mattered was much more likely to be rank, wealth and dynasty.[13] Indeed, idealization was part of the project: the increasingly elaborate tombs that proliferated in the century after about 1550 provided an example for the living by memorializing the virtues of the dead.[14] Monuments depicting families thus give an indication of how the ideal of the family was understood. Tomb sculpture allows us to read what early modern culture perceived to be appropriate relationships between husbands and wives, parents and children.

Figure 13   Monument to Ralph Neville, Earl of Westmorland (d. 1484) and his wife. Brancepeth, County Durham

From the middle ages to 1600 and well beyond, though the materials and the sophistication of the carving varied, the iconography of the traditional English couple changed very little (Figures 13 and 14).

Side by side, serene, pious, and usually open-eyed, though modern restorers are often unwilling to believe it, the horizontal figures face forwards, towards the east, in confident expectation of their ultimate resurrection, apparently ignorant of the death which occasioned their representation. Parallel and stiffly frontal, they attend to each other, if

Figure 14 Monument to Sir Lewis Mansell (d. 1638) and his wife. Margam Abbey, W. Glamorgan

at all, only by clasping hands in evidence of the marital contract which binds them together for life, and perhaps beyond (Figure 15).

The clasped hands, commonly held across the body of the woman without diminishing the distance between the couple, have more to do with property and dynasty, in my view, than with romance.[15] The Savage monument at Elmley Castle in Worcestershire shows their emblematic significance very clearly (Figure 16), though there are late counter-examples from the 1630s, suggesting that by this time romance was recognized as a proper component of marriage.[16] The tombs are exemplary, of course: whatever personal affection may have existed between individual couples, or whatever resentments, come to that, their images do not speak of them. At the beginning of the seventeenth century, funeral monuments in general tend to show as acceptable an alliance which is formal and to a degree detached. Of desire they tell us nothing. The Tudor and Stuart fashion of depicting relatively less

Figure 15 Monument to Ralph Greene (d. 1417) and his wife, Katherine. Lowick, Northamptonshire

Figure 16 Monument to Giles Savage (d. 1631) and his wife, Catherine. Elmley Castle, Worcestershire (detail)

Figure 17 Monument to John Bunce (d. 1611) and his wife, Dorothea (d. 1612). Otterden, Kent

aristocratic couples kneeling in prayer and divided by a prie-dieu reveals the family at a more intimate moment, not on public display, but at their devotions.[17] The emphasis, nevertheless, is still on piety and formality. How different, then, from Shakespeare's plays, where serene decorum seems a long way from the home life of the Macbeths, not to mention the Fords of Windsor, whose households are palpably neither dignified nor devout. There is, of course, a radical difference of genre. Tombs show what the family wanted the world to see: the plays show what they might have preferred to conceal. The tombs are formal, ceremonial: the plays are popular entertainment. But in one sense, the plays and the monuments tell the same story. The project of the tombs is to transcend time and stabilize an ideal in a single image; the plays, by contrast, set out to sustain the attention of an audience by deferring stability for five acts. At the same time, the plays take it for granted that their audiences recognize the values against which deviations from the ideal can be measured.

The tombs traditionally exclude emotion. Dignified, slightly distant, kneeling figures face each other, it appears, only incidentally, in the interests of symmetrical composition, not emotional reciprocity. Their eyes fixed on a world beyond each other, they are untroubled by death. Though mortality is the cause of their tomb, it is represented there emblematically, if at all,[18] often as a way of showing who survives at the moment when the memorial is ordered. The Bunce Monument of 1611, attributed to Issac James, includes a dead daughter in a cradle draped in black: she died in infancy (Figure 17).[19]

The living are represented alongside the dead: as the Duchess of Malfi indicates, widows cut in alabaster kneel at their husbands' tombs. A previous wife, however, was also entitled to her place in the family. When William Knoyle's widow, Grace, commissioned his tomb in 1607 at Sandford Orcas in Dorset, she evidently thought it appropriate to include her predecessor, Fillip, along with her four dead babies (Figure 18). Fillip has her own panel, but she is the same size – and as dignified – as Grace, though she wears the headdress of an earlier date.[20] The tomb of Sir James Deane (d. 1608) in St Olave's, Hart Street, one of the medieval churches that survived the Fire of London, shows three wives. Sir James's widow, Elizabeth, faces him as they kneel at a prie-dieu, and below them two dead infants lean against a skull. Meanwhile, with her back to them, looking east, his first wife, Susanna, kneels with her own dead baby below. On the other side of the couple, also facing east, the monument shows his second wife, another Elizabeth. She had

Figure 18 Monument to William Knoyle (d. 1607) and two wives, Grace and Fillip. Sandford Orcas, Dorset

Figure 19 Monument to Sir Fulke Greville (d. 1559) and his wife, Lady Elizabeth (d. 1562). Alcester, Warwickshire (detail)

no children. Despite three marriages, none of his offspring survived him.

When children do survive, their sorrow is generally strictly formalized. The next generation, who in the sixteenth century replace the mourners on the sides of medieval tomb chests, stand in solemn rows, pious but stoical, resigned to the inevitability of loss, their hands clasped in prayer. Dead infants are included among the living (and are sometimes the same size as their older siblings). Fecundity is evidently a virtue: the Greville tomb of 1559 at Alcester in Warwickshire shows a total of eight daughters and seven sons, in groups according to gender, divided by emblems of dynasty (Figure 19). When the children kneel in imitation of their parents, the same formality generally obtains, and the same gender divisions. Mourning might be indicated by costume, but the children are not generally bowed or wracked by grief. In the context of such representations of filial propriety, Cordelia's refusal to emulate her sisters' extravagant professions of love makes perfect sense – and Lear's demands that she should appear the more absurd.

But just as in painting at this time, fashions in monumental sculpture were changing, and simulation of the living form became an increasingly important value. A tomb in Bath Abbey memorializes a wife and mother. Jane, Lady Waller died in the 1630s and an inscription records her virtues, including her holiness and, perhaps more surprisingly, her learning, wit and wisdom. Sir William Waller went on to command the Parliamentary forces in 1643, and the space for his inscription is blank. He, we may assume, commissioned Lady Waller's monument, which depicts a nuclear family, parents and two children. The Renaissance vogue for showing figures leaning on their elbows has the advantage of making Sir William eminently visible at this dark end of the south transept. It also, and perhaps inadvertently, creates a quite new spatial relationship between the couple. The bodies, that is to say, are now seen as connected with each other. His, turned towards the spectator, also faces hers; she looks up at him. Though they are fully and formally clothed, the respective positions of the figures might permit us to detect a sexual component in what is certainly a romantic interaction. Desire is legitimate within what Milton was to celebrate as 'wedded love'. Sir William's features are defaced: it is impossible to trace the line of his gaze, though his wife's is clearly focused on him. The effigies affirm the intimacy – and the classic gender roles – of the loving nuclear couple (Figure 20).

Figure 20   Monument to Jane, Lady Waller (d. 1630s). Bath Abbey (detail)

Moreover, the children of this newly affective family, rendered in accordance with the equally new ideal of verisimilitude, are childlike,
chubby and engaging. Protected from damage by the classical pillars
supporting the monument, and thus better preserved than their parents, they are visible in clear detail. One child, a boy, but still in
petticoats, leans his head on his left hand in the classic pose of melancholy, while the other hand is idle. Meanwhile, a little girl, evidently
very young, sits on a stool, both hands unoccupied, the corners of her
mouth turned firmly down (Figure 21). Neither infant prays. These
children, we are invited to believe, are sad in a perfectly human and
secular way; they are sorrowing for the loss of their mother.

Though Lady Waller is shown on her tomb as living, not dead, death
is no longer excluded from the representation. It makes its appearance
not in the form of the emblematic paraphernalia of skulls, scythes and
skeletons favoured by the period, however, but in its emotional implications for the children she leaves behind. The affective family is shown
as vulnerable, and the vulnerability is a direct consequence of the affection. The more intimate and the more intense the relationships, the
greater the investment of feeling, the more keenly the pain of loss is

Figure 21 Monument to Jane, Lady Waller (d. 1630s). Bath Abbey (detail)

registered. As eminent modern British examples have so copiously and so notoriously demonstrated, the family based on love is extraordinarily fragile, and the fragility is related to the high expectations the ideal elicits. In practice, the loving nuclear family constitutes a remarkably precarious basis for a stable and well-ordered society.

The historical change marked by the Waller tomb was a gradual one: traditional representations survived alongside this new image of the family. The tomb of Edward and Elizabeth Skynner at Ledbury in Herefordshire reproduces the formal distribution of the conventional kneeling figures, with mourning children in rows below. But between the couple, in place of the prie-dieu, is a dead baby, fully dressed in bonnet and petticoats, leaning on its elbow, its hand resting lightly on a skull. Though the presence of the infant suggests that its death was a cause of sorrow, it lies on the floor in an isolation at once splendid and pathetic, apparently ignored by the rest of the family. No one embraces this child; no one visibly laments its death (Figure 22).

Figure 22 . Monument to Edward Skynner (d. 1631) and his wife, Elizabeth. Ledbury, Herefordshire

Figure 23 Monument to Giles Savage (d. 1631) and his wife, Catherine. Elmley Castle, Worcestershire (detail)

Edward Skynner died in 1631. Meanwhile, however, in January of that year Giles Savage, Esquire, died at Elmley Castle in Worcestershire. His elaborate tomb, carv-ed in the fine detail characteristic of Samuel Baldwin's work, includes an effigy of his father against the far wall. All the heraldic signifiers of dynasty are in evidence, but the tomb also puts on display the pathos of the family divided by death. The inscription, in literary Latin, records that Savage left four sons, of whom the youngest, John, died in August of the same year as his father. All four are seen kneeling at the foot of the tomb (see Figure 29, p. 116). His 'most loving' wife, Catherine, lies beside her husband, although she lived for another forty years and died at the age of 84. Catherine Savage, who took responsibility for raising this 'monument of fidelity and obedience', embraces with both arms a beloved baby daughter whom she bore, the inscription explains, after her husband's death (Figure 23).[21] The precious little girl, a reminder of her lost father, her long dress nearly as elaborately embroidered as Catherine's, is held firmly in her mother's elegant hands. The child, too young to know the meaning of loss, holds a ball in one hand, and fingers the frogging on her mother's bodice with the other. Once again it is the vulnerability of childhood that most clearly indicates the fragility of the family.

III

Like the Waller tomb and the Savage monument, *The Winter's Tale* shows death invading the concord of the family unit, but unlike the tombs, the play locates death at the heart of the intimate relationship between the loving couple. Unpredicted and arbitrary, sexual jealousy dismantles a marriage; the unaccountable rage of Leontes violently displaces parental care, as Mamillius dies of grief and his newborn sister is exposed to die. There is in this instance no external cause, not even a Iago or a Iachimo to blame for the sudden reversal of emotion; Polixenes, the play makes clear, does nothing to provoke it. On the contrary, the murderous passion of Leontes springs from within the loving family itself, wells up at a moment of supreme harmony between the couple and shared courtesy towards their guest, at a time when the meaning of the family as parenthood is most clearly evident in Hermione's pregnancy.

This is a marriage based explicitly on romantic courtship and Hermione's loving response: 'I am yours for ever' (1.2.105).[22] It generates a little boy whose charm springs from his childish mimicry of grown-ups when he teases the ladies-in-waiting, who whispers in his mother's ear a powerful tale of sprites and goblins (2.1.25–8), who softens his father's rage and is the occasion of his temporary restoration to himself (1.2.120–21, 135–7, 153 ff). The play represents childhood as later generations would come to know it: innocent, playful, disarming and, above all, vulnerable. Leontes and Polixenes, who once frisked in the sun like twinned lambs (1.2.67), now share a delight in their own young princes whose 'varying childness' 'makes a July's day short as December' (1.2.169–70). Conversely, it is presumably the more shocking to the audience that Leontes is indifferent to the appeal of Paulina on behalf of his baby daughter as a miniature replica of himself:

> Behold, my lords,
> Although the print be little, the whole matter
> And copy of the father: eye, nose, lip;
> The trick of's frown; his forehead; nay, the valley,
> The pretty dimples of his chin and cheek; his smiles;
> The very mould and frame of hand, nail, finger.
>
> (2.3.97–102)

Subsequently, Paulina's husband, Antigonus, will stress the pathos of
Perdita's exposure, as he reluctantly obeys the instructions of the King:

> Come on, poor babe:
> Some powerful spirit instruct the kites and ravens
> To be thy nurses! Wolves and bears, they say,
> Casting their savageness aside, have done
> Like offices of pity.
>
> (2.3.184–8)

His abandonment of Perdita and the death of Mamillius put on display the
monstrous implications for the loving family of the forgeries of jealousy.

The Victorians, who affirmed the sanctity of family values based on
true love, while incidentally supporting and regulating an unsurpassed
number of prostitutes in nineteenth-century London, regarded unfounded jealousy in marriage as a psychopathology, and looked for
causes in an instability of character. Literary criticism, to the extent
that it is still steeped in Victorian values, continues to seek charactero-
logical or psychopathological explanations for the marital jealousy of
Othello, Posthumus, Master Ford, Oberon, Titania and, of course,
Leontes.[23] The text of *The Winter's Tale*, however, is not helpful here,
since it simply shows Leontes at one moment courtly and romantic,
and at the next, beside himself with grief and rage. Moreover, no one
else in the play seems to think that anything in Hermione's behaviour
justifies the anxiety of Leontes; nothing we know of his past seems to
account for it.

Is it possible that a condition which recurs with varying degrees of
centrality in so many of the marriages Shakespeare depicts is endemic
in romantic love, and not a purely personal idiosyncrasy? Twentieth-
century psychoanalysis would certainly say so. Jacques Lacan, who
reserves his most dismissive moments for the moralizing tendency that
masks desire as true love,[24] places aggressivity at the root of psychic life.
The tormented space of passion is not in psychoanalytic theory a cosy
enclave. Desire, which is absolute, can never believe itself adequately
reciprocated. Young children learn this when they discover that they
cannot have the ceaseless and undivided attention of their carers. Freud
shows little Ernst throwing away the cotton reel when his mother leaves
him, repeating in play his revenge for her necessary absences, which he
experiences as desertion.[25] In so far as every intense interaction repeats

the first, lovers play out repressed relations with each other, which include anger, even if not necessarily on the psychotic scale represented in the *The Winter's Tale*. From a psychoanalytic perspective, the jealousy of Leontes does not need 'explaining': it is a perpetual hazard in the transferential relationship which is affective marriage.

What psychoanalysis theorizes, early modern psychology also observes. Robert Burton's *Anatomy of Melancholy* gives sustained attention to marital jealousy as one of the central dangers of love.[26] It is characteristic of love, Burton explains, to exceed all bounds; passion cannot contain itself, but wanders extravagantly; sometimes it enacts this process of wandering within marriage, and then it is called jealousy.[27] In Burton's description of the jealous person's conduct we can recognize the behaviour of Leontes, who also misinterprets, pries, 'follows close, observes to an hair', and 'through fear, conceives unto himself things almost incredible and impossible to be effected'.[28] Like Leontes, too, Burton's victim of jealousy is deaf to good counsel and impossible to comfort: 'No persuasion, no protestation can divert this passion, nothing can ease him, secure or give him satisfaction.'[29] Much of what follows in *The Anatomy* depicts the familiar type of the jealous husband so common in medieval literature from the *Roman de la rose* and the *Lais* of Marie de France to Chaucer's fabliaux. This figure, often an old man, inadequate, lascivious, possessive and threatened, locks up his wife in order to secure her for his own pleasure.

Descendants of the medieval stereotype survive into early modern drama in *The Merry Wives of Windsor* and *The Changeling*, for instance, but what is new in *Othello*, *Cymbeline* and *The Winter's Tale* (as well as in the figure of Leantio in *Women Beware Women*) is the direct connection between romantic marriage and sexual jealousy. Othello and Desdemona elope together: theirs is, in the first instance, an intensely loving union. The marriage of Imogen and Posthumus is founded on love. Leontes describes his own courtship of Hermione (1.2.102–5), and his first inexplicable outburst occurs immediately after his account of the romance that united them. There is no pause in the action or gap for reflection: only the four lines of Hermione's reply separate his courtship narrative from his agonized exclamation, 'Too hot, too hot!' (1.2.108). For all Burton's dependence on the old stereotype, *The Anatomy* recognizes this connection too. Burton will give jealousy so much attention, he explains, because the condition is virtually coextensive with love itself: 'as Benedetto Varchi holds, no love without a mixture of jealousy, *qui non zelat, non amat*.'[30]

The love depicted in the play belongs at the beginning to Polixenes and Leontes. 'They were trained together in their childhoods, and there rooted betwixt them then such an affection which', Camillo insists in a notorious *double entendre*, 'cannot choose but branch now' (1.1.22–4).[31] Reassigned by means of a figurative and very courtly Fall to women (1.2.71–86) and redeemed by the 'Grace' of marriage (1.2.105), affection becomes the foundation of the nuclear family, where it goes on to constitute, Leontes argues – in a passage many editors have found almost impenetrable – the source of jealous delusions. The speech is addressed, at least ostensibly, to Mamillius:

> Can thy dam? – May't be? –
> Affection! thy intention stabs the centre:
> Thou dost make possible things not so held,
> Communicat'st with dreams; – how can this be? –
> With what's unreal thou coactive art,
> And fellow'st nothing: then 'tis very credent
> Thou may'st co-join with something; and thou dost,
> (And that beyond commission) and I find it,
> (And that to the infection of my brains
> And hard'ning of my brows).
>
> (1.2.137-46)

In the Variorum edition of the play, published in 1898, the note on 'affection' (line 138) already ran to four pages. Capell, the earliest editor cited, in 1767 offered a fairly straightforward explanation of the speech: when 'full bent', that is to say, 'full *intentiveness*', is given to affection, Capell proposed, 'man often receives a stab in his centre, *i.e.* his heart; meaning, that he is in that case subject to jealousy', and jealousy, in turn, makes possible 'things which others hold not so'.[32] Almost at once, however, alternative interpretations of 'affection' began to appear. Steevens thought it must mean 'imagination', presumably on the grounds that the speech makes affection coactive with what's unreal; Steevens was followed in this by Malone, and by Staunton and Keightley in the nineteenth century. In 1876 'affection' was glossed as 'lust',[33] and this version found its way into the Arden edition of 1963, where it becomes the condition Leontes mistakenly attributes to Hermione: *her* lustful fantasies, which fellow nothing, have also co-joined with something, namely Polixenes.[34] The Riverside edition glosses 'affection' as 'jealousy', which might seem to stretch the meaning about as far as it will go, but the *Norton Shakespeare* adds 'rage' and 'suspicion' as well.[35] John Andrews and Stephen Orgel both prefer to attribute the affection to Hermione, on the basis of the punctuation given in the Folio, the only authoritative text ('Can thy Dam, may't be / Affection?').[36] But Jacobean punctuation is not always a reliable guide to syntax, and since our question mark is used in the period to indicate both questions and exclamations, this reading remains to a degree conjectural. Moreover, their version problematizes the referent of 'thy' and 'thou': the delusions affection fosters – and the corresponding possibility that they are not delusions after all – surely belong to Leontes.

Stephen Orgel himself has drawn attention to the way we misread Renaissance texts if we expect them to be transparent, to deliver a single, paraphrasable meaning. Local incomprehensibility was not necessarily a vice in the texts of this period, and it was eighteenth-century editors who taught us otherwise.[37] It is true that this passage is obscure in detail, though not, perhaps, as obscure as some interpreters have made it; it is also true that in the early modern period 'affection' has a wide range of meanings; but what holds a good many of them together is not very different from the modern meaning, or what we might call 'affect', to distinguish the term from the rather watery connotation that now differentiates affection from love. Florizel, loyal to Perdita despite his father's intervention, is heir to his 'affection' (4.4.482), and if this commitment is rash, it is surely not dishonourable but, on the contrary, the evidence that their marriage is based on true love. The monument in the church at Hintlesham, Suffolk, to Captain John Timperley, who died in 1629, records that 'his loving wife caused this memorial too too little to express either his desert or her affection.' Evidently, the term was not necessarily pejorative: Mrs Timperley's devotion was presumably admirable, the proper sentiment of a good wife. Moreover, the childhood affection between Leontes and Polixenes is made synonymous with love (1.1.32).

But like appetite, affection was involuntary, not subject to rational control.[38] In the early seventeenth century affection was also distinguished from love by the essayist William Cornwallis, who saw affection as characterizing the relationship between married people.[39] Affection, Cornwallis elsewhere insists, is not a stable condition: it is partial, irrational, inconstant, and – as if he were anticipating the play's depiction of Leontes – 'All the deformities and misdemeanours of the

world are the children of affection, which binds up our sight in darkness, and leads us blindfolded.'[40]
   In the early modern period blind Cupid, the anarchic, mischievous child-
god, becomes the basis of an allegedly stabilizing institution. Is it possible
that when Leontes rounds on affection, he singles out as the cause of his
torture his own passionate love for his wife, the very basis of romantic
marriage, and the concomitant capacity for imagining improbabilities that
characterizes the lunatic, the lover and the poet,[41] linking them all in an
intensity, or intensification[42] of feeling which is also a kind of madness?
Iago implies a part of this story when he persuades Othello that love itself
is the source of the suspicious husband's torments:

> That cuckold lives in bliss
> Who, certain of his fate, loves not his wronger,
> But O, what damned minutes tells he o'er
> Who dotes, yet doubts, suspects yet strongly loves!
> *Othello* (3.3.169–72)[43]

When Othello is once convinced of Desdemona's infidelity, love explicitly gives way to hatred (3.3.448–52). If love is the cause of jealous
rage and not its cure, is it also possible that from the eighteenth century onwards, it has seemed imperative to find an alternative meaning
for affection in this outburst of Leontes, because it has become un-
thinkable that at the core of family values, there could be something
coactive with what's unreal, a capacity to turn a harmless bush into a
dangerous bear, and a warmth that turns so readily into its murderous
opposite?[44] If in our own culture jealousy is thought to be pathological, how can it reside at the heart of our most precious relationship?
But conceivably Shakespeare's audience was less sentimental about
family values than we are, perhaps because before the institution was
fully sanctified, it was possible to acknowledge the violence that so
commonly occurs behind respectable closed doors. Perhaps, too, in a
world where privacy was less readily available, the violence was correspondingly more visible, as it is at the court of Leontes.
   But if concealment was less easy at this stage, the family had already acquired the beginnings of a sanctity which kept outsiders at
bay. Camillo, Antigonus and Paulina are not entitled to put up a direct
resistance to the folly of Leontes, though, as if anticipating modern
social workers, they try to intervene when his instructions become
homicidal. Contemporary illustrations of the Book of Genesis show

the little family of Adam and Eve entirely alone, surrounded by what
is now a hostile and dangerous world. The isolation of the family, and
its right to privacy and self-determination within the law, combine to
permit the cruelty that family values shelter or even legitimate.

The early modern period brings emotion inside marriage, and it sees
emotion as unstable, unpredictable, arbitrary. Leontes finds it – to the
infection of his brains and the hardening of his supposedly cuckolded
brows. His remorse, when it comes, is equally extreme.[45] For 16 years
Leontes performs a saint-like sorrow (5.1.1–2), daily visiting the chapel
where his wife and child lie buried (3.2.238–9). Hermione herself is
memorialized as a martyr. She appears to Antigonus 'in pure white
robes, / Like very sanctity' (3.3.21–3); her repentant husband alludes
to 'her sainted spirit' (5.1.57). The pain of loss is directly proportional
to the ideal the family represents.

IV

Tombs of the period do not record marital jealousy as a cause of death.
They do, however, on occasions construct a direct relationship between
affection and loss, locating death within the love they celebrate. Lady
Waller's tomb in Bath was put up at least 20 years after the play; Catherine Savage memorialized her family at about the same time. But in
the neighbourhood of London cultural fashions moved faster. The Parish Church at Fulham, then a village on the Thames, houses a tomb of
1603 which is both a monument to motherhood and a record of the
loss that constantly threatens to divide the family. Lady Margaret Legh
sits upright, her head very slightly inclined towards the child in her
arms, one hand supporting the baby, the other against her breast in a
gesture of sorrow. This is an elegant, sophisticated effigy, carved with
the mimetic subtlety emerging in the period (Figure 24).

The details of the story are slightly obscure. Pevsner identifies the
figure as a widow, on account of the hood.[46] This is self-evidently not
right: the inscription makes clear that the monument was put up by her
husband. Arched hoods of this kind were fashionable in the period and
are not necessarily indications of widowhood. Pevsner also draws attention to the stiff babies – like mummies, he comments. Like mummies
indeed, and as if they were encased in lead. My own view is that these
babies are probably dead, like the rigid little corpses pathetically heaped
up behind William Knoyle's first wife on the wall tablet at Sandford

Figure 24 Monument to Lady Margaret Legh (d. 1603). All Saints, Fulham

Orcas (see Figure 18, p. 96), like the infant John Windsor (d. 1588), who has his own incised slab at Stoke-by-Nayland, Suffolk, or like the twins held by their mother, Anne à Wode, on a brass of 1512 at Blickling in Norfolk.[47] The inscription on the Legh monument mentions two daughters and seven sons, of whom three died in infancy. Whether the birth of one, or perhaps two, of the deceased infants mentioned on the inscription, was also responsible for the mother's death is not made clear, but it seems possible.[48] The whole image is in direct contrast to the painting of the Cholmondeley sisters, proud mothers of living and richly dressed babies in their flowing red mantles (Figure 25). The costumes of the women, however unsuitable they might be for sitting up in bed, confirm that this painting dates from roughly the same period as the tomb. The arched hoods, the ruffs and the necklaces are all very similar to those on the Legh monument.

The perils of childbirth made death an ever-present threat to the enclave of the loving family. Margaret Legh's epitaph tells her (short) story:

TO THE MEMORY

OR

WHAT ELSE DEARER REMAINETH OF THE VIRTUOUS LADY, LADY MARGARET LEGH,

DAUGHTER

OF HIM THAT SOMETIMES WAS SIR GILBERT GERARD, KNIGHT AND MASTER OF THE

ROLLS IN THE HIGH COURT OF CHANCERY,

WIFE

TO SIR PETER LEGH OF LYMM IN THE COUNTY OF CHESTER, KNIGHT, AND BY HIM

THE MOTHER OF 7 SONS, PEIRCE, FRAUNCES, RADCLIFFE, THOMAS, PETER, GILBERT,

JOHN, WITH 2 DAUGHTERS, ANNE AND KATHERINE: OF WHICH RADCLIFFE, GILBERT,

JOHN DECEASED INFANTS, THE REST YET SURVIVING TO THE HAPPY INCREASE OF

THEIR HOUSE. THE YEARS THAT SHE ENJOYED THE WORLD WERE 33, THAT HER

HUSBAND ENJOYED HER 17, AT WHICH PERIOD SHE YIELDED HER SOUL TO THE

BLESSEDNESS OF LONG REST, AND HER BODY TO THIS EARTH. JULY 29 1603.

THIS INSCRIPTION IN THE NOTE OF PIETY AND LOVE

BY HER SAD HUSBAND IS HERE

DEVOTEDLY PLACED.

Text and image together constitute a perfect representation of the emergent family, fruitful, pious, loving – and potentially tragic. The serenity of the whole can be read as an affirmation of triumph over loss, but the loss is evident in the sad husband's tribute to motherhood as the patient endurance of sorrow.[49] Daughter, wife and mother, Margaret

Figure 25   The Cholmondeley Ladies, c. 1600–1610

Legh is memorialized as an ideal woman according to family values. Her death, if it occurred while giving birth to her ninth child at the age of 33, is the outcome of marital love, and her loss is experienced as tragic in direct proportion to its cause.

V

Hermione does not die in childbirth, and her husband's behaviour is brutal in a way that Margaret Legh's is apparently not, but her 'death' is also closely related to the affection which makes it so hard to bear. *The Winter's Tale* is fiction, however, and unlike Margaret Legh, Hermione comes back to life. After 16 years of penitence, Leontes, his long-lost daughter miraculously returned, pays homage to his wife's statue in Paulina's chapel. To his astonishment, and presumably that of the audience, the sculpture moves, embraces him and speaks to their child. The family is finally restored.

But what is the nature of this restoration? We do not know how the episode was staged. Simon Forman, who saw the play in May 1611, was largely preoccupied by the details of Autolycus's confidence tricks, and omitted to mention it. But what if the statue of Hermione, which comes alive in the chapel, is not a statue in our sense of the term, but an effigy, and the frame from which it 'descends' (5.3.99) is the marble

and heraldry of a tomb? What if, in other words, the family is saved by
a miracle, an impossibility in nature? This proposition is pure speculation. I am encouraged to put it forward, however, by an essay Bruce
Smith published in 1985, in which he pointed out that there were very
few classical statues in England at this time, and not many surviving
medieval ones: 'Most of the statues that Shakespeare's audiences had
actually seen were tomb sculptures.'[50]

They might, of course, have seen reliefs of classical or allegorical
figures on plaster work, masonry or furnishings, or indeed on funeral
monuments, but there is no real reason to suppose that they would
have thought of these as 'statues'. They might also have seen pictures
of statues – or what appear to be pictures of statues.[51] Engraved title
pages often show figures standing in niches in architectural settings,
commonly standing in statuesque poses. But a closer look indicates
that it is not clear what, in these instances, apart from their locations,
makes us see them as statues, since at the level of detail they bear very
little resemblance to sculpture. Sometimes the figures are to be found
stepping out of their frames; they have precisely etched facial features,
including fully defined eyes; often their garments move in a way that
is far from classical or sculptural. The models for these title pages include pageant-arches constructed for triumphal entries, like James I's
into the City of London, where living actors presented celebratory tab-
leaux.[52] The human forms on the title pages are not copied from existing
sculptures; they are no more 'accurate', or no less inventive, than their
imaginative architectural settings.[53] Among instances more or less contemporary with the play, Hondius's title page for John Speed's *Theatre
of the Empire of Great Britaine* (London, 1611) shows figures with very
non-sculptural plumed hats, while Cornelis Boel's Bible of the same
date puts Moses in a niche, but also makes his two raised locks of hair
glow with light. There seems no particular reason to suppose that an
audience would associate Hermione's statue with these emblematic
and commonly fanciful figures.

One of the first collectors of antiquities in England was Thomas
Howard, 14th Earl of Arundel, seen here in a painting of 1618, displaying his statues, as we understand the term, in an idealized version of his
gallery (Figure 26). Arundel's collection was assembled in the second
decade of the seventeenth century. The Earl travelled in the Low Countries and Italy between 1612 and 1615, and his host in Rome in 1614 was
an Italian collector.[54] *The Winter's Tale*, probably first performed in 1609–
10, precedes by a whisker the fashion Arundel helped to inaugurate.

Figure 26 Thomas Howard, Earl of Arundel (1618) displaying his statues

Smith believes that the likely model for Hermione's statue was tomb sculpture. I want to go further and suggest that the figure might have been represented on stage as an effigy. The words were interchangeable at this time. Certainly, the golden statues promised at the end of *Romeo and Juliet* are monumental.

The hypothesis is not without difficulties. Hermione, Leontes says, 'stands':

> O, thus she stood,
> Even with such life of majesty, warm life,
> As now it coldly stands . . .
>
> (5.3.34–6)

Lady Margaret Legh sits. Most effigies of the period are shown kneeling or recumbent. There are examples of standing male figures in the 1630s,[55] and after the Civil War standing effigies in classical poses are common, but they are unusual, to say the least, in 1609–10. There was always, however, a certain ambiguity about the position of the recumbent figures. As Panofsky pointed out in the 1960s, the medieval tradition in Northern Europe commonly places monumental effigies horizontally, presumably in deference to the shape of the tomb, while requiring them to be read vertically – or, more puzzlingly, vertically *in some respects*.[56] As if their standing figures had been laid down to fit the space available, armed knights draw their swords, placing one leg in front of the other, while apparently lying on their tombs; horizontal couples are found standing under canopies, like the saints in their niches (see Figure 15, p. 93). Brasses, designed to be placed either upright on the wall or flat on the tomb chest indiscriminately, make the position relatively clear: in most instances these figures are decidedly standing (Figure 27).

Figure 27   Brass monument to John Sea (d. 1604) and two wives, Martha and Sara. Herne, Kent

But monuments in three dimensions often present unresolved contradictions. On the tomb of the Earl of Westmorland and his wife at Brancepeth, County Durham, the Countess is provided with a pillow which her head does not fully rest on, possibly because it is not dressed for sleep (Figure 13, p. 91); sometimes a pillow *is* for resting on, despite the headdress, implying a recumbent figure, but at the same time, the canopy indicates that we are to see the figure as if it were standing; in other cases, skirts hang stiffly, as if to the floor, covering feet that are not relaxed, but positioned for standing on (Figure 28). Nor is this attributable, in my view, to incompetence. The Savage monument is sophisticated work. But is Catherine Savage standing or lying on her embroidered pillow, as she holds her daughter at such an awkward angle? No standing figure would clasp a baby against her stomach like this, so we might suppose that she is horizontal, until we reach

Figure 28 Monument to Sir Fulke Greville (d. 1559) and Lady Elizabeth (d. 1562). Alcester, Warwickshire (detail)

Figure 29   Monument to Giles Savage (d. 1631) and his wife, Catherine, with William Savage. Elmley Castle, Worcestershire

her embroidered underskirt, which falls more or less straight, with scarcely a dip between the legs, over feet at right-angles to her body (Figure 29).

These anomalies are not, it seems to me, a cause for anxiety, unless we try to decide whether the figures are to be read as lying or standing. The question, in other words, does not arise unless we ask it. I raise it only because Hermione explicitly stands, and because it is conceivable that Hermione might be an effigy. The tombs do not, in my view, provide an answer. There is, however, among all the undecidable instances, one clear-cut case from the late sixteenth century (Figure 30). It is neither elegant nor sophisticated: the monument to Nicholas Lane, who died in 1595, is primitive work, uninfluenced by London fashion or, indeed, any detectable fashion at all. It is certainly not representative. The tomb is currently placed vertically, but we have no evidence that it occupies its original position in the church. It is clear, however, that Nicholas Lane is standing up. His substantial calves, his shoes with their carefully tied bows, set squarely on their pedestal,

Figure 30   Monument to Nicholas Lane (d. 1595). Alveston, Warwickshire

and the diminutive mourners who kneel in prayer at his feet, are cut from a single block of stone. If Lane is not standing, the mourners are lying on their sides. The Lane monument is in the Old Church at Alveston in Warwickshire, two miles outside Stratford-upon-Avon.[57]

While the tombs do not resolve the question of Hermione's statue, the written texts are not conclusive either. In the source, *Pandosto*, Bellaria dies and is not resurrected. It is perhaps suggestive, but no more, that the text records the inscription on her tomb.[58] The story of Pygmalion is often invoked, for obvious reasons,[59] but in Ovid, as the sculptor bends over the supine body of his ivory simulacrum, she grows warm to his touch, yielding to his fingers.[60] John Marston's witty, erotic poem of 1598, *The Metamorphosis of Pigmalions Image*, seems equally remote from Shakespeare's play: the sculpture he has made comes alive in his bed and in his arms.

Nor are there any obvious dramatic analogues. There is a 'resurrection' in Peele's *The Old Wives Tale* (?1593), but no statue. In *The Second Maiden's Tragedy* (?1611), the Tyrant embarks on a necromantic relationship with the body of the Lady, but here there is neither a statue nor a resurrection. An Echo speaks from the Duchess of Malfi's grave, but the tomb is not described. Lyly's *The Woman in the Moone* (1595–97) offers a possible source. Pandora is an image taken from Nature's workshop and animated on stage, but this is a creation scene, not a resurrection, real or illusory. A closer parallel is Massinger's *The City Madam*, where Plenty and Lacy pretend to be statues and then come alive, as if by magic. They 'descend' (5.3.109) in what might be an allusion to Shakespeare.[61] But there is some uncertainty about what the audience sees here too. The text mainly calls them 'statues' (5.3.80, 91, 99), but it also seems to refer to them as 'pictures' (5.3.2), and comments, 'There they hang' (5.3.80), which is an odd usage for what we think of as statues. In any case, *The City Madam* is perhaps as much as 20 years later than *The Winter's Tale*. Moreover, Plenty and Lacy are not thought to be dead, so the connection is tenuous. In Beaumont's *Masque of the Inner Temple* (1613), animated statues dance, but they do not come alive on stage, and they are understood to be metal, not stone ('nothing seen but gold and silver'[62]). They are only half alive, and the impression is that they 'dance' by striking statuesque poses. The masque tradition in any case offers little evidence for the practice of the public theatres.

But one play supports the possibility I have imagined that

Hermione's statue just might have been an effigy. In the remarkably complicated plot of *The Trial of Chivalry*, printed in 1605, Prince Ferdinand picks a quarrel with his friend, the Earl of Pembroke, over the lady that Ferdinand loves, the aloof Princess Katharine. Ferdinand and Pembroke fight, and 'both fall down as dead'.[63] When each recovers without the other's knowledge, Pembroke builds a tomb for the friend he still supposes dead. The remorseful Ferdinand then reappears at the tomb itself and the friends are reconciled, but not before Katharine has learned to regret her former cruelty to Ferdinand.

How, Pembroke wonders, can he best bring the lovers together? Clearly, Ferdinand must impersonate his own effigy, so that Katharine will reveal her sorrow. 'I told her', Pembroke reports,

> and no more than truth I told,
> A cunning carver had cut out thy shape
> And whole proportion in white alabaster,
> Which I intended here should be set up.
> She earnestly entreated she might have
> A sight of it, and daily be permitted
> To deck thy tomb and statue with sweet flowers.[64]

Ferdinand could hear her lamentations for himself, Pembroke goes on to suggest, if he took the place of the projected 'statue'. Ferdinand kneels on the tomb, encouraged by his friend to obey the conventions of monumental sculpture: 'Soft, there's a cushion: nay, you must be bare [bareheaded, of course], / And hold your hands up, as the manner is.' 'What if I held a book', suggests Ferdinand, 'as if I prayed?' Luckily, Pembroke is able to provide one, and urges him, just in time, to keep still. Katharine agrees that the 'statue' is very like her lost love: 'As like', in fact, 'as if it were himself indeed.' She kneels facing him, wishing that he might come alive, like Pygmalion's image, but since this is impossible, she will kill herself and be united with him in death. At this instant, the effigy speaks. Ferdinand and Katharine agree to marry at once, and the episode inaugurates a happy ending for the elaborate chivalric plot.[65]

In this one clear case of a 'statue' that is apparently reanimated on stage, the figure is explicitly an effigy on a funeral monument. Moreover, the plot concerns friends divided by unfounded jealousy, and the device of the 'statue' permits an encounter between parted lovers and an admission of sorrow which is the prelude to reconciliation. We do not know how the statue scene in *The Winter's Tale* was originally produced, still less what Shakespeare might have had in mind. But what a theatrical coup it would have been to show Hermione, 'wrinkled' (5.3.28) in accordance with an emergent verisimilitude, and painted (5.3.47–8), like most monuments but unlike Arundel's classical statues, coming down from her tomb, resurrected from the dead, restoring her husband's loss, and vindicating Paulina's words:

> 'Tis time; descend; be stone no more; approach;
> Strike all that look upon with marvel. Come!
> I'll fill your grave up: stir; nay, come away:
> Bequeath to death your numbness; for from him
> Dear life redeems you.
>
> (5.3.99–103)

This reading makes no assumptions about whether Hermione 'really' dies or only pretends to. The play, it seems to me, leaves the options open. Paradoxically, critics who interpret *The Winter's Tale* as if it were a Victorian novel prefer the view that Paulina and Hermione colluded in faking the Queen's death and burial, and in inciting Leontes to believe that he had killed her, while the whole kingdom remained oblivious of her secret preservation in seclusion for 16 years.[66] This is surely no more 'realistic' than the alternative, but the play is a romance, not a detective story, and the episode in the chapel is a signifying spectacle addressed to the audience.

The moment would be spectacular indeed if Hermione's monumental body rose from her tomb to be reunited with her husband and child. And what a comment the image would make on family values then or now: they survive after all, but only by a miracle, a resurrection, an impossibility, the effect of a supernatural intervention in the institution our own culture fervently longs to render inevitable and stable by attributing the family to natural causes.

VI

Since Shakespeare, fiction has specialized in unhappy marriages. During the nineteenth century, when the family formed the basis of

Victorian values, Thackeray, George Eliot, Dickens and Trollope, among others, followed by Hardy and Henry James, put on display the damage families can cause. And in this, they did no more than make explicit the anxieties of the class they addressed. Mimetic fiction appealed to its readers to the degree that it seemed to tell a version of the truths they knew. How, then, has the ideal of the family survived? The answer must be that family values represent another instance of the triumph of hope over experience. Marriages fail or go through difficult times; everyone knows that; the early modern Reformers knew it and treated the conjugal relation as a discipline. 'Good' marriages, however, work: a well-founded relationship, so the story goes, one which is based on true love and genuine understanding, will succeed against the odds. Unhappiness in marriage is specific, not structural, we tell ourselves, the result of individual failure, not inherent in the institution itself. The children of unhappily married parents commonly marry with their own ideals intact, at least in the first instance. Jane Austen's novels depict very few happy marriages (the Westons in *Emma* and the Gardiners in *Pride and Prejudice* represent notable exceptions), but marriage, none the less, is synonymous with a happy ending. Families fail, but we continue to believe in the ideal of the family.

The Winter's Tale has been read as confirming this belief. The pastoral episode of Act 4 has been thought to contrast a world of natural, healthy love with the court of Leontes, diseased and deadly in consequence of the pathological condition that afflicts the King. The true love and constancy of Florizel and Perdita have been seen as the source of regeneration for the whole family, a health-giving return of the spring to the court. As the Arden editor puts it,

> After the misery of the hate, strife, death, and decay at the court in the first part of the play, it is with masterly rhythm that the play moves on to happiness in the love, life, youth, growth, and power of beauty in the floral countryside in the second part. Here the young are shown as having grown by nature . . .

There are darker notes in Act 4, he concedes, but 'it is Florizel's constancy in love which makes the last act possible.'[67] The marriage of the children, it is implied, grounded in nature and mutual respect, will succeed where their parents failed. This time family values will work.

Possibly. We have no way of knowing. Happy endings are precisely endings and happy perhaps because they arrest the action at a moment of joy, without making promises for a conjectural future. Only fairy tales (and *Jane Eyre*) categorically record that the protagonists lived happily ever after. But it is equally possible that the play's own account of desire in Act 4 is less optimistic, or perhaps less naive, than a criticism steeped in family values has wanted to recognize.

To test this possibility, we might examine the case of Perdita's lost daffodils, and the desire inscribed in a speech that anthologies have rendered so familiar as to be almost inaudible. At the midsummer sheepshearing feast in Act 4 Perdita, playing Flora, wishes she had spring flowers to distribute to her young and virginal guests. What follows associates love in the most lyrical terms with the brightly lit pastoral landscapes of Ovid's *Metamorphoses* and the wild flowers of the English countryside:

> O Proserpina,
> For the flowers now that, frighted, thou let'st fall
> From Dis's waggon! daffodils,
> That come before the swallow dares, and take
> The winds of March with beauty.
>
> (4.4.116–20)

The brave – or perhaps foolhardy – daffodils, exposed to the blustering winds of March, are a fitting parallel, of course, for Perdita herself, a shepherdess who wants to marry a prince, threatened more immediately than she yet knows with the danger of discovery, the rage of his loving father, Polixenes, and a decisive separation from Florizel (4.4.16–40).

But the image is also one of desire, as the daffodils take the winds with beauty. 'Take' means charm or captivate: the flowers evidently seduce the winds. But the verb is also more explicitly sexual. There appears at first glance to be a puzzle over the question of what it is that takes what (or who takes whom), if the daffodils with their (perhaps phallic) trumpets are swept back and forth by the fierce March winds. But 'take' meaning 'take sexual possession of' is a twentieth-century term: the first author to use it seems to have been D. H. Lawrence.[68] Paradoxically, in a previous usage it meant 'admit sexually': sixteenth-century mares 'take' horses.[69] (A whole history of sexuality might be implied by the regendering of the term.) The seductive daffodils presumably surrender, then, to the fierce sexuality of the winds.

Like the daffodils, the flowers that follow in Perdita's list are commonly either subjects or objects of desire:

> ... violets, dim,
> But sweeter than the lids of Juno's eyes
> Or Cytherea's breath; pale primroses,
> That die unmarried, ere they can behold
> Bright Phoebus in his strength (a malady
> Most incident to maids); bold oxlips and
> The crown imperial; lilies of all kinds ...
>
> (4.4.120–26)

And they represent a variety of relations to the sexual, from the anaemic, loveless primroses to the forward oxlips. It is difficult to know where to place the daffodils on this continuum. Autolycus's song has earlier associated them with doxies (the female companions of vagrants, or prostitutes), while also stressing their connection with the return of sexual desire in spring, when 'the red blood reigns in the winter's pale' (4.3.4). The flower imagery embraces a range of possibilities, not all of them happy, none of them domestic.

Moreover, if the speech draws a parallel between the brave daffodils and the shepherdess's daring love, it surely presents another between the lost daughter of Hermione and the lost daughter, Proserpina, who, in Milton's later words, 'cost Ceres all that pain / To seek her through the world'.[70] According to Ovid's version of the story, the girl was gathering flowers in a grove of perpetual spring, filling her basket and her lap with violets and lilies, when, in an instant, Dis saw, loved and snatched her up. He swept her onto his chariot and plunged her into the underworld to be his bride. In her fright, the flowers fell from her torn tunic, and such was the innocence of her childish years, that this loss intensified her grief.[71]

As Ovid's sophisticated text so commonly permits, we can find any number of displacements here, but in its allusion to the story of Dis's plunging horses and Proserpina's torn clothing, Shakespeare's play silently invokes another narrative of desire, this time an account of rapè, familiar to a substantial proportion of the early modern audience from their grammar-school primer, the *Metamorphoses*.[72] Ovid recounts how Cupid shoots an arrow into the heart of Dis on the instructions of Venus, in order to reaffirm the sovereignty of love. Already, Venus complains, Athena and Diana have revolted against her, and the daughter of Ceres aspires to emulate them.[73] Helplessly enthralled, the god of the underworld sees, wants and takes her, so 'hasty, hot and swift' is love, in Golding's sixteenth-century translation.[74] The rest of the story is well known. Jove promises that Proserpina shall be returned to her mother on condition that she has consumed nothing in Pluto's kingdom. But she has eaten seven pomegranate seeds, so Jove divides the year into two equal halves, creating the seasons, and Proserpina spends the winter underground and the summer with the goddess of plenty. Thus, like so many of Ovid's tales of transformation, the story of Proserpina is also a fable of origins. For Proserpina, and for the sublunary world, just as it does for Hermione, as it does for Leontes, an arbitrary, anarchic passion brings about a state of loss – of innocence, stability, wholeness. It inaugurates division.

The Ovidian frame of Perdita's catalogue of flowers encourages a return to the puzzling gender of the (possibly phallic) daffodils. In Ovid, there are no daffodils in this story: Proserpina loses violets and lilies. The violets and lilies duly reappear in Shakespeare's account, but preceded by the most explicitly sexual of all the images in the speech. The daffodils come first in Perdita's reinscription of the Ovidian narrative and actively seduce the winds in the elusive signifier 'take'. 'Take' is one of the most equivocal words in English, its two oldest senses diametrically opposed to each other. It means both to appropriate, seize, on the one hand and to receive or accept on the other. To take money, for instance, might be to steal or to be duly rewarded. To take a lover is to leave open the question of who makes the running. Shakespeare's daffodils both captivate and submit to the winds. 'Take' creates the possibility of a radical contrast between the innocent Proserpina and the seductive daffodils.

The daffodils play no part in Ovid's story of Proserpina, but an earlier book of the *Metamorphoses* tells the influential tale of a beautiful boy, loved by a nymph, but himself in love with a beautiful boy, his own image. He despaired – and became a daffodil.[75] Narcissus surely stands as the prototype of all those early modern boys,

Marlowe's Leander and Shakespeare's Adonis, not to mention his 'Ganymede' and 'Cesario', whose physical perfections enable them to stand as objects of sexual desire for both men and women indiscriminately. A daffodil is now a yellow narcissus, but the distinctions were not so sharply defined in the seventeenth century. Early attempts to differentiate one term from the other led a horticultural text of 1629 to insist, rather irritably, that narcissus was simply the Latin name and daffodil the English 'of one and the same thing'.[76] A certain uncertainty about the gender of Proserpina's daffodils, which might once have been beautiful boys, distinguishes this early modern anatomy of love from the Victorian taxonomies we have inherited, with their clear oppositions between masculine and feminine, wholesome and perverse sexuality.

Narcissus also represents the paradigm case of a hopeless, impossible longing, predicated on the imaginary presence of his own image mirrored in the pool, and he has given his name to a critical category in the twentieth-century psychoanalytic understanding of desire. In Lacan's work, as in Freud's, narcissism constitutes the primary motive for love in the longing to return to the imagined full identity experienced by what Freud calls his Majesty the Baby, autonomous, imperious, held, cared for, recognized.[77] For psychoanalysis, identity itself is never full, riven as it is by the division between the imperatives of the human organism and the signifying system in which we struggle helplessly not only to name, but also to live them. As organisms-in-culture, we are always other than we are, and desire is born in the rift that divides us. Desire meets, in Lacan's account, only absence, lack: there is, he insists, no sexual relation.[78]

Perdita's speech is also predicated on longing. It begins, 'O ... For the flowers' (4.4.116–17) and ends, 'O, these I lack, / To make you garlands of' (127–8). The lost daughter, who wants flowers to scatter over the body of her lover (129), in turn invokes a lost daughter and the flowers whose loss intensified her grief. And Perdita herself, the desiring speaker in the guise of Flora, is other than she is, not fully present in her own identity:

> Methinks I play as I have seen them do
> In Whitsun pastorals: sure this robe of mine
> Does change my disposition.
> *The Winter's Tale* (4.4.133–5)

And yet the speech itself is densely populated with deferred, figurative subjects and objects of desire: daffodils, violets that evoke the Queen of Heaven and the goddess of love, as well as 'Bright Phoebus in his strength', the lover denied to the dead primroses. In this it strikingly resembles postmodern love, a *fort / da* game of presence glimpsed and closed off. According to Jacques Derrida's *The Post Card*, a text which contests Lacan's metaphysics of absence, (?reciprocal) love subsists as a repetition of the child's desire for perfect and total presence; always dissatisfied, however close the beloved, it seeks a completeness beyond what is possible, deconstructing the opposition between lack and possession. 'Even before abandoning me you lose me at every instant', exclaims the writer of Derrida's sequence of passionate postcards.[79] And at the same time, this lyrical, sexy, philosophical text is always other than it is, at once a love story (inconclusive, of course) and a sceptical analysis of Western metaphysics.

As I read Perdita's speech, it calls into question any simple polarity between the court and nature, true love and blindness, pathology and health. The desire it invokes is variously exhilarating, frightening, violent, divisive, blatant, thwarted, as well as irresistibly seductive; it is driven by lack and precipitates loss. If it is also daring, perhaps that too is a kind of folly, a willing suspension of common sense. We could, of course, interpret this in terms of character, explaining it as Perdita's anxiety motivated by her own precarious situation, but it is worth noting that Florizel's most lyrical contribution to this dialogue also formulates a longing for a perfect and impossible presence, an ultimately self-defeating stasis:

> When you do dance, I wish you
> A wave o'th'sea, that you might ever do
> Nothing but that; move still, still so,
> And own no other function.
>
>   (4.4.140–43)

There is, of course, a radical difference between the court scenes and the pastoral episode, between the two locations, generations and love stories in the play, but there are resemblances too. In both cases the play's account of desire seems a good deal more equivocal in every sense than critics have been willing to suppose. Colluding with what's unreal, love conjures fears as well as romantic fantasies; privation is inextricable from fulfilment. The text we have gives no indication that, even in its pastoral mode, love is a sure guarantee of the stability of the nuclear family. Indeed, desire seems an improbable basis for the discipline that marriage is expected to entail.

As *The Winter's Tale* indicates, the most helpless victims of parental love-turned-to-hate are the children, who cannot be held to blame. Mamillius, allowed to charm the audience at the beginning of the play, is not restored to life at the end. A culture that chooses to ground the family on romantic love risks revealing the unpredictability at the heart of its plan to regulate the future. Only unremitting reaffirmation of the utopian ideal, it appears, can deflect the anxieties its adherents continue to experience.

Chapter Five
Sibling Rivalry: 'Hamlet' and the First Murder

I

 frieze of stories from Genesis decorates the mid-sixteenth-century tomb of Henry Fitzroy Duke of Richmond and his wife, Lady Mary Howard, in the Parish Church at Framlingham in Suffolk. These tiny images show the conventional sequence of events leading to the construction of the first human family. The earliest panel depicts Eve emerging from Adam's rib, while God watches approvingly. In the next scene, the couple are ushered into a garden where two trees, one bearing apples, tower above the corner turrets of this sheltered enclave, which is fortified in vain, as it turns out, against the intrusion of evil. There follows the Fall and then the Expulsion. In the depiction of their banishment from Eden, the Garden is behind them, with only one tree now visible above the walls, its apples sharply defined.

As the pictorial story continues, Cain and Abel, children of the first marriage, offer sacrifices to God. Flames rise from their respective altars. Abel, the shepherd, burns a lamb, anticipating, in the conventional Christian account, the sacrifice of Christ,[1] while Cain, the firstborn and a farmer, comes bearing a sheaf of corn. According to the Old Testament narrative, God accepts Abel's sacrifice and refuses Cain's. Bitterly resentful at this arbitrary rejection, envious of the love accorded to his younger brother, Cain takes Abel out into the fields and kills him.

The Framlingham panel is defaced: Cain has lost a leg; it is impossible to identify his weapon; his face is damaged. Even so, something of the violence of the image is still visible: Cain seems to be holding his brother by the hair; Abel, taken by surprise, is at a disadvantage: already on the ground, he holds up a hand in an effort to defend himself. The first family is seen to be the location of the first murder. Adam and Eve were punished by the introduction of human mortality, but the death in question was not in this initial instance their own. Instead, they lived to see their elder son kill his brother, learning in the hardest possible way the meaning of death and the effects of mortification.[2] The skeleton that hounds them out of Paradise in Holbein's and Salomon's images of the Expulsion has designs on them in the long term, but its first victim is their son, and so too is the assassin. Holbein's next woodcut after the Expulsion shows the first family with Adam delving, while Eve suckles the infant Cain. The skeleton digs alongside Adam, mocking his efforts to ensure the survival of his wife and child (see Figure 12, p. 87). God's gift of the nuclear family, its tenderness and reciprocity a compensation for the loss of security in the Garden, led directly to murder. Abel's offering was favoured by God, and Cain's homicidal envy could find no satisfaction short of death.

The image of the first murder was remarkably familiar in early modern culture. A spangled needlework picture of 1628, now at Parham Park, West Sussex, shows Abel under an apple tree, surrounded by fluffy, glittering sheep (Figure 31). In the foreground Cain drives a pair of horses pulling a plough. Further back, on the left of the picture, the brothers offer their respective sacrifices, while opposite this image, Cain wields a cudgel over the prostrate body of his brother. In this paradoxically engaging depiction of the biblical story, the images follow no narrative sequence, and the spaces between them are filled with decorative plants: immediately behind Cain's lethal club stands a much larger flower. Evidently, the story of Cain and Abel had permeated early-seventeenth-century gentry culture in England.

Indeed, it had been familiar for hundreds of years from illuminated manuscripts, church iconography and, more recently, illustrated Bibles. At the head of Chapter 4 of the Book of Genesis in the popular 'Bishops" Bible of 1568, a muscular Cain stands with his foot on Abel's chest; Abel raises his hand to ward off the blow as his brother swings a stout club. In Bernard Salomon's widely circulated mid-century Bible pictures, the violence is equally forcibly portrayed, and this time the weapon is apparently the traditional jawbone of an ass. The jawbone, familiar since

Figure 31   Cain and Abel, needlework picture, 1628

the middle ages, had already been popularized in sixteenth-century England by a woodcut printed in the first edition of Coverdale's Bible in 1535, and in more than one of the subsequent 'Matthew' Bibles (Figure 32). Several 1570s editions of the 'Bishops'' Bible enclose the opening woodcut of Adam naming the animals in a pictorial narrative of the main events recounted in the Book of Genesis. The story begins with the sacrifices and the first murder. Abel's hands are joined in prayer, while smoke rises from his altar and the Tetragrammaton appears in a cloud above. Cain's smoke, however, billows sideways; he spreads his arms in frustration and despair. The next image shows him beating his defenceless brother with an animal's jawbone (see Figure 1, p. 37).

The conventional visual sequence in representations of the Fall, both medieval and early modern, makes a direct link between the Expulsion and the first murder, and what follows is the entire history of violence and destruction which constitutes the Old Testament. Four seventeenth-century embroidered bed-pillow covers, currently in the Victoria and Albert Museum, each show four Old Testament scenes, 16

Figure 32   The first murder, 'Matthew' Bible, 1537

episodes in all. Five images tell the story of the Fall. The fifth, derived
from Holbein, which shows Adam delving and Eve breastfeeding, is
immediately followed by the contest for God's favour between Cain
and Abel, and Abel's death. Murder takes place within the family unit
as a result of sibling rivalry, when the Father accepts Abel's sacrifice
but not Cain's. The iconographic sequence that leads from the Fall to
the family and on to murder is traditional: it repeats the pattern of the
mystery cycles and countless medieval representations of the Old Testament stories.

   The first family, I have suggested, is offered as a consolation for the
loss of Eden, and the image of Eve breastfeeding properly evokes the
mother of Christ, the second Eve who inaugurates the reversal of the
Fall. At Framlingham, however, the child on Eve's lap is evidently Abel
(Figure 33). His older brother stands beside them, and in his right hand,
by the baby's head, he holds an apple. With his left he picks another,
iconographically preparing to repeat the sin of his parents. It is impossible to trace the line of Cain's gaze since his head is damaged again.

Figure 33   The infant Cain. Framlingham, Suffolk

The consistent defacement of these images of Cain on the Framlingham tomb suggests to me that it is not accidental: it seems that the first murderer elicited the rage of at least one spectator.

In his Creation drawings Jan Wierix depicts the new family as apparently tranquil: Adam builds a house, and Eve holds her baby in her arms as she watches the cooking-pot (see Figure 11, p. 86). But there are signs of anxiety too: Cain is struggling to climb down from his mother's lap. Eve holds his arm firmly in a restraining gesture. Is the child's behaviour to be read as merely playful, or is there an anarchic element here, an indication of the conflict to come? Cain, conceived after the Fall, is heir to original sin.

The next drawing in the Wierix sequence shows Adam beginning to cultivate a space in front of the shelter. There are domestic animals, and beyond the clearing wild creatures are to be seen, no threat at the moment, but a reminder of the forces that civilization needs to keep at bay. Time has evidently passed: Eve now has two children. The three extant versions of this drawing differ slightly. One shows the domestic space enclosed by a neat fence (Figure 34). Eve sits in a kind of porch holding the younger child upright on her lap. He looks back at her, as if for approval of a developing ability to stand up. The older child can do this already: Cain stands facing his younger brother with an expression that is hard to interpret. The little boy who will grow up to cultivate the fruit of the ground (Genesis 4.3) holds an apple, again repeating the choice of evil in an act of inherited, original sin. The following picture shows their contrasting sacrifices, Abel's welcomed by God, Cain's a failure. In the background Cain beats his brother to death with a club.[3] Murderous hatred begins with sibling rivalry.

Figure 34   Jan Wierix, The infant Cain, 1607–8

Cain's apple is widely found in continental images of the first nuclear family.[4] A Swiss bed valance of 1604 reproduces from Holbein its embroidered rendering of domesticity after the Expulsion: Eve spins and nurses a baby; Adam and Death delve (Figure 35). But the bed-hanging adds details which naturalize the nuclear family: beside Eve a bitch nurses two pups and at her feet is a hen with chicks. Moreover, the valance introduces a new figure. At the centre of the tableau, Cain,

Figure 35 Cain and Abel, bed valance, 1604

now apparently about three or four years old, sits behind a rock which forms a table bearing an array of fruit. He devours an apple and stares intently at his baby brother at the breast. This image of the infant Cain, already possessed by the sin of envy, as well as the animals with their young, are copied from Tobias Stimmer's *Neue künstlicher Figuren biblische Historien* (1576). Stimmer includes a makeshift shelter, with chickens perched on the crossbeam.[5]

Although the jealousy of the infant Cain is depicted relatively rarely in English culture of the period, the image has a long ancestry. An illumination, one of a sequence illustrating the Book of Genesis, in *The Bohun Psalter*, a manuscript apparently made for Humphrey de Bohun, Earl of Hereford, in the 1370s, tells the story of Cain in five miniature scenes. The first of these shows Adam, and Eve with Abel on her lap, while Cain watches, devouring a fruit.[6]

II

Meanwhile, Shakespeare's *Hamlet* includes a scene which, by a kind of visual synecdoche, has become virtually synonymous for many with the play itself. Parodying legal argument, two clowns debate the meaning of suicide. They go on to consider the political consequences of hierarchy in a fallen world, and the durability of death. The Prince, who happens to find himself in the graveyard with his friend, picks up a succession of skulls and reflects ironically on mutability and human values, the implications of mortality and the ultimate irrelevance of hierarchy in a world bounded by death. After 210 lines of exchanges which have no obvious bearing on the events of the play and advance the action not at all, a procession of the King, Queen and attendant lords comes on bearing the coffin of Ophelia.

The scene with the gravediggers constitutes an extended interlude in the long play of *Hamlet*; it could easily be cut to abridge the performance; and yet it is among the most familiar moments in a text so well known to a modern audience that at times every other line sounds proverbial. For the Romantic critics and, indeed, well into the twentieth century, Hamlet is consistently recognizable as a figure holding a skull. Even during its own period, the image apparently possessed an emblematic quality for the audience. Although at the time of the play it was already conventional to portray young men contemplating this reminder of mortality, thus emphasizing the mutability of youth,[7] *Hamlet* (or the ur-*Hamlet*) evidently modified the traditional meaning of the representation, so that by the time of *The Revenger's Tragedy*, it is the death's head in his hand that immediately indicates the protagonist's avenging mission in the opening scene.

As Hamlet and Horatio enter, the Gravedigger's song is about the fecklessness of youth and love, eclipsed in due course by old age. Hamlet complains that he seems to have 'no feeling of his business' since he 'sings in gravemaking' (5.1.65–6),[8] but as the original audience would have known, this song about mutability has a direct relevance to the Gravedigger's trade. Whether in the portraits of young men, in the *carpe diem* convention of contemporary love poetry, or in the ascetic tradition of contempt of the world inherited by the early modern period from the middle ages, it is death that puts the joys of youth in perspective, for better or worse.[9] Death followed on from the Fall and, in the process, rendered human happiness finite.

The stage direction indicating that the Gravedigger turns up a death's head is a conjectural emendation, but it seems justified by Hamlet's comment: 'That skull had a tongue in it, and could sing once.' And he adds, 'How the knave jowls it to th' ground, as if 'twere Cain's jawbone, that did the first murder' (5.1.74–6). He could count on the audience to recognize his allusion to 'Cain's jawbone, that did the first murder', even if there is some confusion here between Cain's skull and the traditional version of his weapon, the jawbone of an ass. The story ensures that from its inaugural moment the family is seen as the site of jealousy and violence. Worse even than simple murder, fratricide is doubly tragic: as a crime against the family, it is nevertheless one that only the family permits, or perhaps incites. The stakes of the rivalry between brothers are intrinsic to the institution: the breast, the mother's love, inheritance, the father's (or Father's) blessing. Nor is the story of Cain and Abel an isolated instance. This originary moment in Genesis leads on to other fraternal rivalries, between Jacob and Esau, and then between Joseph and his brothers.

According to the Lacanian account of aggressivity, infant rivalry is an inevitable stage in the formation of identity. The self, in Lacan's story, begins to come into being as a result of identification with another child: we assume an alienating image, an identity that belongs to another. The other child's wishes become our wishes, the other child's toys more desirable than our own. To that extent, the other who constructs my identity is also my rival. The playful struggles of young children are a form of imitation and also of retaliation: children copy their playfellows – and strike them.[10]

The invocation of Lacanian psychoanalysis would throw a whole new light on the frisking of young Polixenes and Leontes, twin lads, it could be argued, in lamb's clothing. But it might seem anachronistic to invoke Lacan's very specific account of the formation of identity here, were it not for the role of 'emulation' in early modern educational theory. The young, it was supposed, might develop good qualities by emulation. But as the duality of the word implies, admiration and imitation are hard to distinguish from their opposites, competitiveness and jealousy, so that the practice of emulation is at once valuable and dangerous, a source of instruction and a rivalry to be feared.[11] William Cornwallis's essay 'Of Emulation' first equates the term with envy, and then paradoxically goes on to advise parents to encourage their children to learn by means of it.[12] Conversely, Francis Bacon points to the foolish practice of parents and schoolteachers in 'creating and breeding an emulation between brothers during childhood, which many times sorteth to discord when they are men, and disturbeth families'.[13]

Moreover, Lacan gives as an instance of infant rivalry St Augustine's account of the pallid fury that characterizes a child who sees another at the breast that nurses him too. 'I have seen with my own eyes,' Augustine records, 'and known very well an infant in the grip of jealousy: he could not yet speak, and already he observed his foster-brother, pale and with an envenomed stare.'[14] The context of this account in the *Confessions* is Augustine's affirmation of infant depravity: 'may this pass for innocency,' he asks rhetorically, 'that a baby full fed, should not endure a poor foster-child to share with him in a fountain of milk plentifully and freshly flowing?'[15] Though Augustine does not use the word in this context, Lacan reads astutely when he names the event he cites as an instance of 'original' aggression.[16]

In the early modern period there coexisted with the emerging picture of childhood innocence and vulnerability a directly contrary view of children. Few writers exercised a greater influence on Reformation values than St Augustine. Through Luther and Calvin, the theory of infant depravity progressively drove out humanist educational theory and practice from the schools of Tudor England. Is it fanciful to suppose that the traditional image of the infant Cain eating an apple, his eyes fixed on Abel at his mother's breast, alludes to the passage from the *Confessions*? In any case, as countless illustrations of the period make clear, the nuclear family, offered as a kind of compensation for the loss of Eden, is also the location of homicidal jealousy.

The closest analogue in Shakespeare's works to the story of Cain and Abel is the rivalry in *As You like It* which prompts Oliver to plot the murder of his innocent younger brother, Orlando. Oliver's motive, the play indicates, is his own misprision: in what might easily be a humanist secularization of the story of Cain's arbitrary resentment, Oliver claims that Orlando's virtues attract the love of the world, and make him correspondingly ugly (1.1.162–9).[17] St Augustine accounts for the first murder in similar terms. Like the rage of the fully fed infant, Cain's rivalry is not a desire to seize something Abel possesses. On the contrary, he explains, since Abel has nothing, 'Cain's envy was rather of that diabolical sort that the wicked feel for the good just because they *are* good, not wicked like themselves.'[18] Cain and Abel are not mentioned in *As You Like It*, but the analogy with the familiar story gives added point to the archetypal name of old Adam ('Adam Spencer' in Lodge's *Rosalynde*, the play's main source). Adam behaves in many ways like a stand-in for Orlando's dead father, and elicits in turn a filial courtesy which demonstrates to the audience the piety that helps prove Orlando a worthy husband for Rosalind. Although the villain's prototype in Lodge's source-narrative is not a family member, the play also includes in Duke Frederick one of Shakespeare's usurping brothers, like Antonio in *The Tempest*, Richard III and, of course, Claudius in *Hamlet*.

Hamlet originates in fratricide, and invokes the parallel with the death of Abel. 'O, my offence is rank', exclaims Claudius, 'it smells to heaven; / It hath the primal eldest curse upon't – / A brother's murder' (3.3.36–8). And the motive, he himself confesses in his effort to pray, was envy, though this time of his brother's power and his wife: after all, he still possesses

> those effects for which I did the murder –
> My crown, mine own ambition, and my queen.
>
> (3.3.54–5)

Attempting to reconcile Hamlet to his father's death, Claudius invokes 'the first corse' (1.2.105). Ironically, the first corpse was Abel's, and his blood cried out to God for vengeance (Genesis 4.10).[19] Sibling rivalry leads to the death of old Hamlet, and inaugurates the sequence of killings which eventually destroy Rosencrantz and Guildenstern, Polonius, Ophelia and Laertes, as well as Gertrude, Claudius, and Hamlet himself. In consequence of family violence, the play opens on to a world of death both within the family unit and beyond it.

III

The skulls Hamlet addresses sceptically, scathingly, wittily in the grave-yard are introduced as a succession of social types: a politician, a courtier, a lawyer, and then – the only named figure – Yorick, the fool. 'Now get you', he urges Yorick's skull, 'to my lady's chamber and tell her ... to this favour she must come' (5.1.186–8). His allusion to the lady as yet another representative figure immediately prompts a new association: 'Dost thou think Alexander look'd o' this fashion i'th' earth?' (191–2): the conqueror of the known world himself conquered by death in due course. Alexander is evidently there to represent a further estate of the realm, this time the highest: 'Imperious Caesar, dead and turn'd to clay, / Might stop a hole to keep the wind away' (206–7). From the emperor to the fool, no one escapes the corruption of death. Hamlet's final words, as the procession arrives, are perhaps in the context more ominous than he knows – for Claudius, and also, perhaps, for Gertrude and Laertes: 'Here comes the King, / The Queen, the courtiers' (210–11).

A woodcut of about twenty years earlier shows a bishop preaching to a line of figures, first a king, then a woman, a lawyer and a labourer (Figure 36). Each claims to be more powerful than the last: 'I pray for you four', the prelate affirms. 'I defend you four', asserts the king, fully armed and pointing to the plumes in his helmet. The woman, richly dressed, with a feathered fan, holds a little dog under her arm: 'I vanquish you four', she insists. According to the verse below:

> The smiling quean, the harlot called by name,
> Stands stiff upon the blaze of beauty brave.
> To vanquish all she makes her prized claim,
> And that she ought the golden spurs to have;
> For by her sleights she can bewitch the best,
> The strong, the Lawyer and the rest.

The lawyer himself, who carries a parchment, urges, 'I help you all to your right'. Behind him the labourer, spade in hand, and seed pouch and pruning hook at his belt, lays claim to true supremacy on the grounds that he feeds them all. But a thin hand on his shoulder makes clear where true power lies:

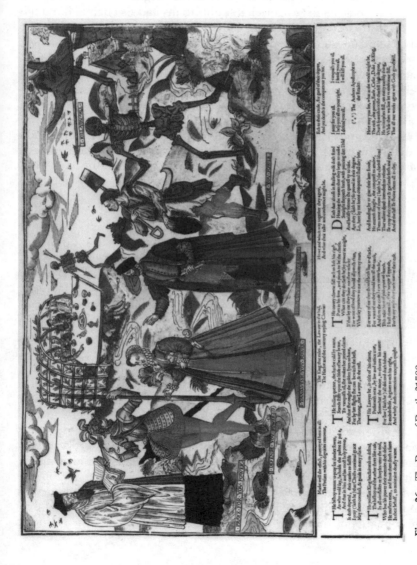

Figure 36 *The Dance of Death*, ?1580

> Death, that aloof in stealing wise doth stand,
> Hearing the vaunts that they begin to make,
> Straight steppeth forth, with piercing dart in hand,
> And boldly seems the quarrel up to take.
> Are they (saith he) so proud in their degree?
> Lo, here by me soon conquered shall they be.

'I kill you all', announces the skeleton in the woodcut.[20]

Both the broadside and the play constitute reinscriptions of the Dance of Death, a tradition familiar all over Europe since at least the early fifteenth century.[21] In the oldest versions of the Dance, emaciated corpses, who draw a succession of reluctant figures into the ring, make no distinction between wealth and poverty. They seize representative types from the Emperor to the Fool and coax them into the Dance. The great leveller is unimpressed by privilege. According to the broadside,

> Here may you see what as the world might be,
> The rich, the poor, earl, Caesar, duke and king;
> Death spareth not the chiefest high degree;
> He triumphs still on every earthly thing.[22]

All human beings are descendents of Adam, though in the woodcut only the labourer still follows Adam's trade. This is part of the message of the scene from *Hamlet* too, but the play adds gardeners, ditchers and gravemakers, and claims, in an allusion to the rhyme that played a part in the Peasants' Revolt, that Adam was the first gentleman and bore arms: 'The Scripture says Adam digged. Could he dig without arms?' the Gravedigger insists, unanswerably (5.1.36–7). 'When Adam delved and Eve span, / Who was then the gentleman?' asked John Ball. The second clown has already addressed the Gravedigger as 'Goodman Delver' (5.1.14), and it is between this interpellation and the Gravedigger's affirmation of Adam's gentility that they confirm each other's resentment of the privileged right of 'great folk' 'to drown or hang themselves more than their even-Christen' (5.1.27–9).

An egalitarian thread runs all the way through the scene in the churchyard: skulls have no status and mere gravediggers lord it over the remains of the powerful. 'This might be the pate of a politician which this ass now o'er-offices' (76–8), Hamlet comments; 'Here's fine revolution and we had the trick to see't. Did these bones cost no more the breeding but to play at loggets with 'em? Mine ache to think on't' (89–91);[23] and finally, as if alluding to a procession like the one in the woodcut, 'the age is grown so picked that the toe of the peasant comes so near the heel of the courtier he galls his kibe' (scrapes his chilblain, 135–8). Kings, we are invited to recognize, can die; but so too can the prince who assassinates them in an act of revenge; and as little as eight or nine years on (161–2), there is nothing to choose between them and the court jester.

In the rest of Act 5 Death, so grimly visualized as the officer who places his hand on the shoulder of the insouciant labourer in the woodcut, becomes a spectral, figurative character in the play that is performed before the court of Denmark. He is invoked by the dying Hamlet as the remorseless agent of a law that permits no delay:

> You that look pale and tremble at this chance,
> That are but mutes or audience to this act,
> Had I but time – as this fell sergeant, Death,
> Is strict in his arrest – O, I could tell you –
> But let it be.
>
> (5.2.339–43)

Conversely, Fortinbras sees him as a murderous host:

> O proud Death,
> What feast is toward in thine eternal cell,
> That thou so many princes at a shot
> So bloodily hast struck?
>
> (5.2.369–72)

The woodcut also shows a feast, though this time Death is a visitor and the banquet takes place in an arbour. While plants curl round a trellis, the king entertains the harlot, the lawyer and the bishop. The table rests on the back of the labourer who feeds them, and bears wine and grapes, meat and spice. Lowering his spear, Death fingers the food, no doubt preparing to poison it.

The broadside printed by John Awdely in 1569 is closer to the traditional images of the Dance of Death, but each new representation

Figure 37 *The Dance and Song of Death*, 1569

offers scope for invention (Figure 37). Here dancing skeletons pull into a circle pairs of antithetical representative types: a king and a beggar, an old man and a child, a wise man and a fool. In this instance, too, what is at stake is Death's indifference to the status, age and attributes of his victims. At the centre of the circle Sickness, Death's minstrel, pipes a tune. His flesh marked with sores, Sickness is poised over an open grave; the bones that support his seat rest on the handles of a spade and pickaxe, tools of the gravedigger.

Images in the corners of the woodcut allude to the *ubi sunt* tradition, which points the vanity of worldly values. 'Where now', so the conventional rhetorical question goes, 'is youth, beauty, pleasure?' The bottom right-hand corner shows another feast in another arbour. This time lovers, enclosed by a trellis, only have eyes for each other, as yet unaware that the figure of Death sits beside them, urging them to join the Dance. The Fool, meanwhile, looks back longingly at the world he has lost. 'Where be your gibes now, your gambols, your songs, your flashes of merriment, that were wont to set the table on a roar?' Hamlet asks the skull of Yorick. 'Not one now to mock your own grinning? Quite chop-fallen?' (5.1.183–6). And in the case of the lawyer, 'Where be his quiddities now, his quillities, his cases, his tenures, and his tricks?' (5.1.97–8). In the woodcut the judge, at the top right, is intercepted at the moment of delivering judgment. Where now, the image implicitly asks, is the judge's power of life and death over others?[24]

Hamlet's mockery is consonant with the tradition. The Dance of Death was always a vehicle of social satire. Lydgate's Catholic translation of the text from the French, reprinted by Tottel in 1554,[25] with its fat abbot and well-dressed abbess, its dissolute monk and its worldly parson, could easily be reread for Protestantism when the moment came, as could Holbein's famous woodcuts, reprinted by a Reformation press in Lyons in 1542.[26] Perhaps the durability of the tradition owes something to the ambivalence it evokes. There is a *frisson* of horror, certainly, at the gloating, capering figures of the Dead, but a sense of triumph too, as pretension is brought down and pride laid low.

> To what base uses we may return, Horatio! Why, may not imagination trace the noble dust of Alexander till a find it stopping a bung-hole?
>
> (*Hamlet* 5.1.196–8).

This is a major theme of the ballad, *Death's Dance*, printed in about 1625, which proposes that there would be radical changes if Death would only make his presence felt at every corrupt transaction, all unjust judgments, each instance of ill-founded pride. The illustrations show dancing skeletons, a parade of citizens, and the arrival of Death at a sickbed, an image derived from the *Ars Moriendi* tradition.

Evidently the Dance and its variants were still a recognizable component of popular culture a quarter of a century after the first performance of *Hamlet*.[27] But the play, like the earliest recorded visual representations, sets the Dance in a graveyard. The most famous Dance of Death, painted in 1424, was depicted on the south wall of the Cimetière des Saints Innocents in Paris. That Dance was destroyed in 1699, but not before Guyot Marchant had produced in 1485 a best-selling book based on the images. Marchant's first edition showed 15 pairs of figures, preceded by a woodcut of the group providing the music. Here, in a setting which evokes the cloister where the Dance was originally painted, figures of the Dead offer to partner alternating religious and lay figures, beginning with the Pope and the Emperor, and descending through the estates (Figure 38). These are not skeletons: the anatomy theatres had not yet impressed the bone structure of the human frame on the popular imagination. But the cadaverous mummies, back from the dead, are no less uncanny for that. They

Figure 38   Guyot Marchant, The Pope and the Emperor, *La Danse macabre*, 1485

closely resemble the shrouded corpses widely displayed on *transi* tombs from the mid-fourteenth century onwards as a reminder of the fate of the body weeks or months after death. The Dance in book form was so successful that in 1486 Marchant produced a new and enlarged edition. A month later he followed this with a *Danse Macabrè des femmes*. Meanwhile, London had its own representation of the Dance. And like the Grossbasel Dance, painted on the outer wall of the lay cemetery of the Dominican Friary in Basle, the London version, too, was located in a graveyard – at St Paul's. Here is Stow's account (printed, it should be borne in mind, nearly 50 years after the walls of the churchyard were pulled down in 1549, but two or three years before the conjectural first performance of *Hamlet*):

> There was also one great cloister on the north side of this Church, environing a plot of ground, of old time called Pardon Churchyard . . . . About this cloister was artificially and richly painted the Dance of Machabray, or Dance of Death, commonly called the Dance of Pauls, the like whereof was painted about S Innocents' cloister at Paris in France. The metres or poesie of this Dance were translated out of French into English by John Lydgate, the monk of Bury, and with the picture of Death leading all estates painted about the cloister . . . . In the cloister were buried many persons, some of worship and others of honour, the monuments of whom, in number and curious workmanship, passed all other that were in that church.[28]

Many less illustrious bodies were buried without monuments, however, in medieval cemeteries. Indeed, they were often laid directly in the earth with no coffin. Subsequently they might be dug up to make way for new corpses, and the bones and skulls, returned from their graves, would be assembled in a charnel house.[29] Whether by accident or design, Shakespeare's play locates its own variant of the Dance in an altogether appropriate setting.

IV

The Dance of Death was extraordinarily popular in England. Traces of it survive even now at Hexham Priory in Northumberland, in Newark Parish Church, as part of an early-sixteenth-century window at St Andrew's, Norwich, and as misericords in St George's Chapel, Windsor. Until the Second World War St Michael's Cathedral in Coventry had figures from the Dance on three misericords; a handwritten note in Stow's copy of Leland's *Itinerary* refers to a Dance of Death in the Parish Church at Stratford-upon-Avon. Similar images also appeared in print, sometimes without obvious motivation. For example, they decorate the pages of Richard Day's *Book of Christian Prayers*, printed in London in 1578. The woodcuts, repeated three times with variations, show skeletons, shrouds and charnel houses, as well as the Dance itself, and fill the margins of the pages in the manner of a medieval psalter. They bear no obvious reference to the prayers in question. Some of the large capitals (A, I, T) in a Bible printed by James Nycolson in 1537 show Death and a partner.

The Dance was also popular all over Northern Europe.[30] Basle had two, the first in Kleinbasel in a nunnery, and the second an appropriation of the same images by Dominican friars in Grossbasel on the other side of the river. It was after moving to Basle in 1515 that Holbein completed the designs which were finally printed as woodcuts in Lyons in 1538. These *Pictures of Death* begin with the Creation and Fall, and go on to depict Death's consequent presence in the lives of a succession of representative social types, including the Emperor, the King, the Queen, the Lawyer and the Lady, figures who also feature, in one way or another, in the graveyard scene in *Hamlet*. Holbein's woodcuts were famous all over Europe by the time he died five years later; they were copied and pirated endlessly in the course of the sixteenth century.

Some of this popularity may be attributed, I have suggested, to an undecidability in the effect of the Dance. The horror spectators might be expected to feel in the contemplation of their inevitable destiny, and the sense of the uncanny prompted by the grotesque images of dancing revenants, is legitimately accompanied by a certain triumph in the spectacle of pride, complacency or corruption brought low, as the mighty are put down from their seats and the rich are sent empty away. Populism is a strong element of Christian culture from the *Magnificat* on. To the degree that the spectator shares the point of view of the living in the Dance, the image is a source of fear, but from the perspective of the Dead, the Dance is a promise of mastery. The animated corpses are remorseless: without souls, they are also without pity.[31] Resistance is vain: they have nothing to offer their victims but mockery. This perspective is also available to a spectator – and, of course, to Hamlet, whose corrosive wit in the graveyard is also an assertion of command: 'Now get you to my lady's chamber and tell her, let her paint an inch thick, to this favour she must come. Make her laugh at that' (*Hamlet* 5.1.186–9).

Our own death is a chastening thought, but the mortality of others can be, paradoxically, reassuring, an affirmation of our own survival. There is also an erotic element, however, in the appeal of the Dance.[32] Marchant's woodcuts, however, attribute all the vitality, ironically, to the sinewy figures of the Dead. The Squire, meanwhile, hangs back coyly; the Bishop does his best to ignore the corpses before and behind him. Only the Fool is fool enough to join in willingly. The Dead hold the hands of the living, or take their arms; they do not use force. They hardly need to. Instead, they smile as they welcome their partners into

Figure 39   Guyot Marchant, The Lawyer and the Minstrel, *La Danse macabre*, 1485

the Dance. They tease the Lawyer, while they invite him to plead in his own defence before the Great Judge: one of the Dead arrests him, taking the part of the fell sergeant, and the other nonchalantly twitches his scarf (Figure 39). When the living are women, the element of seduction is more pronounced. The single new illustration in Marchant's *Danse des femmes* leaves out the traces of the cloister (Figure 40). In a setting that in consequence more closely resembles a Garden of Love, one of the Dead takes the arm of the Queen firmly, but without malice, while the other prances engagingly before the Duchess. The living are

Figure 40 Guyot Marchant, The Queen and the Duchess, *La Danse des femmes*, 1486

courtly ladies, appropriately distant; whether anxious or aloof, they hold back before they succumb. No matter that the corpses are identified in the text as feminine ('*la morte*'): this dark, narcissistic desire is prohibited on all counts.

The erotic element, which is no more than a possibility in the traditional versions of the Dance, was more fully developed by the sixteenth-century painters in the Northern European tradition, where the personification of Death seems to have taken deeper cultural hold and to have lasted longer. Niklaus Manuel Deutsch shows a nubile young woman surrounded by the imagery of desire (Figure 41). But her lover is the familiar protagonist of the Dance of Death, mimetically portrayed, his cadaverous body only partly covered by the tattered remnants of his shroud. The painting would have made sense to Shakespeare's Romeo. 'Shall I believe', he asks rhetorically over the body of Juliet in the tomb,

> That unsubstantial Death is amorous,
> And that the lean abhorred monster keeps
> Thee here in dark to be his paramour?
> *Romeo and Juliet* (5.3.102–5)

Figure 41   Niklaus Manuel Deutsch, *Death and a Young Woman*, 1517

Niklaus Manuel was responsible for the Bern *Totentanz* in the cloister of the Dominican Friary, and this too developed the erotic possibilities of the Dance. Kaspar Meglinger's version, painted in Lucerne more than a century later, includes a Prioress. Behind her Death raises the curtain of her bed, clambering over rumpled sheets towards her un-suspecting back. Meanwhile, in a picture of *Death and a Woman* (one of several) by Hans Baldung Grien, the appeal to the spectator combines the erotic with the uncanny, as Death ignores the fabric that fails to cover the woman's naked body (Figure 42). His grasp is greedy, de-vouring (literally: he is about to bite her); her expression is one of helpless terror, or perhaps ecstasy. Like a duck-rabbit, or a vase that is also two faces, the picture stresses now mortality, now the sexual, or perhaps both at once. Death and desire meet as the woman's covering, which might be either a bedsheet or a shroud, falls away in a setting that appears to be a cemetery.[33] The image depicts an intensity of emo-tion beyond pleasure.

In English drama *The Revenger's Tragedy* reverses the sex-roles to show a death's head seducing the Duke and poisoning him with a kiss, in the form of the 'bony lady', who 'has somewhat a grave look with her'. This figure is all that remains of Vindice's lost love.[34] The tyran-nical villain of *The Second Maiden's Tragedy* (1611–12) dies kissing the poisoned lips of the Lady he has abducted. Paradoxically, it is a dead body which most decisively elicits Hamlet's desire: 'I lov'd Ophelia', he declares, as he leaps into the grave in imitation of her brother's last embrace (5.1.264, 243).[35]

Baldung's image of *Death and a Woman* is remodelled in the paint-er's own later depiction of the archetypal ideal sexual relationship – appropriately, since the Fall brought death into the world (Figure 43). Here the serpent is poised menacingly behind Eve, who clasps the Tree of Knowledge and holds in her hand the fatal apple. The less than in-nocent eroticism of the central couple is framed by darkness, already marked out for mortality. Elsewhere, in a picture now in the National Gallery of Canada, Ottawa, Baldung conflates Adam and Death in a single figure: the first man becomes an emaciated corpse at the very moment that he takes the apple. The serpent bites Adam's other desir-ing hand as it grasps Eve's arm, linking the three figures in a knot of sexuality and death which forms the centre of the image.[36] From this moment on, we are invited to suppose, Death shadows all human en-deavour – and all living passion. The point is most fully developed in Holbein's *Pictures of Death* where, after four woodcuts of the Creation

Figure 42   Hans Baldung Grien, *Death and a Woman*

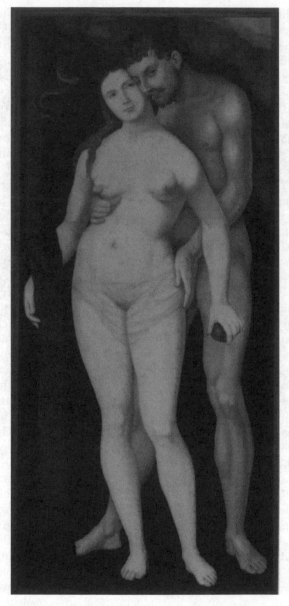

Figure 43   Hans Baldung Grien, *Adam and Eve*, 1531

and Fall, the skeleton who dances triumphantly at the Expulsion goes on to reappear as a dancing partner for the Pope, the Emperor and the other representatives of the estates, including a pair of lovers and a nun who turns from her prayers to greet a young man.

What is the moment of these images, or what is the location of the Dance of Death? If in one sense the Dance brings home to the spectator the horror that awaits all human beings, it also contradicts the meaning of that horror. The Dead are uncannily possessed by an urgent, hectic energy, while the living are precisely living: not, that is to say, in the process of expiring, not at their last gasp, but immersed in the pleasures of life. A sixteenth-century French Book of Hours depicts Death and the Emperor. At the foot of the page a lover shows his mistress her own beauty in a mirror. On the opposite page Death, grotesquely parodying the god of love, shoots an arrow at the couple as they walk together.[37] The Dance does not dramatize the instant of death itself, but the energetic intrusion of death into life. It thus represents a moment of recognition, whose real destination is the spectator, when human beings acknowledge death's mastery – and its consequent power to seduce. As organisms-in-culture, we are not only subject to death, but aware of it too. We are always, the iconography of the Dance seems to urge, dancing with death, called into a dance which is life-in-the-consciousness-of-death. As signifying subjects, we come to inhabit the sphere of difference, a world inhabited and defined by the threat of loss and absence, including the ultimate absence; in human life the recognition of death is always a possibility, as the trace of the differentiating other. It is our knowledge of death, the Dance paradoxically suggests, which gives life its intensity, including sexual intensity. A trace of death affirms the presence of the living present.[38] The Epicureans were believed to bring their skeletons to the feast not to quell the appetite, but to enhance it. In this sense, the dancing Dead, otherworldly visitants whose huge eye-sockets mark them as subject to an avid, insatiable longing, at the same time present themselves as objects of a desire that reaches beyond pleasure.

Death 'itself', the state of being dead, is non-existence (anything else is life, or life-after-death) and, as such, death is unknowable.[39] Freud maintained that it was impossible to imagine our own death as an experience – 'and whenever we attempt to do so we can perceive that we are in fact still present as spectators'.[40] Hamlet cannot imagine it either: 'To die – to sleep . . . .. To sleep, perchance to dream' (*Hamlet* 3.1.60–65): it is the thought of life after death that inhibits action, makes 'cowards of us all' (3.1.83). By definition, death exceeds what we can know empirically:

> Fundamentally one knows perhaps neither the meaning nor the referent of this word. It is well known that if there is one word that remains absolutely unassignable or unassigning with respect to its concept and to its thingness, it is the word 'death'. Less than for any other noun, save 'God' – and for good reason, since their association here is probably not fortuitous – is it possible to attribute to the noun 'death', and above all to the expression 'my death', a concept or a reality that would constitute the object of an indisputably determining experience.[41]

The Dance of Death does not represent the state of being dead. On the contrary, the encounter between the living and their unearthly but agile partners takes place on a terrain at the limits of life and knowledge, the zone where death invades the familiar world of the living and invests it, ironically, with additional intensity.[42] The Dance offers to lure the spectator on to this liminal terrain, presenting the avid, desiring Dead as returned from the grave and thus possessed of a knowledge impossible for us, but exerting an attraction beyond pleasure, the pull of a secret. Frightening, triumphant and seductive all at once, the spectacle of the Dance of Death thus 'dances' with the spectator.

V

Hamlet also inhabits this same terrain where death invades the world of the living, lured there by an otherworldly visitant who is himself motivated by an insatiable desire. The Ghost, Hamlet affirms, unsettles mortal convictions, 'With thoughts beyond the reaches of our souls' (1.4.56). When this revenant beckons, the Prince is powerless to resist, despite the repeated efforts of Horatio and Marcellus to restrain him, by force when it seems necessary. 'My fate cries out,' Hamlet insists, and follows the Ghost (1.4.81). It is midnight (1.1.7), the moment that deconstructs the opposition between life and death, 'When churchyards yawn, and hell itself breathes out / Contagion to this world' (3.2.380–81).[43] In darkness and 'bitter cold' (1.1.8) Old Hamlet, duly clothed for burial, 'hearsed' and 'quietly inurn'd' (1.4.47, 49), has returned from his marble tomb to terrify the living. Beneath his armour, the text affirms, is a 'dead corse' (1.4.52), bones that have burst their shroud (1.4.47–8).

Guyot Marchant's French text of the Dance of Death names each interlocutor of the living as '*le mort*' or '*la morte*', the dead person, not '*la mort*', death. The Basle Dance in the Dominican Friary, though it designates each figure '*der Tod*' (Death), shows the mummy sharing some of the properties of its victim, a haggard, attenuated simulacrum of its living partner: the women dance with female figures, the 'cripple' with a mutilated corpse; the Knight's partner wears a breastplate and carries a sword.[44] Although Lydgate translates '*le mort*' into English as 'Death', Sir Thomas More perceives the corpses of the Dance at St Paul's as a mirror for the spectators, 'the loathly figure of our dead bony bodies bitten away the flesh.'[45] In Shakespeare's play, the living Hamlet meets a revenant who shares his name and who impels him towards his own death.

From its first entrance, the Ghost enacts a grim parody of seduction, teasing, tantalizing, enigmatic. It appears, but does not speak; in an elaborate game of *fort/da*, it comes and goes mysteriously, unaccountably. How do we understand a ghost? The text is evasive: 'What, has this thing appear'd again tonight?' Horatio asks (1.1.24). The figure of the Ghost, more commonly referred to as 'it' than 'he', is an 'apparition' (line 31), perhaps a 'fantasy' (line 26). Is this the dead King, Old Hamlet, the Prince's father? But a spectre and a person are not the same thing; they are divided by death, which distinguishes the revenant from its living predecessor, renders the ghost inhuman. '*It is*', Derrida argues, 'something that one does not know . . . .'

One does not know: not out of ignorance, but because this non-object, this non-present present, this being-there of an absent or departed one no longer belongs to knowledge. At least no longer to that which one thinks one knows by the name of knowledge.[46]

The apparition in *Hamlet* comes from elsewhere, from beyond a determinate boundary; it alludes to the secrets of the grave that must not be revealed (1.5.13 ff). The Ghost beckons from an unbridgeable distance. Nevertheless, it delivers its appeal to Hamlet as a father, in the name of familial love (1.5.23), and Hamlet responds in kind (1.5.30). Like the dancing Dead, the Ghost is driven by an insatiable desire – to be remembered and avenged. Michael Neill brilliantly makes the case that, when Protestantism outlaws the traditional chantry masses for the souls of the dead, the obligation to remember and, indeed, appease them is borne the more intensely by those who survive. Revenge tragedy, he argues, in the same way as the Dance of Death, represents an engagement with the anxiety of remembrance.[47] The Ghost's tale is one of desire thwarted, of family values destroyed by Gertrude's infidelity and Claudius's 'luxury and damned incest' (1.5.83). But the spectral father's command is deadly: 'Revenge his foul and most unnatural murder' (1.5.25).

By speaking in the name of the father, the spirit lays claim to the authority of the paternal law. Fathers, who socialize and civilize their sons, who, by inculcating the proprieties of their culture, prepare little boys to take their own place in due course, are entitled to expect obedience. Filial piety consists in a proper respect for the father and his surrogates, the tutor, the teacher. When Hamlet indicates, by promising to 'sweep' to his revenge, that he has duly internalized his lesson, the Ghost comments approvingly, 'I find thee apt' (1.5.31), for all the world as if it were delivering a school report. Eager to act, the pupil, we are invited to believe, is neither lazy nor stupid. On the contrary, but then

> duller shouldst thou be than the fat weed
> That roots itself in ease on Lethe wharf,
> Wouldst thou not stir in this.
>
> (1.5.32–4)

The educational authority of the father is reinforced by the love that is due within the family, and the Ghost invokes that emotion as well as Hamlet's duty: 'If thou didst ever thy dear father love . . ..' (1.5.23). To this day, family values have not lost their rhetorical power. The Ghost of Hamlet's father can count on filial and familial feeling to motivate a son who has been brought up to recognize the authority of nature in allegedly creating a relation of love between parents and children, and between the siblings who share their blood. Even now, despite any number of counter-examples, we continue to suppose that genetic inheritance must produce affection as well as obligation. Claudius contravenes the law of nature in repeating the sin of Cain: fratricide is 'foul and most unnatural murder' (1.5.25); he also breaks it by seducing his brother's wife. By contrast, the Ghost wants Hamlet to act in accordance with his natural impulses, in order to prevent the criminal's continued enjoyment of the fruits of his unnatural deeds:

> If thou hast nature in thee, bear it not,
> Let not the royal bed of Denmark be
> A couch for luxury and damned incest.
>
> (1.5.81–3)

Hamlet *has* nature in him, and passion too: 'O most pernicious woman! / O villain, villain, smiling damned villain!' (1.5.105–6). And as the Ghost darts back and forth, coming and going under the stage, the son 'dances' in response, skipping backwards and forwards across the acting space: 'Art thou there, truepenny?'; '*Hic et ubique*? Then we'll shift our ground. / Come hither, gentlemen'; 'Well said, old mole. Can'st work i'th' earth so fast? / O worthy pioner! Once more remove, good friends' (1.5.158; 164–5; 170–71).

In the intensity of the moment, Hamlet responds eagerly to the Ghost's seduction and undertakes to 'sweep' to an act of vengeance which risks his own death (1.5.31). But the remainder of the play replicates the ambiguity of the Dance itself for the spectator: the living Hamlet hangs back after all, resists his own seduction, fears the death he also embraces. His soliloquies are preoccupied with what seems an unaccountable anxiety: 'Am I a coward?' he asks (2.2.566);

> it cannot be
> But I am pigeon-liver'd and lack gall
> To make oppression bitter, or ere this
> I should ha' fatted all the region kites
> With this slave's offal.
>
> (2.2.572–6)

The play registers Hamlet's ambivalence in the imagery of its period, the effect of centuries of Christian iconography. What it withholds – both from the hero and from the audience – is the place of origin which would specify the moral identity of the Ghost. At its first appearance to Hamlet, he approaches it in the explicit recognition of this uncertainty:

> Be thou a spirit of health or goblin damn'd,
> Bring with thee airs from heaven or blasts from hell,
> Be thy intents wicked or charitable,
> Thou com'st in such a questionable shape
> That I will speak to thee.
>
> (1.4.40–44)

What is a 'questionable shape'? A shape, perhaps, which prompts a question, a signifier whose significance is unknown? Does the term 'shape' imply the possibility of alternatives, of other shapes? Has a shape no shape of its own, no proper shape? Or might this figure change its shape at will, on the basis that there is behind the appearance a substantial, if immaterial, identity, whether angel or demon?

The Romantic critics, locating the cause of Hamlet's delay in the character of the sensitive prince – too imaginative, too intellectual, too 'poetic', as, indeed, they were themselves, to be capable of direct intervention in the affairs of a violent world – tended to disregard the questionable shape of a spectral figure from outside the frame of what it is possible for human beings to know. And Hamlet, caught up in the immediate intensity of filial propriety and family values, at the moment of the encounter disregards it too, accepting the spectral father's injunction as precisely *un*questionable. But his first anxiety recurs throughout the play, as the hero repeatedly reopens the 'question' of an injunction from the Ghost of a loving father who, apparently, commands an action which might incur his son's damnation. 'The spirit that I have seen', he reflects,

> May be a devil, and the devil hath power
> T'assume a pleasing *shape*, yea, and perhaps,
> Out of my weakness and my melancholy,
> As he is very potent with such spirits,
> Abuses me to damn me. I'll have grounds
> More relative than this.
>
> (2.2.594–600)

What kind of father would expose his son to the possibility of damnation? Why Adam, of course, and in Adam all his descendants. As Thomas Peyton rhetorically asks,

> Adam, what made thee wilfully at first
> To leave thy offspring to this day accursed,
> So wicked, foul and overgrown with sin;
> And in thy person all of it begin?[48]

The play reduplicates fathers who seem to risk their sons' immortal souls by demanding acts of violence as proof of love: Old Fortinbras;

Achilles, whose blood incites the rugged Pyrrhus to kill Priam; and finally Hamlet's own victim, Polonius. Claudius, who speaks on Polonius's behalf, repeats the appeal of the Ghost: 'Laertes, was your father dear to you?' And he adds, as if he has learnt from Hamlet's affirmation of the difference between appearance and 'that within', 'Or are you like the painting of a sorrow, / A face without a heart?' (4.7.106–8) Challenged to demonstrate filial love, Laertes offers the most sacrilegious of murders: 'To cut his throat i'th' church' (4.7.125). Fortinbras, however, restrained by his uncle, relinquishes the attempt to recover the lands his father lost. And Hamlet, too, on reflection withholds the blind, hectic and deadly obedience that filial love seems to require. He seeks 'grounds', and to know the 'nobler' course. Hamlet, in other words, wants to make up his own mind.

An analysis of the play as a record of Hamlet's quest for the grounds on which to base an ethical decision represents an alternative reading to the Romantic story of the sensitive, suicidal Prince. As a filial avenger, ready to act in the familial name of nature, love and duty, Hamlet confronts an objection, which paradoxically reproduces with a difference, which is to say repeats, the very terms of his obligation. His immediate, passionate response to the Ghost's appeal involves turning against his mother: 'O most pernicious woman' (1.5.105). Revenge means killing her husband, his uncle and his King; it entails a breach of both family values and the authority structure of a patriarchalist Renaissance regime, where the king lays claim to the obedience due precisely to a father. Uncles in general, as everyone knows, are (or ought to be) indulgent incarnations of family feeling, embodiments of the father's affection, without his fearful power to prohibit. And the Claudius of Act 1 outwardly conforms to type, even though his sulky nephew refuses to respond (1.2.106–12). But if the murder of an uncle is villainy, regicide is high treason and is deadly to the soul as well as the body.[49] Half a century after the first performance of the play, Cromwell was to experience the greatest difficulty in inducing his Parliamentarian colleagues to sign the death warrant of Charles I, even though the law had been rewritten to legitimate the King's legal execution as a traitor to the people of England. The Ghost confronts Hamlet with an impossible dilemma: nature, love and duty require an act which constitutes the repudiation of nature, love and duty.

The question whether it is nobler to endure wrongs or to act poses the alternatives sharply: 'to suffer / The slings and arrows of outrageous fortune, / Or to take arms' (3.1.57–9). In reformulating the

problem, Hamlet counterposes Stoical endurance of injustice with violent resistance. The choice of action against such overwhelming odds
is also and inevitably a choice of death: 'To take arms against a sea of
troubles / And by opposing end them. To die . . .' (3.1.59–60). The treason the Ghost requires of Hamlet is no small crime, and regicide can
hardly be kept secret. But death itself is not the problem: 'To die – to
sleep, / No more' (3.1.60–61). Hamlet, who repeatedly castigates himself for cowardice, is not afraid of dying. In a Christian cosmos,
however, if treason is not justified, and at this historical moment there
is some debate about whether it ever is,[50] the penalty remains to be
paid beyond execution – in the dreams that disturb the sleep of death
(3.1.66). The Ghost withholds the secrets of its prison-house from ears
of flesh and blood (1.5.13–22), but Hamlet confronts the likelihood that
the price he would pay for ethical miscalculation is not loss of integrity, but the sacrifice of his immortal soul. Hamlet's hesitation is
motivated by 'the dread of something after death' (3.1.78), which 'puz-
zles the will' (3.1.80) and makes us cowards in all conscience (3.1.83).
The anxiety he feels concerns 'The undiscover'd country' (3.1.79), the
truth of the grave that the Ghost is forbidden to tell, a knowledge beyond what can be known. And yet, 'Examples gross as earth exhort
me' (4.4.46): Fortinbras and his army are willing to expose 'what is
mortal and unsure' 'Even for an eggshell' (4.4.51, 53).

> How stand I then,
> That have a father kill'd, a mother stain'd,
> Excitements of my reason and my blood,
> And let all sleep, while to my shame I see
> The imminent death of twenty thousand men
> That, for a fantasy and trick of fame,
> Go to their graves like beds ....
>
>   (4.4.56-62)

They die with pleasure, go to the grave to sleep, or perhaps to make
love ... But for Hamlet, nevertheless, the fear of the knowledge beyond what can be known remains unmastered.

The proximity, in Hamlet's Renaissance account, of the secular question and the theocratic order may be read as hinting at the degree to
which the Enlightenment project of finding grounds of right action
independent of Christianity will continue to bear the trace of religion,

in its allusion to an independent moral law, which defines what ought to be done or specifies the ethical imperative. Inscrutability simply shifts from the eternal consequences to the nature of the imperative itself, which is, after all, where in practice it was to begin with. Hamlet faces damnation if he kills Claudius *and* if it is wrong to kill a usurper and a murderer who is also a king. The Romantic critics, who interpreted the 'To be or not to be' speech as a meditation on suicide by a prince too sensitive to act, inadvertently revealed in the process their own understanding of right action: two revolutions had by now demystified monarchy; regicide was no longer quite so special; and evidently it was obvious to them that real men do not hesitate to solve moral problems by violence. At the same time, their intense sympathy with Hamlet surely also implies a more complex, if unacknowledged, reading of the play. 'I have a smack of Hamlet myself, if I may say so', Coleridge famously commented,[51] distancing himself in the process from the violent imperatives of his culture. The ethical problem posed by the questionable shape, which they seem to disregard, returns to inform the ambivalent relationship of nineteenth-century poets and painters to the prince they both despise and identify with.

Hamlet does not give up the ethical struggle easily. Just how resolutely he pursues it is in practice partly a textual question. Modern editions have tended to conflate three distinct texts, the first quarto of 1603, the second, much longer quarto of 1604, and the Folio (F).[52] No wonder Hamlet's delay seems protracted: it is, in the versions we read, more prolonged than it probably was in any early modern performance. Among other differences, his self-castigating soliloquy over Fortinbras's army ('How all occasions do inform against me' 4.4.33–66) is omitted from F, leaving a correspondingly more decisive figure at the centre of the play. Meanwhile, F develops the case for action in more specific detail by adding four critical lines in the final act (5.2.67–70). Hamlet's renewed attempt to formulate the question posed by the questionable shape of the Ghost is addressed to Horatio, in the light of the new evidence that the King has tried to have his nephew killed in England. 'Does it not', Hamlet asks – and the modality remains interrogative –

> Does it not, think thee, stand me now upon –
> He that hath kill'd my king and whor'd my mother,
> Popp'd in between the election and my hopes,
> Thrown out his angle for my proper life

And with such coz'nage – is't not perfect conscience
To quit him with this arm? And is't not to be damn'd
To let this canker of our nature come
In further evil?

(5.2.63–70)

The reference to conscience and the lines that follow are new. If, as seems possible, F is closer to the text that was actually performed in the theatre, the early modern stage Hamlet was a good deal less indecisive than the Romantic Prince. The framework of his reflections is still Christian and eschatalogical, though both conscience and damnation have changed sides in F's reformulation of the question. The case against Claudius is no longer familial, however, but political. The issue is justice: as the Folio formulates the question, is it not more than perfect conscience in the light of such crimes, but actually an obligation, to quit him (requite him, bring about a situation in which to call it quits)? In addition, the issue is also the prevention of crime. The question posed by the questionable shape from the past also bears on the future, as Claudius threatens to come in further evil. And furthermore, the issue is collective: no longer a matter of personal revenge or individual integrity, the question concerns public safety, 'our nature', which faces the possibility of evil still to come.[53] Redefined in this way, the question – and it remains a question – is one of intervention to prevent a tyrant's misuse of power.

In the Folio version of the play, Hamlet has found possible grounds for action, for killing Claudius with a clear conscience, but the grounds are tentative, rather than total or conclusive, and they may not be decisive. Politically, however, as Ernesto Laclau has argued, we make decisions in a framework of 'constitutive incompletion', acknowledging undecidability, while not investing it with an alternative metaphysics of ground*lessness*.[54] Hamlet does, in the event, kill Claudius, urgently, imperatively, in the instant after he has received his own death wound, and without, therefore, the opportunity for further reflection. But we are not necessarily invited to see the action, decisive though it is, as the outcome of his deliberations, in the sense that the moment of decision is incommensurable with the thought that leads up to it. Urgency, Derrida argues, in a passage that might serve as a commentary on *Hamlet*, is the law of the decision: 'Centuries of preparatory reflection and theoretical deliberation – the very infinity of a knowledge – would change nothing in this urgency. It is absolutely cutting, conclusive, decisive, heartrending; it must interrupt the time of science and conscience, to which the instant of decision will always remain heterogeneous.'[55] We cannot be sure, in other words, whether the grounds he has identified determine the act. Nor is it certain whether the act is ethically right, whether Hamlet is *entitled* to a clear conscience, and to the angelic 'rest' that Horatio wishes for him (5.2.365). On this issue, the play as a whole retains, I believe, the questionable shape imposed on it by the apparition in Act 1: the undecidable Ghost inhabits the decision it prompts, deconstructing any certainty we might lay claim to.[56]

For all the contradictions of his ethical situation, however, Hamlet apparently retains a strong sense of the antithesis between himself and his wicked uncle, Claudius the traitor, who contravened both family values and the law by poisoning his brother, the King. Hamlet identifies himself and Claudius as 'mighty opposites' (5.2.62). And yet, in the event, he kills his uncle, amid accusations of treason (5.2.328), with the poisoned sword he snatches from Laertes the revenger: 'The point envenom'd too! Then, venom, to thy work' (5.2.327). And to make doubly sure, he compels Claudius the poisoner to drink poisoned wine. These are not the conventional actions of a political hero with a clear conscience. They are, however, quite possibly, and always questionably, the best he can do in the circumstances.

The villain of *The Mousetrap*, the play that Hamlet stages to catch the conscience of Claudius, poisons the King and marries the Queen. He is, as Hamlet triumphantly explains to the stage audience, the King's nephew (3.2.239). In the play within the play, poisoner and nephew are one and the same. In Shakespeare's tragedy uncle and nephew are antagonists. But as he pursues the ethical question posed by the Ghost's absolute and unconditional identification of his enemy, Hamlet, who is responsible, directly or indirectly, for the deaths of Polonius, Rosencrantz and Guildenstern, Ophelia, Laertes and Claudius, comes to bear an uncanny resemblance to the antagonist whose violence initiates the entire sequence of events that constitutes the action of the play.

VI

In consequence of sibling rivalry that leads to murder, and the call for vengeance on the part of a loving father, Hamlet becomes Death's reluctant living partner in a Dance initially brought into existence for all human beings within the first marriage, and inaugurated by the first instance of sibling rivalry leading to murder. Ancestral sin, in other words, is visited upon the children in a line of descent from family to family. The nineteenth century was surely right to single out the scene in the graveyard, though mistaken in supposing, however ambivalently, that the problem confronting Hamlet was the weakness of his own character.

On the contrary. Paradoxically, as a revenger, Hamlet also plays the part of Death. In the graveyard the living Hamlet is the active partner in the miniature Dance of Death he performs with the politician, the courtier, the lawyer, the lady, the emperor and the fool: the figure the nineteenth century so commonly represents as emaciated,[57] picks up their skulls[58] with relish, challenges, teases and mocks them. Verbally, figuratively, Hamlet dances. In the plot of the play, moreover, he causes, directly or indirectly, the deaths of a politician, two courtiers, a lady and a gentleman, before he finally reaches the King.[59] As Death, Hamlet masters the skulls in a grim symbolic rehearsal of his ultimate and deadly mission. He *plays* at death, and in the process he both recognizes death's mastery and asserts his own.

In this respect, we may attribute to Hamlet a distant and very youthful descendant, who also reluctantly learns to recognize the inevitability of loss and asserts his mastery of it in play. Freud's grandson, little Ernst, the diminutive hero of the most familiar (and familial) narrative moment of *Beyond the Pleasure Principle*,[60] learns to renounce his mother's company without protesting, by symbolizing her disappearance. And in the process, he constitutes himself as a revenger.

According to Freud's account, this 'good little boy', who was 'greatly attached to his mother', repeatedly threw a cotton reel on a string into his curtained cot, thus making it disappear.[61] As he did so, he uttered a sound which his mother and his admiring grandfather interpreted as '*fort*' ('gone'). The word was 'accompanied by an expression of interest and satisfaction'. He then pulled the cotton reel back again with a joyful '*da*' ('there'). Though the greater pleasure was evidently attached to the triumphant recovery of the cotton reel, it was the act of throwing it away that was repeated 'untiringly' and 'far more frequently'. How, Freud's text asks, can we account for the pleasure of this game which 'stages' what must have been a distressing experience, the necessary absences of the mother he loves? (A footnote reveals that later, when his mother died, when she was really 'gone', the little boy showed no signs of grief. But by then the birth of a baby brother had roused him to violent jealousy.) Is it possible, Freud wonders, that the *fort/da* game yields a 'pleasure of another sort' for the unhappy child?

> At the outset, he was in a *passive* situation – he was overpowered by the experi-ence; but, by repeating it, unpleasurable though it was, as a game, he took on an *active* part. These efforts might be put down to an instinct for mastery that was acting independently of whether the memory was in itself pleasurable or not.

But there is more. 'Throwing away the object,' Freud continues, 'so that it was "gone" might satisfy an impulse of the child's, which was suppressed in his actual life, to revenge himself on his mother for go-ing away from him.' Children often re-enact frightening events as games, the text affirms, and derive from this transferential repetition the satisfaction of passing on the disagreeable experience to a play-mate, revenging themselves on a substitute.

By analogy, we might see Hamlet, lured by the Ghost on to the ter-rain of death, commanded by a dead father to perform an act which entails his own death, gratifying the impulse to revenge for *this* dis-tressing experience by playing the part of Death in the graveyard. We might also see him, in his drive to master the knowledge beyond what can be known, repeatedly bringing about the deaths, in a succession of transferential repetitions, of figures who are not the object of the Ghost's injunction: Polonius, Rosencrantz and Guildenstern, Ophelia, Laertes.

But the psychological processes of the sensitive Prince have prob-ably elicited quite enough critical attention in the two centuries since Goethe, Schlegel and Coleridge, and I have no wish to add to the list of tributes to Shakespeare's insight into universal human nature. On the contrary, my main interest in the episode from *Beyond the Pleasure Principle* is elsewhere. Freud's text goes on to consider tragedy as a kind of grown-up game:

> Finally, a reminder may be added that the artistic play and artistic imitation carried out by adults, which, unlike children's, are aimed at an audience, do not spare the spectators (for instance, in tragedy) the most painful experi-ences and can yet be felt by them as highly enjoyable.

Does tragedy appeal as another kind of play which also yields a satis-faction beyond pleasure? What is the seduction of tragedy for an audience?

A. D. Nuttall's book, published in 1996 by Oxford University Press, explicitly addresses the question, *Why Does Tragedy Give Pleasure?* In the course of composing an answer, Nuttall invokes an extremely unsympathetic and profoundly reductive version of Freud, who is duly dismissed, and Nietzsche, who does a little better. But in the end, he repudiates them both for Aristotle, whose main interest lay, he explains, in what happened next, the audience's 'state of mind when the play was over, after the lucid demonstration of a probable or necessary sequence of events leading to the dreadful death of the protagonist.' Tragedy, in Nuttall's account, delivers closure, and this means understanding: 'the special pleasure ... that we feel when all is done, when we have followed the sequence to its terrible end and understood.' And the consequent knowledge, however complex, however difficult to come by, is ultimately moral: 'The words "good" and "evil"', he concludes, 'mean not less but more to one who has just watched *King Lear*.'[62]

I do not want to raise hopes that I have an alternative answer to Nuttall's question. It might, in my view, be overambitious to address the issue of tragic enjoyment at quite such a level of generality. But his account does not seem to explain whatever it is that draws audiences to *Hamlet* in particular. What exactly is it that we turn out to have 'understood' when the performance of *this* play is over?[63] Answers have, of course, been put forward, but they do not seem to satisfy: the critical mill grinds on. And do good and evil mean more at the end of *Hamlet*? Are they more clearly differentiated, or *less*? Was the Ghost good or evil? Is revenge good or evil? Is it 'nobler' to act or to suffer? And, since the tragedy displays an intimate concern with death, is death good or evil? What would such a question mean?

Moreover, in the end, Nuttall's account bypasses the process of the play in favour of the end-product. The pleasure lies in having been there. Is this a case of extremely deferred gratification – you buy a ticket for the pleasure of coming out of the theatre afterwards? Is the assumption that we go to the play because tragedy is so nice when it stops, but we need to find an uplifting way of explaining why we bought the ticket in the first place? Like so much traditional criticism, Nuttall's view seems to substitute moral profit for textual experience, valuing metaphysics at the expense of the signifier.

VII

In the hope of reaffirming the textuality of the text, reinvesting seduction in the signifier, I want to go back to *Beyond the Pleasure Principle*. This is Freud's most extensive account of death, or more specifically, of the death drive, that elementary and primitive impulse that entices human beings beyond pleasure. The text sets out to explain this drive, to link it with the compulsion to repeat, and to show how it overrides the life instincts in mortal combat with the libido. *Beyond the Pleasure Principle* promises, in other words, to put the reader in a position of mastery. But it never does. Derrida's brilliant reading of the book demonstrates how the 'a-thetic' working of Freud's text[64] withholds at least as much as it delivers, plays with its readers, luring us down the path of speculation towards a prohibited knowledge, which is a knowledge of what cannot be known. 'If there is no thesis in this book, it is because its proper object cannot be the object of any thesis', Derrida insists.[65] There is no moral profit here, no final truth of death or the death drive, no metaphysical reward at the end of the reading process.

And yet the reading process has proved itself powerful: this is among the most widely read of all Freud's writings, one of the best known works in the psychoanalytic canon. Why? Because it plays a kind of *fort / da* game with the reader. The elusive death drive repeatedly comes and goes in the text, appears only to be banished again at the moment when we imagine we might grasp it, take hold of it finally, master it. Little Ernst, the infant protagonist, seeks to master in play the departures of the mother he loves. With the cotton reel, he re-enacts at a symbolic level his mother's unintended seduction of the child himself, the comings and goings that keep him guessing, and in the process confirm his longing. Meanwhile, the text repeats, in another symbolic form, at a (?)higher level of symbolization, the comings and goings of the cotton reel, offers to keep the reader guessing, sets out to deliver a knowledge of the death drive and thus promises mastery only, in the end, ironically, to master *us*. *Beyond the Pleasure Principle* constitutes itself for the attentive reader as an object not so much of knowledge as of desire.

The scene in the graveyard shows Hamlet seeking to master death in play. And in the soliloquies he pursues another form of mastery at a (?)higher level of symbolization. The soliloquies seek a knowledge of death, 'The undiscover'd country', and an ethical reason to kill Claudius. Prompted to act by heaven and hell (2.2.580), by both heaven

and hell at once, he tries to disentangle the moral imperatives of revenge, to find firm grounds for action. Filial love seems to demand
murder, but might not Stoical patience be 'nobler'? *Fort/da*. The ethical positions come and go. In the soliloquies Hamlet re-enacts at a
symbolic level the seductive comings and goings of the Ghost, the spectre of the loved father whose commands initiate his deliberations. In
the end, Hamlet relinquishes the desire for the closure of certainty and
mastery over his own death: 'Since no man, of aught he leaves, knows
aught, what is't to leave betimes? Let be' (5.2.218–20).

At the end of *Beyond the Pleasure Principle*, Freud too gives up the
struggle to be sure, to establish a clear antithesis between the pleasure
principle and the death drive. He does not know, he announces, how
far he believes in his own conclusions; his attitude towards the results
of his 'deliberations' is one of 'cool benevolence'; 'we must be patient
and await fresh methods and occasions of research.' The effort to distinguish the two drives leads to an unexpected realization. If the death
drive is the desire of the organism to die in its own way and its own
time, to follow its own path to death, the pleasure principle, which
seeks to ward off danger, is not its opposite but its ally: 'The pleasure
principle seems actually to serve the death instincts.' It follows, the
text concludes, that we are left with a host of unresolved questions. In
consequence: 'We must be ready ... to abandon a path that we have
followed for a time, if it seems to be leading to no good end.'[66]

Beyond the Pleasure Principle advances, or rather fails to advance, by a
succession of 'steps': 'Let us make a bold attempt at another step forward', it proposes; and the discussion that follows is defined in terms of
a series of further 'steps'.[67] Exploiting the pun on the French *pas*, as the
step which both proceeds and prohibits, Derrida reads the book as a
text which sets out to step beyond where it is possible to go. In the event,
it advances without advancing, 'without ever advancing anything that
it does not immediately take back;'[68] 'Despite several marching orders
and steps forward, not an inch of ground is gained', he points out.[69]

Derrida's reading quite properly treats these steps which fail to
step into the impossible, forbidden realm of death, as steps in a logical argument, along a path which might lead to a conclusion. But are
they not also steps in an elaborate signifying dance? (Freud 'pirou-
ettes', Derrida concedes at one point.[70]) The text advances and retreats,
moves back and forth, repeats with a difference the patterns it sets
up. This book, which turns coyly away from the impossible knowledge it glimpses, which offers the reader a *frisson* and promises the

possibility of mastery, is surely Freud's own version of the Dance of Death. Of course, Freud the modern scientist would repudiate the medieval analogy. But *Beyond* plays with (speculates on) a more elusive knowledge than science (or indeed philosophy) permits. Coming and going, brilliantly masterful and yet forever desiring a mastery it cannot attain, promising a gratification it does not deliver, and for all these reasons seductive, *Beyond the Pleasure Principle* dances with the reader.

And *Hamlet*? Does not the play too offer to dance with the audience? Located, from the opening scene on the guarded walls, at the liminal place where what is beyond is always only just kept at bay, and dramatizing the intensity of the will to live when confronted by the imperative to experience whatever death entails, the tragedy shares something of the attraction beyond pleasure of the Dance it also incorporates. The play repeatedly promises and withholds action. The text, meanwhile, promises and withholds explanation, the possibility of mastery by the audience, and constitutes itself in the process as an object not primarily of knowledge, but of desire, teasing, enigmatic, seductive.[71]

Critics have longed to fill the gap that is the cause of this desire, to pluck out the heart of the play's mystery by supplying the missing thematic content, most commonly in the form of a defect in the hero's character: an excess of intellect, an overdeveloped sensibility, the desolation of world-sorrow.[72] And Freud, ironically, joined them. 'The conflict in *Hamlet*,' he announced complacently in an essay on stage psychopaths, 'is so effectively concealed that it was left to me to unearth it.'[73] The secret he unearthed, of course, was that Hamlet's delay is a consequence of the guilt which stems from a forbidden desire. Claudius takes his father's place with his mother, thus showing him 'the repressed wishes of his own childhood realized'.[74] In Freud's account, Hamlet is the victim of an unresolved Oedipus complex, a prohibited, incestuous passion generated within the family.

Freud does not go into textual detail, but the play indicates rather that the incest consists in Gertrude's marriage to her husband's brother (1.5.42), once prohibited in canon law,[75] and that Hamlet is propelled towards vengeance by love of his father, not his mother. Furthermore, whatever the moral ambiguities of revenge as murder, and specifically here as regicide, the filial love which impels it is not only legitimate but required by family values:

Ghost	If thou didst ever thy dear father love –
Ham.	O God!
Ghost	Revenge his foul and most unnatural murder.
Ham.	Murder!
Ghost	Murder most foul, as in the best it is,
	But this most foul, strange and unnatural.
Ham.	Haste me to know't, that I with wings as swift
	As meditation or the thoughts of love
	May sweep to my revenge.
Ghost	I find thee apt.

                                                    (1.5.23–31)

The intensity of family feeling, which generates on the one hand a
brother's rivalry, and on the other a son's revenge, precipitates Hamlet into the realm of mortality, which is an altogether more enigmatic
location than criticism has been willing to recognize. The tragedy takes
place on the terrain where life comes face to face with its indissociable
other. It presents this terrain to the audience in play, in a manner which
is as grimly playful as the Dance of Death. And it shows it to be at once
– and undecidably – frightening, paradoxically reassuring, strangely
seductive. Death is a secret which alarms and attracts, the inevitable
trace of absence that gives meaning to the living present. As the history of criticism shows, we can pick up the challenge of *Hamlet* by
supplying the thematic content it withholds, telling the *play's* secret,
mastering the text to prevent it mastering us. Metaphysics is always
ready to supplant the signifier. A possible alternative, however, is to
relinquish the desire for closure and to follow the dance-steps of the
signifier, permitting the text to take the lead. By this means, we allow
the play, like the mortality it depicts, to retain its mystery, its a-thetic
knowledge, its triumphant undecidability – and its corresponding
power to seduce.

VIII

In *Hamlet*, as in the Book of Genesis, death is in the first instance a
family affair. Fratricide, the primal sin, leads on to a world of death,
where innocence is no longer an option. All intimate relationships
are problematic, and the most problematic are named love. For love,

Gertrude marries her husband's brother, who is also his murderer; the Ghost of Old Hamlet bitterly incites his son to murder in the name of love; the son, who does his loving, pious, scrupulous best to make ethical sense of the Ghost's command, casually eliminates a succession of collaborators in a series of transferential repetitions, before finally killing his uncle with a poisoned sword.

Hamlet does not get married. The precise nature of his relationship with Ophelia is one of the unresolved mysteries of the play. He seems to have loved her, or at least, Ophelia believes so (1.3.110–14), but the taunts and torments he subjects her to in the course of the play go way beyond sexual teasing. Only her corpse elicits his direct avowal of love – in, of course, the past tense:

> I lov'd Ophelia. Forty thousand brothers
> Could not with all their quantity of love
> Make up my sum.
>
> (5.1.264-6)

In practice, surely, marriage is simply irrelevant to his main design. 'I say we will have no moe marriage. Those that are married already – all but one – shall live; the rest shall keep as they are' (3.1.149–51). From the moment Hamlet follows the Ghost, he is wedded to death itself, caught up in the erotics of a dance which proffers an uncanny alternative to love. The revenger seeks an object beyond pleasure.

The quest of revenge reaches beyond death, too. If we take Hamlet seriously in the prayer scene, and there seems no good reason not to, he aims not just to kill his uncle, but to damn him (3.3.88–95). As in the parallel cases of Laertes and Pyrrhus, the depth of family feeling and the intimacy of family relations invest familial violence with an intensity in excess of mere hire and salary (3.3.79). In the nineteenth century, the great age of the family, critics habitually blamed Hamlet for his delay; what makes Hamlet heroic in our own period is surely his reluctance to regard as absolute a murderous imperative delivered in the name of the dead father.

Whatever made us think of marriage as closure, or associate the parental relationship with the promise of security? The family is a place of passion, and on the evidence of Shakespeare's plays, that passion remains resolutely unresolved. Family values, the proper love of a son for his father, enmesh Hamlet in a web of anxiety, deceit and death: tragedy stems from the commitment the family elicits. Both in Genesis and in Shakespeare, love and hate are inextricably entwined; and the greater the emotional investment, the greater the potential disruption of the security and stability, the compensation for hardship, that the family conventionally promises to deliver. From its first moment, the family, as a place of passion, is also, and correspondingly, the source of our greatest peril.

Chapter Six
Postscript: Passion and Interpretation

he effect of the Fall is a profound uncertainty at the heart of human existence. This perplexity concerns life's differentiating other, the unknown condition of death, brought into being by the first couple, and violently introduced into the first family. In Shakespeare the family, loving, unpredictable, vulnerable, homicidal, is variously material for comedy, romance and tragedy. Family values are both life-giving and deadly.

As information comes out about domestic violence in our own period, we are relearning this empirically, at the level of social practice. The early modern period, as is widely documented, also knew a good deal about familial violence in practice. But my contention has been more specific: that in its representation of an emergent pattern of values, sixteenth- and seventeenth-century culture identified, whether consciously or not, contradictory possibilities, of constraint as well as contentment, at the heart of the model itself. Officially loving, family relationships can instead (or as well) be possessive, proprietary, coercive; family values, designed to cement society, can also be profoundly antisocial. Cultures have their own imperatives and later, as the model became more fully consensual, it would be in the interests of our culture to efface these contradictions. But at the inaugural moment of family values, I have wanted to indicate, the problematic character of the new ideal is sharply on display in the popular texts of the period, and available for recognition at the level of the signifier.

For better or worse, the family is a place of passion. But my narrative itself, this textual history, is also a place of passion. 'The signifier', Lacan maintains, 'has an active function in determining certain effects in which the signifiable appears as submitting to its mark, by becoming through that passion the signified.'[1] Lacan's words do full justice to the etymology of passion. It denotes love, certainly, in its most intense form, but also suffering, and most commonly, the suffering of Christ on the cross. If the family is a place of passion, textuality is too. The signifiable, translated to the realm of signification and momentarily, provisionally and ultimately ineffectually 'fixed' as the signified, undergoes the pain of a loss, a kind of death; the experience of the past reappears in the present text as merely differential and differentiated, other than it is, no more than the lost cause of its own representation.

But it is important to remember that the experience was always differential and differentiated, since the represented could never be recognized or acknowledged independently of representation. Passion, and this is Lacan's point, is the human condition. As signifying subjects, we have no access to the signifiable, the as-yet-unsignified, the imagined simplicity of the way things are or were. What we interpret may have existed outside our interpretation, but it was never experienced independently of interpretation itself, however inadequate the account seems or may have seemed.

To say this is not to deny the existence of the event. But we do not know the event-in-itself. For human beings caught up in signification there is no 'in-itself', no access to the pure signifiable. This makes interpretation precarious, uncertain, provisional, but it also makes it a necessity, and as all Lacanians know, what is lost when a need is formulated as a demand reappears as desire. Unnamed residues remain: a single reading is never the whole story.

An essay in cultural history, this book can be no more than one reading of the past, as perceived from the present. It is put forward as a reservation about the call for the restoration of family values in our own society. My account of the early modern representation of the family, of the delights and dangers of passion, has attempted to draw attention to the inclusion of the other in the selfsame: the tragic element in true love; the proprietariness that inhabits the proper; the destructive capabilities of the claims parents make; the rivalry that subsists where affection is expected. This record of the past is self-evidently a product of our own historical moment, overtly sceptical about the stability we still both long for and distrust. But my readings are also motivated by a passion which belongs in the present, and specifically the human passion to interpret, which is among the most powerful determinations of the signifier. To interpret is to know, to take possession of the texts we read. It is impossible to do so with any finality, of course, but the imperative is no less pressing – and no less consequential – for that. The sense we make of the past has material implications for the way we live now, at a moment in history. A passion for interpretation can be experienced only in – and perhaps for – history itself.

Notes

CHAPTER 1   READING CULTURAL HISTORY

1. Michel de Certeau, *The Writing of History*, trans. Tom Conley (New York: Columbia University Press, 1988), p. 3.
2. Hayden White, *Tropics of Discourse: Essays in Cultural Criticism* (Baltimore: Johns Hopkins University Press, 1978), pp. 84–5 and *passim*.
3. Cf. Certeau, *The Writing of History*, p. 287.
4. For an excellent example of the social history of the family in the period, see Susan Dwyer Amussen, *An Ordered Society: Gender and Class in Early Modern England* (Oxford: Blackwell, 1988). Amussen analyses texts, including advice manuals, as well as the economy and demography of the Norfolk villages she discusses, and she recognizes that there may be a gap between beliefs and practices. Where they differ, it is the practices she pursues.
5. Louis Althusser, *Lenin and Philosophy and Other Essays*, trans. Ben Brewster (London: New Left Books, 1971), pp. 156–8.
6. 'Fiction' is itself a problematic term, of course. I use it here, for want of a better, in order to avoid the value judgement commonly implied by 'literature', but the category rarely exists in pure form. Mimetic fiction, not self-evidently an independent mode until the nineteenth century, depends on (the illusion of) reference to what is perceived as fact (human psychology, social convention, etc.). Meanwhile, epic, chronicle drama, and even romance, were not usually offered as pure invention. Current categories of 'faction' and drama-documentary also deconstruct the opposition between fact and fiction. I owe this reservation to a conversation with Martin Kayman.

7. Clifford Geertz, '"From the Native's Point of View": On the Nature of Anthropological Understanding', *The Interpretation of Cultures: Selected Essays* (New York: Basic Books, 1973), ch. 3.

8. Certeau, *The Writing of History*, p. 33. Certeau is concerned here primarily with previous historical debates, but the point also holds for the material they consider.

9. See, for example, Richard J. Evans, *In Defence of History* (London: Granta, 1997). For a much more thoughtful account of the limitations of constructivism, see Michel-Rolph Trouillot, *Silencing the Past: Power and the Production of History* (Boston, MA: Beacon, 1995).

10. Jacques Derrida, 'Differance', *'Speech and Phenomena' and Other Essays on Husserl's Theory of Signs*, trans. David B. Allison (Evanston, IL: Northwestern University Press, 1973), pp. 129–60.

11. As Patricia Parker points out, there is no shortcut to the process of learning the language(s) of the past. See her *Shakespeare from the Margins: Language, Culture, Context* (Chicago: University of Chicago Press, 1996), pp. 18–19.

12. Kiernan Ryan, ed., *New Historicism and Cultural Materialism: A Reader* (London: Arnold, 1996), p. xviii.

13. These questions are not always so easily answered, of course (see Jacques Derrida, *Limited Inc* (Evanston, IL: Northwestern University Press, 1988)), but that does not, in my view, legitimate ignoring them.

14. See, for example, Stephen Greenblatt, 'Fiction and Friction', *Shakespearean Negotiations: The Circulation of Social Energy in Renaissance England* (Oxford: Clarendon Press, 1988), pp. 66–93.

15. James Fernandez, 'Historians Tell Tales: Of Cartesian Cats and Gallic Cockfights', *Journal of Modern History*, 60 (1988), pp. 113–27 (p. 118). I am grateful to Stuart Clark for this reference.

16. C. S. Lewis, *The Allegory of Love: A Study in Medieval Tradition* (Oxford: Oxford University Press, 1936).

17. William and Malleville Haller, 'The Puritan Art of Love', *Huntington Library Quarterly*, 5 (1941–42), pp. 235–72.

18. Robert Crofts, *The Lover: or, Nuptiall Love* (London, 1638), sigs A7v–A8r. Cf. Robert Burton, *The Anatomy of Melancholy*, ed. Thomas C. Faulkner, Nicholas K. Kiessling and Rhonda L. Blair (Oxford: Clarendon Press, 3 vols, 1989–94), 3.2.1.2 (vol. 3, pp. 52–3).

19. See, for example, Lena Cowen Orlin's dense and compelling analysis of conflicts of power in the early modern household (*Private Matters and Public Culture in Post-Reformation England* (Ithaca, NY: Cornell University Press, 1994). I have written of the ambiguities of early modern

marriage in *The Subject of Tragedy: Identity and Difference in Renaissance Drama* (London: Methuen, 1985), pp. 129-221. See also Catherine Belsey, 'Disrupting Sexual Difference: Meaning and Gender in the Comedies', *Alternative Shakespeares*, ed. John Drakakis (London: Methuen, 1985) pp. 166-90.

20. Thomas Becon, *Worckes* (London, 1560-64), vol. 1, fol. 616r.
21. Thomas Becon, Preface to H. Bullinger, *The Christen State of Matrimonye*, trans. Miles Coverdale (London, ?1546), sig. A3v.
22. Rachel Speght, *A Muzzle for Melastomus, The Women's Sharp Revenge*, ed. Simon Shepherd, (London: Fourth Estate, 1985), pp. 57-83 (p. 71).
23. Josuah Sylvester, trans., *The Divine Weeks and Works of Guillaume de Saluste Sieur du Bartas*, ed. Susan Snyder, 2 vols (Oxford: Clarendon Press, 1979), 1.6.1055-9.
24. Frances E. Dolan, *Dangerous Familiars: Representations of Domestic Crime in England, 1550-1700* (Ithaca, NY: Cornell University Press, 1994).

CHAPTER 2   DESIRE IN THE GOLDEN WORLD: *LOVE'S LABOUR'S LOST* AND *AS YOU LIKE IT*

1. William Shakespeare, *As You Like It*, ed. Agnes Latham, The Arden Shakespeare (London: Methuen, 1975).
2. William Shakespeare, *Love's Labour's Lost*, ed. H. R. Woudhuysen, The Arden Shakespeare (Walton-on-Thames: Nelson, 1998).
3. Frances A. Yates, *The French Academies of the Sixteenth Century* (London: Warburg Institute, 1947).
4. Andrew Gurr, *Playgoing in Shakespeare's London* (Cambridge: Cambridge University Press, 1987), pp. 147-53.
5. 'Loving in truth, and fain in verse my love to show . . .'(Philip Sidney, *Astrophil and Stella*, 1.1, *The Poems of Sir Philip Sidney* , ed. William A. Ringler, Jr. (Oxford: Clarendon Press, 1962), p. 165).
6. William Shakespeare, *A Midsummer Night's Dream*, ed. Harold F. Brooks, The Arden Shakespeare (London: Methuen, 1979), 4.1.213.
7. William Shakespeare, *The Merry Wives of Windsor*, ed. H. J. Oliver, The Arden Shakespeare (London: Methuen, 1971), 2.1.14-18; 1.1.179-80.
8. See Catherine Belsey, *Desire: Love Stories in Western Culture* (Oxford: Blackwell, 1994), pp. 81-6 and *passim*.
9. In this instance 'faining' also means 'soft' (a soft voice).
10. For a sophisticated account of the racial implications of 'fair' in the period, see Kim Hall, *Things of Darkness: Economies of Race and Gender*

in Early Modern England (Ithaca, NY: Cornell University Press, 1995), pp. 62–122.

11. Q and F give 'affection', but most modern editors amend this to 'affectation'.

12. G. K. Hunter, 'Poem and Context in *Love's Labour's Lost*', *Shakespeare's Styles: Essays in Honour of Kenneth Muir*, ed. Philip Edwards, Inga-Stina Ewbank and G. K. Hunter, (Cambridge: Cambridge University Press, 1980), pp. 25–38 (p. 36).

13. Ibid., p. 33.

14. *The Holie Bible* [Bishops' version] (London, 1572).

15. See, for example, Martin Luther, *Lectures on Genesis (Chapters 1–5)*, trans. George V. Schick, *Luther's Works*, ed. Jaroslav Pelikan, vol. 1 (Saint Louis, MI: Concordia, 1958), p. 115, but the point is confirmed in most discussions of the issue.

16. John Calvin, *A Commentarie of John Calvine, upon the first book of Moses called Genesis*, trans. Thomas Tymme (London, 1578), pp. 71, 73.

17. Luther, *Lectures on Genesis*, p. 67.

18. Nicholas Gibbens, *Questions and Disputations Concerning the Holy Scripture* (London, 1601), p. 83.

19. Andrew Willet, *Hexapla in Genesin* (Cambridge, 1605), p. 39.

20. Gervase Babington, *Certaine Plaine, brief, and comfortable Notes, upon every Chapter of Genesis* (London, 1596), p. 24.

21. Henoch Clapham, *A Briefe of the Bible* (Edinburgh, 1596), p. 18.

22. John Carey and Alastair Fowler, eds, *The Poems of John Milton* (London: Longman, 1968).

23. John Wing, *The Crowne Conjugall or, The Spouse Royall* (Middelburgh, 1620), pp. 27–32.

24. Ibid., p. 28.

25. Ibid., p. 29.

26. Thomas Gataker, *A Good Wife Gods Gift. A Marriage Sermon on Prov. 19.14, Two Marriage Sermons* (London, 1620), p. 9.

27. Ester Sowernam, *Ester Hath Hang'd Haman* (1617), *The Women's Sharp Revenge*, ed. Simon Shepherd, (London: Fourth Estate, 1985), pp. 85–124 (p. 93). Jane Anger had argued that Eve's creation out of flesh rather than dust demonstrated the superior excellence of women, (*Jane Anger her Protection for Women* (1589), *The Women's Sharp Revenge*, pp. 29–51 (p. 39).

28. Henry Smith, *A Preparative to Mariage* (London, 1591), p. 25.

29. Josuah Sylvester, trans., *The Divine Weeks and Works of Guillaume de Saluste Sieur du Bartas*, ed. Susan Snyder, 2 vols (Oxford: Clarendon

Press, 1979), 1.6.959–66.

30. Ibid., 1.6.1003–18. Cf. Calvin: Adam lost a rib, 'but for the same a greater reward was given unto him, when he got a faithful companion of life: yea, when he saw himself to be perfect and complete in his wife, *who before was but as an half creature* (my italics)' (*A Commentarie upon Genesis*, p. 76).

31. See, for example, ibid., 2.1.2.269–72.

32. Ibid., 1.6.1044–54.

33. Luther, *Lectures on Genesis*, p. 133.

34. See, for example, Thomas Peyton, *The Glasse of Time in the First Two Ages* (London, 1620), *The Second Age*, p. 22.

35. George R. Potter and Evelyn M. Simpson, eds, *The Sermons of John Donne*, 10 vols (Berkeley: University of California Press, 1955), vol. 2, p. 336.

36. William Perkins, *Christian Oeconomie*, trans. Thomas Pickering, *Works*, vol. 3 (Cambridge, 1618), p. 671. Cf. John Milton, *The Complete Prose Works*, vol. 2, ed. Ernest Sirluck (London: Oxford University Press, 1959), p. 447.

37. Marjorie Garber, 'The Education of Orlando', *Comedy from Shakespeare to Sheridan: Change and Continuity in the English and European Dramatic Tradition*, ed. A. R. Braunmuller and J. C. Bulman, (Newark: University of Delaware Press, 1986), pp. 102–12.

38. Patricia Parker, *Shakespeare from the Margins: Language, Culture, Context* (Chicago: University of Chicago Press, 1996), pp. 30–32.

39. At the beginning of Marlowe's *Dido Queen of Carthage*, Ganymede sits on Jupiter's knee and coaxes jewels out of the King of the gods.

40. Jacques Lacan, *The Four Fundamental Concepts of Pyscho-analysis* (London: Penguin, 1979), p. 107.

41. *OED*, 2.1

42. Babington, *Certaine Plaine … Notes*, p. 23.

43. Gibbens, *Questions and Disputations*, pp. 82–92. According to Calvin, 'solitariness is not good, but in him whom God hath exempted by a special privilege' (*A Commentarie upon Genesis*, p. 72).

44. Babington, *Certaine Plaine … Notes*, p. 23.

45. Willet, *Hexapla in Genesin*, p. 41. Cf. Gibbens, *Questions and Disputations*, pp. 84–5.

46. Martin Luther, *The Estate of Murriage*, trans. Walther I. Brandt, *Luther's Works*, ed. Helmut T. Lehmann, vol. 45 (Philadelphia, PA: Muhlenberg, 1962), pp. 11–49 (p. 19).

47. R. B., *A Watchword for Wilfull Women* (London, 1581), sig. F7r.

48. *As You Like It*, 3.3.47–57; 4.1.54–9; 4.1.159–60; 4.2.14–17.

49. John Lyly, *Loves Metamorphosis, The Complete Works of John Lyly*, ed. R. Warwick Bond, 3 vols (Oxford: Clarendon Press, 1902), vol. 3, 1.1.14–20.

CHAPTER 3 MARRIAGE: IMOGEN'S BEDCHAMBER

1. William Shakespeare, *Cymbeline*, ed. J. M. Nosworthy, The Arden Shakespeare (London: Methuen, 1955).
2. For cuckoldry as a pervasive theme of the plays, see Coppélia Kahn, *Man's Estate: Masculine Identity in Shakespeare* (Berkeley: University of California Press, 1981), pp. 119–50.
3. See, for example, 3.7 1–12.
4. William Shakespeare, *The Winter's Tale*, ed. J. H. P. Pafford, The Arden Shakespeare (London: Methuen, 1963).
5. This is a commonplace in the sermons of the period. See, for instance, Roger Hacket, *Two Fruitful Sermons* (London, 1607), p. 1 and *passim*.
6. For extant representations of the marriage of Adam and Eve, see Louis Réau, *Iconographie de l'art chrétien*, 3 vols (Paris: Presses Universitaires de France, 1955–59), vol. 2, Pt 1, pp. 81–2.
7. H. Diane Russell, ed., *Eva/Ave: Woman in Renaissance and Baroque Prints* (New York: National Gallery of Art, Washington, with The Feminist Press at the City University of New York, 1990), pp. 114–15.
8. See, for example, John Calvin, *A Commentarie of John Calvine, upon the first booke of Moses called Genesis*, trans. Thomas Tymme (London, 1578), pp. 73–4, 76.
9. Margaret H. Swain, *Historical Needlework: A Study of Influences in Scotland and Northern England* (London: Barrie and Jenkins, 1970), p. 23.
10. Izaak Walton, *The Lives of John Donne, Sir Henry Wotton, Richard Hooker, George Herbert and Robert Sanderson* (London: Oxford University Press, 1927), pp. 27–8. It might be worth noting that a further piece of furniture inscribed with the joint names of Walton and his wife (in this case his second wife, Anne) also survives, this time a richly carved cabinet with a top centre panel in bold relief showing the Last Judgement (E. Marston, *Thomas Ken and Izaak Walton, A Sketch of Their Lives and Family Connection* (London: Longman, Green, 1908), pp. 170–2).
11. Walton, *Lives*, pp. 178–9.
12. The full text reads, 'Feare god and sleepe in peace: That thou in

chryste mayste reste: To passe theis dayes of sinne: And raigne with him in blisse: Where angells do remayne: And blesse and praise his name: With songes of joy and happines: And live with him for ever: Therefore o lord in thee: is my full hope and truste: That thou wilt me defend: From sinne the worlld and Divel: who goeth about to catch: Poore sinners in their snare: And bringe them to that place: Where greefe and sorrowes are Soe now I end my lynes: And worke that hath beene longe: to those that do them reade: In hope they will be pleasd by me: Dorithy Davenporte-: 1636.'

13. I owe this discovery to Lena Cowen Orlin.

14. See Swain, *Historical Needlework*, pp. 25, 32.

15. In one remarkably vivid French instance, the figure of Death triumphantly holds aloft the apple that brought about his existence: see the tomb of Count René de Chalons at Bar-le-Duc. I owe this reference to Jonathan Dollimore.

16. The details of the relationship between the New York valance and Salomon's woodcuts were first traced by Nancy Graves Cabot, 'Pattern Sources of Scriptural Subjects in Tudor and Stuart Embroideries', *Bulletin of the Needle and Bobbin Club*, 30:1–2 (1946), pp. 3–57, (pp. 7–17). The Capesthorne tapestry is a cruder copy of Salomon, but the debt accounts for the odd stance of several of the figures. For the woodcuts, see Claude Paradin, *The True and lyvely historyke purtreatures of the woll Bible* (Lyons, 1553), sigs A2r–A5r. Anthony Wells-Cole assesses the effects of European prints and woodcuts on early modern visual culture in *Art and Decoration in Elizabethan and Jacobean England: The Influence of Continental Prints, 1558–1625* (New Haven: Yale University Press, 1997).

17. Hans Holbein, *Les simulachres & historiees faces de la mort* (Lyons, 1538), sigs C1v–C2r.

18. *De Conceptu et Generatione Hominis* (Frankfurt, 1580), sig. A1r. I owe this reference to Georgianna Ziegler. Michael Neill reproduces a lithograph in which a dancing skeleton also forms the trunk of the tree of knowledge (Michael Neill, *Issues of Death: Mortality and Identity in English Renaissance Tragedy* (Oxford: Clarendon Press, 1997), p. 6.

19. Jakob Rüff, *The Expert Midwife, or An Excellent and most necessary Treatise of the generation and birth of Man* (London, 1637), sig. A2v.

20. Henry Smith, *A Preparative to Mariage*, (London, 1591), pp. 31–2.

21. Heinrich Bullinger, *The Christen State of Matrimonye* (London, 1546), fol. 16v.

22. William Whately, *A Care-cloth: Or A Treatise of the Cumbers and Troubles of Marriage* (London, 1624), p. 74.

23. John Wing, *The Crowne Conjugall or, The Spouse Royall* (Middelburgh, 1620), p. 32.
24. Ibid., p. 95.
25. Ibid., p. 62.
26. Ibid., pp. 95–6.
27. Augustine, *The City of God*, trans. Philip Levine, The Loeb Classical Library (London: Heinemann, 1966), 14.15.
28. Michel de Montaigne, 'Upon Some Verses of Virgil', *Montaigne's Essays: John Florio's Translation*, ed. J. I. M. Stewart, 2 vols (London: Nonesuch, 1931), vol. 2, pp. 233–98 (p. 255).
29. Ibid., pp. 243–8.
30. Ibid., p. 269.
31. Ibid., p. 296.
32. Ibid., pp. 259–70.
33. Both Montaigne and Bacon are indebted, of course, to Plutarch, whose essay 'Of Love' in the *Moralia* also stresses the anarchic character of love (though without concluding that it is incompatible with marriage): see Plutarch, *The Philosophie, commonlie called, The Morals*, trans. Philemon Holland (London, 1603), pp. 1138–9.
34. Francis Bacon, 'Of Love', *The Essayes or Counsels, Civill and Morall*, ed. Michael Kiernan (Oxford: Clarendon Press, 1985), pp. 31–3.
35. Bacon, 'Of Marriage and Single Life', *The Essayes*, pp. 24–6.
36. Robert Burton, *The Anatomy of Melancholy*, ed. Thomas C. Faulkner, Nicholas K. Kiessling and Rhonda L. Blair, 3 vols (Oxford: Clarendon Press, 1989–94), 3.2.1.1 (vol. 3, pp. 40–41).
37. Ibid., 3.2.1.2 (vol. 3, p. 55).
38. Ibid., 3.2.3.1 (vol. 3, pp. 149, 162).
39. Ibid., 3.2.1.2 (vol. 3, p. 54).
40. Ibid., 3.2.5.3 (vol. 3, pp. 232–3).
41. Ibid., 3.2.1.2 (vol. 3, p. 52).
42. The first edition is dated 1620 and appeared in 1621. Thereafter, *The Anatomy* was revised and greatly expanded in editions of 1624, 1628, 1632 and 1638, and further modified until Burton died in 1640.
43. Burton, *Anatomy of Melancholy*, 3.2.3.1 (vol. 3, p. 148).
44. Mary Beth Rose, *The Expense of Spirit: Love and Sexuality in English Drama* (Ithaca, NY: Cornell University Press, 1988).
45. Whately, *A Care-cloth*, sig. A3v.
46. Jacques Lacan, *Ecrits*, trans. Alan Sheridan (London: Tavistock, 1977), p. 245.

CHAPTER 4 PARENTHOOD: HERMIONE'S STATUE

1. The text also lists *'Boulime'* and *'Anorexie'* (Josuah Sylvester, trans., *The Divine Weeks and Works of Guillaume de Saluste Sieur du Bartas*, ed. Susan Snyder, 2 vols (Oxford: Clarendon Press, 1979), 2.1.3.439.)
2. Ibid., 2.1.4.143–4.
3. Ibid., 2.1.4.188.
4. Jan Wierix, *The Creation and the Early History of Man, 1607–8*, ed. Carl Van de Velde, (London: Feigen, 1990). Spain took Antwerp in 1585. Wierix thus worked under a Catholic regime.
5. Ibid., p. xi.
6. J. M. Clark, *The Dance of Death by Hans Holbein* (London: Phaidon, 1947), p. 32.
7. Thomas Harriott, *A Brief and true report of the new found land of Virginia* (Frankfurt, 1590).
8. For further continental examples, see Diane Kelsey McColley, *A Gust for Paradise: Milton's Eden and the Visual Arts* (Urbana: University of Illinois Press, 1993), figs 9, 20, 51.
9. The title page of William Lawson's popular gardening book shows men working in an orchard enclosed by a picket fence. The woodcut has the caption: 'Skill and pains brings fruitful gains.' Lawson insists on the importance of the fence, and also draws attention to the parallel between gardens or orchards and Paradise (*A New Orchard and Garden* (London, 1618), pp. 13, 56).
10. Martin Luther, *Lectures on Genesis (Chapters 1–5)*, trans. George V. Schick, *Luther's Works*, ed. Jaroslav Pelikan, vol. 1 (Saint Louis, MI: Concordia, 1958), p. 133.
11. William Shakespeare, *Cymbeline*, ed. J. M. Nosworthy, The Arden Shakespeare (London: Methuen, 1969).
12. Cf. Stephen Orgel, 'Prospero's Wife', *Representing the English Renaissance*, ed. Stephen Greenblatt, (Berkeley: University of California Press, 1988), pp. 217–29 (p. 222).
13. Jean Wilson, *The Archaeology of Shakespeare: The Material Legacy of Shakespeare's Theatre* (Stroud: Sutton, 1995), pp. 55–6.
14. Nigel Llewellyn, 'Honour in Life, Death and in the Memory: Funeral Monuments in Early Modern England', *Transactions of the Royal Historical Society*, ser. 6, vol. 6 (Cambridge: Cambridge University Press, 1996), pp. 179–200 (pp. 180–81).
15. For the view that the medieval examples of clasped hands may indi-

cate an increasing idealization of emotional closeness, though in conjunction with the emerging legal practice of jointure (property held
jointly by the couple), see Peter Coss, *The Lady in Medieval England 1000–
1500* (Stroud: Sutton, 1998), pp. 84–110.

16. See John Rudhall (d. 1636) and his wife, Mary at St Mary's, Ross-on-
Wye, and George Monox (d. 1638) and his wife, Cirencester. Both
tombs may be by Samuel Baldwin.

17. Wilson, *Archaeology of Shakespeare*, p. 90.

18. For instance, the monument to Robert Suckling (d. 1589) and his wife
in St Andrew's Church, Broad St, Norwich, displays skulls on either
side of the couple. Though they are relatively rare at this late date,
transi tombs also introduce the theme of death by depicting an emaciated cadaver in a state of decomposition. *Transi* tombs are shocking
to the degree that they introduce notions of time and decay into the
timeless serenity of conventional monumental sculpture. On the other
hand, as Paul Binski points out, the cadaver itself is often artfully
displayed. Desexed, desocialized and differentiated from the figure
commemorated by clothing or indications of office, the shrouded
corpse becomes an object of aesthetic interest in its own right (Paul
Binski, *Medieval Death: Ritual and Representation* (London: British Museum Press, 1996), p. 150). *Transi* tombs usually commemorated single
individuals rather than families.

19. I am grateful to Geoffrey Fisher for information about this tomb.

20. The inclusion of a previous wife was entirely conventional from the
middle ages on. A brass to John Hauley (d. 1408) at St Saviour's,
Dartmouth, shows two wives. Though he holds the hand of one, they
are virtually indistinguishable in all other ways. A brass of 1481 at
Morley, Derbyshire, shows Henry Stathum with three wives. Thomas
Inwood of Weybridge has three in 1586. Sir Richard Fitzlewes, d. 1528
at Ingrave, Essex, has four, differentiated by the heraldry shown on
their mantles. In 1470 the will of Sir Thomas Stathum specified that
his marble tombstone should show brass images of himself and his
two wives (quoted in Coss, *The Lady in Medieval England*, p. 105).

21. 'Hic iacet Egidius Savage Armiger filius Gulielmi Savage Armig Dns
de Elmeley Castle Iusticarius Pacis et Quorum Supraefectus Comita-
tus Wigorn qui diem clausit supremum 31 die Ianuarij Anno Doni
1631, in cuius memoriam amantissima ipsius coniunx Catherina filia
Ricardi Daston Armig iuxta posita una cum quattuor filijs Thoma,
Gulielmo, Egidio, Johanne, quorum Johes minimus natu obiit 13
Augusti eode quo pater anno et dilecta filiola quam post obitum ipsius

est enixa et utrisque ulnis amplectitur hoc monumentum fidelitatis et obedientiae ergo extrui curavit.'

22. William Shakespeare, *The Winter's Tale*, ed. J. H. P. Pafford, The Arden Shakespeare (London: Methuen, 1963).

23. B. J. Sokol attributes the rage of Leontes to the couvade syndrome, which in the 1950s was shown to afflict American men when their wives were pregnant. See *Art and Illusion in 'The Winter's Tale'* (Manchester: Manchester University Press, 1994), pp. 42–9.

24. Jacques Lacan, *Ecrits*, trans. Alan Sheridan (London: Tavistock, 1977), p. 245.

25. Sigmund Freud, *Beyond the Pleasure Principle*, The Penguin Freud Library, vol. 11, *On Metapsychology*, ed. Angela Richards (London: Penguin, 1984), pp. 269–338 (pp. 284–6).

26. Robert Burton, *The Anatomy of Melancholy*, ed. Thomas C. Faulkner, Nicolas K. Kiessling and Rhonda L. Blair, 3 vols (Oxford: Clarendon Press, 1989–94), 3.3 (vol. 3, pp. 273–329).

27. Ibid., 3.2.1.2 (vol. 3, p. 54).

28. Ibid., 3.3.2.1 (vol. 3, pp. 297–8).

29. Ibid., 3.3.2.1 (vol. 3, p. 299).

30. Ibid., 3.3.1.1 (vol. 3, p. 273).

31. M. M. Mahood, 'Wordplay in *The Winter's Tale*', *Shakespeare's Later Comedies*, ed. D. J. Palmer (London: Penguin, 1971), pp. 346–64 (p. 347).

32. H. H. Furness, ed., *A New Variorum Edition of Shakespeare*, vol. 11, *The Winter's Tale* (London: Lippincott, 1898), p. 27.

33. Ibid., pp. 27–9.

34. Shakespeare, *The Winter's Tale*, p. 166. Henry N. Hudson glosses it as 'lust', 'After a great deal of thought spent on this line' in his edition, in *The Windsor Shakespeare*, vol. 7 (Edinburgh: T. C. and E. C. Jack, n.d.). Arthur Quiller-Couch gives 'instinct (sexual), desire', but does not say whose, in his Cambridge University Press edition of 1931. S. C. Boorman glosses it as 'lust' (Hermione's) in his University of London Press edition of 1964. Ernest Schanzer in the Penguin edition of 1969, after weighing the options, settles for 'sexual desire' (Hermione's). Most modern editions stay broadly within this frame: affection is generally pathological if attributed to Leontes, or lascivious if it is seen as belonging to Hermione.

35. G. Blakemore Evans et al., eds, *The Riverside Shakespeare* (Boston, MA: Houghton Mifflin, 1974), pp. 1565, 1571; Stephen Greenblatt et al., eds, *The Norton Shakespeare* (New York: Norton, 1997), p. 2878.

36. William Shakespeare, *The Winter's Tale*, ed. John Andrews (London:

Dent, 1995); William Shakespeare, *The Winter's Tale*, ed. Stephen Orgel (Oxford: Oxford University Press, 1996).

37. Stephen Orgel, 'The Poetics of Incomprehensibility', *Shakespeare Quarterly*, 42 (1991), pp. 431–7.
38. David Ward, 'Affection, Intention, and Dreams in *The Winter's Tale*', *Modern Language Review*, 82 (1987), pp. 545–54 (p. 546).
39. 'I hope I shall not offend Divinity if I say the conjunction of man and wife is not love. It is an allowance of God's, and so good, and the name of it, I think, two honest affections united into one.' Don Cameron Allen, ed., *Essayes by Sir William Cornwallis, the Younger* (Baltimore: Johns Hopkins University Press, 1946), p. 20.
40. Ibid., p. 81. Cf. Ben Jonson, 'blind affection, which doth ne'er advance / The truth, but gropes, and urgeth all by chance' (Pafford, *The Winter's Tale*, p. 166).
41. Cf. Howard Felperin, '"Tongue-tied our Queen?": The Deconstruction of Presence in *The Winter's Tale*', *Shakespeare and the Question of Theory*, ed. Patricia Parker and Geoffrey Hartman, (New York: Methuen, 1985), pp. 3–18 (p. 11).
42. Ward, 'Affection, Intention, and Dreams', p. 549.
43. William Shakespeare, *Othello*, ed. E. A. J. Honigman, The Arden Shakespeare (Walton-on-Thames: Nelson, 1997).
44. Ward defends the Folio punctuation, which aligns 'what's unreal' with 'dreams'. He takes 'coactive' to mean 'coercive': Leontes is driven by an uncontrollable feeling ('Affection, Intention, and Dreams', p. 552). His reading differs from mine in detail, but points in a similar direction.
45. Cf. William Shakespeare, *The Merry Wives of Windsor*, ed. H. J. Oliver, The Arden Shakespeare (London: Methuen, 1971), where Page reproaches Ford because his 'submission' is as 'extreme' as his previous jealousy (4.4.10–12).
46. Nikolaus Pevsner, *London, Except the Cities of London and Westminster*, The Buildings of England (London: Penguin, 1952), p. 129.
47. John Page-Phillips, *Children on Brasses* (London: Allen and Unwin, 1970), fig. 31. The inscription states that they died suddenly, after a hazardous birth. Fig. 32 shows Dorothy Parkinson holding twins who closely resemble the children on the Legh monument. She died in childbirth in 1592 at Houghton-le-Skerne in County Durham, but in this case it is not clear whether the twins also died.
48. Katharine A. Esdaile, *English Church Monuments 1510–1640* (London: Batsford, 1946), p. 122. Nicholas Stone's monument to Arthur Croke

(d. 1629) at Bramfield, Suffolk, shows his wife Elizabeth holding the baby whose birth caused her own death in 1627. Stone's workshop made the tomb of Lady Coventry (d. 1634) at Croome d'Abitot (Worcs). She leans on her elbow, holding a baby in the crook of her arm. In 1634 Sir John St John set up his own monument at Lydiard Tregoze (Wilts). The tomb, probably by Samuel Baldwin, shows two wives, the second living. The first wife, Anne Leighton, died giving birth to her thirteenth child. She clasps the baby, who survived, in her arms.

49. Lady Dorothy Allington died in 1613 at Horseheath in Cambridgeshire. Her tomb records that she married Sir Giles Allington and 'made him a joyful father of ten children', all named. The inscription adds: 'To whose dear memory her sorrowful husband, mindful of his own mortality, erected this monument.'

50. Bruce R. Smith, 'Sermons in Stones: Shakespeare and Renaissance Sculpture', *Shakespeare Studies*, 17 (1985), pp. 1–23 (p. 20). Manuela Rossini drew my attention to this essay.

51. Malcolm Baker drew my attention to this possibility.

52. Margery Corbett and Ronald Lightbown, *The Comely Frontispiece: The Emblematic Title-page in England 1550–1660* (London: Routledge and Kegan Paul, 1979), p. 7. See also Wilson, *Archaeology of Shakespeare*, pp. 48, 52.

53. Corbett and Lightbown, *The Comely Frontispiece*, p. 5.

54. Karen Hearn ed., *Dynasties: Painting in Tudor and Jacobean England 1530–1630* (London: Tate Gallery, 1995), p. 208.

55. See, for example, John Coke (d. 1632) at St Mary's, Ottery St Mary, Devon; Sir William Slingsby (d. 1634), Knaresborough, Yorkshire.

56. Erwin Panofsky, *Tomb Sculpture: Its Changing Aspects from Ancient Egypt to Bernini*, ed. H. W. Janson (London: Thames and Hudson, 1964), pp. 47–59.

57. Captain John Timperley stands at Hintlesham, Suffolk. This much later image (d. 1629) is engraved on slate and placed vertically in the wall.

58. Pafford, *The Winter's Tale*, p. 199.

59. See, for instance, ibid., p. xxxiv.

60. Ovid, *Metamorphoses*, 10.247–97.

61. Philip Massinger, *The City Madam*, ed. Cyrus Hoy, Regents Renaissance Drama Series (London: Edward Arnold, 1964). I owe this comparison to Alan Dessen.

62. Francis Beaumont, *The Masque of the Inner Temple*, ed. Philip Edwards, *A Book of Masques in Honour of Allardyce Nicoll* (Cambridge: Cambridge University Press, 1967), pp. 125–48, lines 202–6.

63. *The History of the Tryall of Chevalry* (London, 1605), sig. E3r SD.

64. Ibid., sig. H1v.
65. Ibid., sigs H1v–2r.
66. 'Either Hermione died and was resurrected in marble, or else she spent 16 years in a garden-shed on the grounds of her husband's palace, a solitude broken only by daily visits from her protectress – or jailer? – Paulina, all the while that this same worthy lady was encouraging Leontes into deeper paroxysms of grief over having in effect killed his wife.' Leonard Barkan, '"Living Sculptures": Ovid, Michelangelo, and *The Winter's Tale*', *ELH*, 48 (1981), pp. 639–67 (p. 640).
67. Shakespeare, *The Winter's Tale*, pp. lxix–lxx.
68. *OED*, 14.
69. *OED*, 39b, 70c.
70. *Paradise Lost*, 4.271–2. The implied parallel in Milton's text is with Eve, who is to be partly ensnared by the monarch of Hell, but the play of ideas here too depends on lost and desired flowers: 'Proserpine gathering flowers / Herself a fairer flower by gloomy Dis / Was gathered' (John Carey and Alastair Fowler, eds, *The Poems of John Milton* (London: Longman, 1968).
71. Ovid, *Metamorphoses*, 5.385–424.
72. Florizel has already invoked other Ovidian 'transformations' (4.4.27–32). It is worth remembering that the mechanicals of *A Midsummer Night's Dream* also draw on this text for their play, however inadequate Peter Quince's memory – or his Latin. The stories it tells were not regarded as esoteric knowledge.
73. Ovid, *Metamorphoses*, 5.371–84.
74. John Frederick Nims, ed., *Ovid's Metamorphoses, The Arthur Golding Translation* (London: Collier Macmillan, 1965), 5.496.
75. Ovid, *Metamorphoses*, 3.339–510. Ovid's transformations are often visually motivated: Niobe, 'all tears', becomes a fountain; Clytie, in love with Apollo, is turned into a heliotrope, her face following his chariot as it moves; a pining boy becomes a daffodil.
76. John Parkinson, *Paradisi in Sole Paradisus Terrestris* (London, 1629), p. 9 (*OED*, 'daffodil' 2).
77. Sigmund Freud, 'On Narcissism: An Introduction', *On Metapsychology*, pp. 59–97 (p. 85).
78. Jacques Lacan, 'God and the Jouissance of The Woman', *Feminine Sexuality: Jacques Lacan and the Ecole Freudienne*, ed. Juliet Mitchell and Jacqueline Rose, (New York: Norton, 1985), pp. 138–48 (p. 143 and *passim*).

79. Jacques Derrida, *The Post Card: From Socrates to Freud and Beyond*, trans. Alan Bass (Chicago: University of Chicago Press, 1987), pp. 120–21.

CHAPTER 5   SIBLING RIVALRY: *HAMLET* AND THE FIRST MURDER

1. For evidence that this instance of medieval typology survived the Reformation, see Alexander Ross, *The First Booke of Questions and Answers upon Genesis* (London, 1620), p. 75.
2. This interpretation is St John Chrysostom's (see Joseph Leo Koerner, 'The Mortification of the Image: Death as a Hermeneutic in Hans Baldung Grien', *Representations*, 10 (Spring 1985), pp. 52–101 (pp. 52–3).
3. Jan Wierix, *The Creation and the Early History of Man, 1607–8*, ed. Carl Van de Velde, (London: Feigen, 1990), figs 11–13.
4. Jan Sadeler, in an engraving published by Gerard de Jode in 1585, has Cain apparently trying to feed an apple to a sheep, while Eve feeds Abel and Adam leans on a pick. Jacob Floris van Langeren and William Slatyer, in their Genesis series of 1635, more intelligibly show young Abel playing with a lamb, while Cain holds an apple triumphantly above his head. Adam digs; Eve spins under a sloping roof. Jan Saenredam's Genesis series of 1604 depicts the children struggling over an apple, while their parents toil, against a background which includes their thatched shelter. For all three images, see Diane Kelsey McColley, *A Gust for Paradise: Milton's Eden and the Visual Arts* (Urbana: University of Illinois Press, 1993), figs 9, 20, 51.
5. Tobias Stimmer, *Neue kunstliche Figuren biblischer Historien* (Basel, 1576), sig. A3r. The image was evidently influential: all four figures from Stimmer reappear against a wilder, less domestic setting in Melchior Küsel, *Icones Biblicae Veteris et Novi Testamenti* (Vienna, 1679), p. 5.
6. *The English Bohun Psalter*, Bodleian MS. Auct. D. 4. 4, fol. 40. A capital in the cloister at Tarragona shows the infant Cain trying to snatch Abel from his mother's arms as she feeds him (Louis Réau, *Iconographie de l'art chrétien*, 3 vols (Paris: Presses Universitaires de France, 1955–59), vol. 2, pt 1, p. 94).
7. Roland Mushat Frye, 'Ladies, Gentlemen, and Skulls: *Hamlet* and the Iconographic Traditions', *Shakespeare Quarterly*, 30 (1979), pp. 15–28. See also Frye, *The Renaissance Hamlet: Issues and Responses in 1600* (Princeton, NJ: Princeton University Press, 1984), pp. 205–53, which includes a brief account of the Dance of Death (pp. 237–43).
8. William Shakespeare, *Hamlet*, ed. Harold Jenkins, The Arden Shake-

speare (London: Methuen, 1982).

9. The song is a garbled version of a text by Thomas Lord Vaux, printed as 'The Aged Lover Renounceth Love' in *Tottel's Miscellany* (1557) (Shakespeare, *Hamlet*, pp. 548–50).

10. Jacques Lacan, *Ecrits*, trans. Alan Sheridan (London: Tavistock, 1977), pp. 8–29.

11. For an account of the homicidal possibilities of emulation, see Wayne A. Rebhorn, 'The Crisis of the Aristocracy in *Julius Caesar*', *Renaissance Quarterly*, 43 (1990), 75–111.

12. Don Cameron Allen, ed., *Essayes by Sir William Cornwallis, the Younger* (Baltimore: Johns Hopkins University Press, 1946), pp. 26–7.

13. Francis Bacon, *The Essayes or Counsels, Civill and Morall*, ed. Michael Kiernan (Oxford: Clarendon Press, 1985), p. 24.

14. Lacan, *Ecrits*, p. 20.

15. *St Augustine's Confessions*, with an English translation by William Watts, 1631, The Loeb Classical Library, 2 vols (London: Heinemann, 1912), vol. 1, 1.7 (pp. 21–3).

16. Lacan, *Ecrits*, p. 20.

17. William Shakespeare, *As You Like It*, ed. Agnes Latham, The Arden Shakespeare (London: Methuen, 1975).

18. *The City of God*, trans. Philip Levine, The Loeb Classical Library, 7 vols (London: Heinemann, 1966), vol. 4, Bks 12–15, 15.5 (p. 429).

19. Donald V. Stump, 'Hamlet, Cain, Abel, and the Pattern of Divine Providence', *Renaissance Papers* (1985), pp. 27–38 (p. 30).

20. Cf. 'Your worm is your only emperor for diet: we fat all creatures else to fat us, and we fat ourselves for maggots. Your fat king and your lean beggar is but variable service – two dishes, but to one table. That's the end' (*Hamlet* 4.3.21–5).

21. For recent accounts of the implications of the *danse macabre* for the English stage, see Phoebe S. Spinrad, *The Summons of Death on the Medieval and Renaissance Stage* (Columbus: Ohio State University Press, 1987); and Michael Neill, *Issues of Death: Mortality and Identity in English Renaissance Tragedy* (Oxford: Clarendon Press, 1997). For its relevance to the play in particular, see also Elizabeth Maslen's excellent 'Yorick's Place in *Hamlet*', *Essays and Studies*, 36 (1983), 1–13.

22. [*Dance of Death*] 'Marke well the effect' (London, ?1580).

23. Kiernan Ryan makes the point that though 'revolution' at this moment does not carry the political significance it now has, the play in effect anticipates something of the later meaning. (Paper given at the Solothurn Symposium, September 1996.)

24. *The Daunce and Song of Death* (London, 1569).
25. *The Daunce of Machabree* accompanies Boccaccio's *De Casibus illustrium virorum* (London, 1554). A crude woodcut at the head of the Dance shows the Dead and the estates in procession.
26. See Natalie Zemon Davis, 'Holbein's *Pictures of Death* and the Reformation at Lyons', *Studies in the Renaissance*, 3 (1956), pp. 97–130.
27. A '*Roll of Daunce of Death*, with pictures and verses upon the same' was entered in the Stationer's Register in 1597. This was possibly a copy of the St Paul's Dance. (Florence Warren ed, *The Dance of Death* (London: EETS, OS 181, 1931), p. 108.)
28. Warren, ed., *The Dance of Death*, pp. xxii–xxiii.
29. Philippe Ariès, *Images of Man and Death*, trans. Janet Lloyd (Cambridge, MA: Harvard University Press, 1985), p. 23. See also Paul Binski, *Medieval Death: Ritual and Representation* (London: British Museum Press, 1996), p. 55.
30. For examples, see Hélène and Bertrand Utzinger, *Itinéraires des Danses macabres* (Paris: Garnier, 1996). An exhibition of the Dance at the Museum für Sepulkralkultur, Kassel, in 1998 collected a great deal of material from the German-speaking countries. The catalogue was published as *Tanz der Toten – Todestanz: der monumentale Totentanz im deutschsprachigen Raum* (Dettelbach: Verlag J. H. Röll, 1998).
31. Binski, *Medieval Death*, p. 158.
32. Cf. Neill, *Issues of Death*, pp. 74–7.
33. For a brilliant reading of this picture and others on the theme of death, see Koerner, 'The Mortification of the Image'.
34. Cyril Tourneur, *The Revenger's Tragedy*, ed. R. A. Foakes, (London: Methuen, 1966), 3.5.121, 137.
35. For evidence of Hamlet's action see Shakespeare, *Hamlet*, note on 5.1.252.
36. Koerner, 'The Mortification of the Image', p. 90.
37. Bodleian Library, MS Douce 225.6, fols 3v–4r.
38. Jacques Derrida, *Of Grammatology*, trans. Gayatri Chakravorty Spivak (Baltimore: Johns Hopkins University Press, 1976), p. 71.
39. As Michael Neill argues, the iconography of death in the early modern period, including the theatrical iconography, is a way of attempting to map this unknowable territory (Neill, *Issues of Death*, pp. 1–48).
40. Sigmund Freud, 'Thoughts for the Times on War and Death', *Civilization, Society and Religion*, ed. Albert Dickson, The Penguin Freud Library (London: Penguin, 1985), vol. 12, pp. 57–89 (p. 77).
41. Jacques Derrida, *Aporias*, trans. Thomas Dutoit (Stanford, CA: Stanford

University Press, 1993), p. 22.

42. This is the zone where Jacques Lacan locates *Antigone* (*The Ethics of Psychoanalysis*, ed. Jacques-Alain Miller (London: Tavistock-Routledge, 1992), pp. 241–87). Antigone 'incarnates' the desire of death, Lacan argues (p. 282), longing for life from the place where it is already lost (p. 280). We know death only in the signifying chain, from which we (learn we) can disappear (p. 295). *Jouissance* (coming, enjoyment, possession) depends on oblivion of death, and yet, since *jouissance* mimics rejoining the Real, paradoxically desire 'at fleeting moments carries us beyond the encounter that makes us forget it' (p. 298). For an account of the 'puzzle' which intensifies the fear of death in the period, see Duncan Harris, 'Tombs, Guidebooks and Shakespearean Drama: Death in the Renaissance', *Mosaic*, 15 (1982), pp. 13–28.

43. It is also, of course, a moment associated with sexual exploits, see, for example, *Macbeth*, 2.1.49–56.

44. I am grateful to Balz Engler for a copy and an exposition of the Basle Dance. A representation was made in 1806, the year after the wall had been demolished. By this time the images had been heavily restored and perhaps remodelled.

45. Sir Thomas More, *A Treatise Unfynyshed* [*The Four Last Things*], *The Workes of Sir Thomas More Knyght ... wrytten by him in the Englysh tonge* (London, 1557), pp. 72–102, (p. 77).

46. Jacques Derrida, *Specters of Marx: The State of the Debt, the Work of Mourning, and the New International*, trans. Peggy Kamuf (New York: Routledge, 1994), p. 6.

47. Neill, *Issues of Death*, pp. 243–61.

48. Thomas Peyton. *The Glasse of Time, in the Two First Ages* (London, 1620), *The First Age*, p. 5.

49. In Beaumont and Fletcher's *The Maid's Tragedy* (1610) Amintor, however wronged, cannot contemplate killing the King.

50. See Quentin Skinner, *The Foundations of Modern Political Thought*, 2 vols (Cambridge: Cambridge University Press, 1978), vol. 2; Catherine Belsey, *The Subject of Tragedy: Identity and Difference in Renaissance Drama* (London: Methuen, 1985), pp. 93–125.

51. S. T. Coleridge, *Table Talk, Collected Works*, 14, ed. Carl Woodring, 2 vols (Princeton, NJ: Princeton University Press, 1990), vol. 2, p. 61.

52. The parallel texts are laid out clearly in Paul Bertram and Bernice W. Kliman, eds, *The Three-text 'Hamlet'* (New York: AMS Press, 1991).

53. The audience already knows, though Hamlet does not, that the further evil takes the form of suborning Laertes to kill Hamlet.

54. Ernesto Laclau, *Emancipation(s)* (London: Verso, 1996), p. 79.
55. Jacques Derrida, *Politics of Friendship*, trans. George Collins (London: Verso, 1997), p. 79. Cf. Jacques Derrida, *The Gift of Death*, trans. David Wills (Chicago: University of Chicago Press, 1995), p. 77.
56. Cf. Jacques Derrida, 'Force of Law: "The Mystical Foundation of Authority"', *Deconstruction and the Possibility of Justice*, ed. Drucilla Cornell, Michel Rosenfeld and David Gray Carlson, (New York: Routledge, 1992), pp. 3–67 (pp. 24–5).
57. I owe this point to Jacquie Hanham.
58. The stage directions do not specify this, but it is difficult to make sense of the scene without that assumption.
59. Helen Cooper calls him 'a serial killer' in an important historicization of the play, '*Hamlet* and the Invention of Tragedy', *Sederi*, 7 (1996), pp. 189–99 (p. 189).
60. Jacques Derrida, 'To Speculate – on "Freud"', *The Post Card from Socrates to Freud and Beyond*, trans. Alan Bass (Chicago: University of Chicago Press, 1987), p. 257–409 (p. 369).
61. The story and its interpretation appear in Sigmund Freud, *Beyond the Pleasure Principle, On Metapsychology: The Theory of Psychoanalysis*, ed. Angela Richards, The Penguin Freud Library, (London: Penguin, 1984), vol. 11, pp. 269–338 (pp. 283–7).
62. A. D. Nuttall, *Why Does Tragedy Give Pleasure?* (Oxford: Clarendon Press, 1996), pp. 104–5.
63. For a subtle account of the enigma staged by the play, see Bill Readings, 'Hamlet's Thing', *New Essays on 'Hamlet'*, ed. Mark Thornton Burnett and John Manning (New York: AMS Press, 1994), pp. 47–65.
64. Jacques Derrida, 'To Speculate', p. 261.
65. Ibid., p. 370.
66. Freud, *Beyond the Pleasure Principle*, pp. 332–8.
67. Ibid., p. 322. Cf. pp. 324, 325, 332, 333.
68. Derrida, 'To Speculate', p. 293.
69. Ibid., p. 294.
70. Ibid., p. 297.
71. Cf. Pierre Iselin, 'The Enigmas of *Hamlet*,' *William Shakespeare, 'Hamlet'*, ed. Pierre Iselin (Paris: Didier, 1997), pp. 9–35.
72. Francis Barker made a similar but more specific point, of course, about the hero's historically premature subjectivity (*The Tremulous Private Body* (London: Routledge, 1984), pp. 36–7).
73. Sigmund Freud, 'Psychopathic Characters on the Stage', *Art and Literature*, ed. Albert Dickson, Penguin Freud Library (London: Penguin,

1985), vol. 14, pp. 119–27 (p. 126). Jacques Lacan develops Freud's account, though with a specifically Lacanian inflection, of course, in 'Desire and the Interpretation of Desire in *Hamlet*', *Literature and Psychoanalysis: the Question of Reading: Otherwise*, ed. Shoshana Felman, (Baltimore: Johns Hopkins University Press, 1982), pp. 11–52.

74. Sigmund Freud, *The Interpretation of Dreams*, ed. Angela Richards, Penguin Freud Library (London: Penguin, 1976), vol. 4, p. 367.

75. See Shakespeare, *Hamlet*, note on 1.2.157.

CHAPTER 6   POSTSCRIPT: PASSION AND INTERPRETATION

1. Jacques Lacan, *Ecrits*, trans. Alan Sheridan (London: Tavistock, 1977), p. 284.

Index